"Julia," Brand said, the use of her given name an unmistakable challenge

His eyes glinted. Ignoring the people around them, he held out his hand.

The gesture was a command. One that almost any other woman in that room, regardless of her age or marital status, would have responded to with alacrity. But Julia wasn't *any* woman. She was completely and uniquely herself.

Her head tilted to one side, and she regarded him with a slight smile. "Have you met Mr. Barton, the Viscount—"

"No," Brand responded, making it clear that he did not wish to. The social pleasantries were completely beyond him. Let them gossip all they liked about his extraordinary rudeness. They would talk no matter what he did. It meant nothing. All that counted was Julia. And the moment...!

Dear Reader,

With over sixty novels to her name and more than five million of her books in print, Maura Seger is familiar to all but a few readers. But whether you are a longtime fan, or are picking her up for the first time, I hope you will enjoy *The Tempting of Julia*. The book is part of the Belle Haven Saga, set in a fictional town in Connecticut. It is the story of a self-proclaimed spinster and the dashing rogue who finally wins her heart.

Also this month, Harlequin Historicals is very pleased to present *Fire and Sword*, Theresa Michaels's first medieval romance, a classic tale of desire and revenge. And from the very talented Nina Beaumont comes *Tapestry of Fate*, a passionate story set against the backdrop of a dangerous world. Last is *Angel*, a warm-hearted tale of a Montana Christmas, from author Ruth Langan.

We hope you'll keep a lookout for all four titles wherever Harlequin Historical books are sold.

Sincerely,

Tracy Farrell
Senior Editor

Please address questions and book requests to:
Harlequin Reader Service
U.S.: 3010 Walden Ave., P.O. Box 1325, Buffalo, NY 14269
Canadian: P.O. Box 609, Fort Erie, Ont. L2A 5X3

MAURA SEGER

THE TEMPTING OF JULIA

Harlequin Books

TORONTO • NEW YORK • LONDON
AMSTERDAM • PARIS • SYDNEY • HAMBURG
STOCKHOLM • ATHENS • TOKYO • MILAN
MADRID • WARSAW • BUDAPEST • AUCKLAND

ISBN 0-373-28844-1

THE TEMPTING OF JULIA

Books by Maura Seger

Harlequin Historicals

Light on the Mountain #107
The Lady and the Laird #127
*The Taming of Amelia #159
*The Seduction of Deanna #183
*The Tempting of Julia #244

*The Belle Haven Series

Harlequin Books

Harlequin Historical Christmas Stories 1992
"Miss Montrachet Requests"

MAURA SEGER

began writing stories as a child and hasn't stopped since. Her love for history is evident in the many historical romances she has produced throughout her career. But her interests are not confined to the early periods of history. She has also written romances set in the more recent eras of World War II, the sixties and contemporary times.

A full-time writer, Maura experienced her very own romance in her courtship and marriage to her husband, Michael, with whom she lives in Connecticut, along with their two children.

Prologue

The moon had risen several hours before. It rode in a cloudless sky, bathing the slumbering earth in molten silver.

Julia Nash stood at the window of her bedroom and stared out at the scene. The night air was cool. She was glad of the lacy shawl she wore over her nightgown. It trailed almost to the floor and smelled slightly of the dried lavender she used to scent her drawers.

It was very quiet beyond the house. There was only the gentle, rhythmic whoosh of the waves on the nearby beach and the muted sound of the wind in the pine trees.

A deep sigh of contentment escaped her. In the three months since she had moved to her grandmother's house, she had come to feel a sense of belonging unlike any she had ever known.

That was surprising, given that she had only the happiest memories of growing up in the Marlowe country house, nestled among sylvan acres north of Belle Haven, and equally delightful recollections of frequent visits to the Virginia estate, called Holycroft, that had come into the family in the previous century.

Then there was the town house in New York; in fact there were any number of places where she could feel at home. But it was this house, rough-beamed and weathered, set by itself far out on the point of land known as Daniels' Neck, that most called to her.

Her grandmother, Sara, had suspected it would. "It's a special place," she'd told Julia as they sat together in the gazebo behind the family's country house.

Illness and old age were forcing Sara to give up her own home and come to live with her son and daughter-in-law. They were happy to have her, and determined to do everything possible to make her final years both comfortable and loving. Much as Sara appreciated that, she couldn't help but miss the house far out on Daniels' Neck where she had lived so long.

Sitting in the sun, her favorite granddaughter at her side, Sara had spun a tale that Julia had heard many times before but which never failed to fascinate her.

"Long ago," Sara began, "when this country was still a collection of colonies, people came here in search of freedom. They were led by your ancestress, Amelia Daniels, and your ancestor, Captain Garrick Marlowe."

She chuckled to herself. "Oh, how those two fought. Oil and water they were, her so fiercely independent and determined to do what no woman had ever done—found her own colony—and him not liking taking orders from a female for a moment, and anxious to be on his way as soon as he collected what was due him."

"Then why didn't he?" Julia asked, though she knew the answer as well as her own name.

"They fell in love, that's why. Right there on Daniels' Neck. Garrick built the house for Amelia, and they came to it as husband and wife. A long and happy life together. But that isn't the end of the story."

"Tell me the rest," Julia asked, as she always did.

"Many years later, more than a century later, Deanna Marlowe live in that house. She was Amelia and Garrick's great-granddaughter. During the Revolution, she met Edward Nash. She thought he was a British spy, and didn't they have a fine to-do over that. But it all worked out in the end. He was from Virginia, from Holycroft, and they spent part of their time down there, but they always returned to Daniels' Neck, and Amelia's house.''

"You were born there, weren't you?" Julia asked, though she knew full well.

Sara smiled as she remembered. "It was always my favorite place. I had my own babies there, your father among them, and laid my dear husband to rest in the nearby graveyard."

She sighed deeply and looked out across the neat, rolling lawns of the country house to where horses could be seen grazing.

"This is a beautiful place, make no mistake, but Amelia's house is where we began. It's our roots, the source of our strength."

She turned and laid her hand over Julia's, old to young, past to future. "Now I want it to be yours. Of all my grandchildren, you're the most suited to take Amelia's house into the new century. I will rest easy knowing you are there."

Tears blurred Julia's eyes. The mere thought of losing her grandmother was enough to make her weep, but she understood the inevitability of such things.

Amelia and Deanna had understood it, too. Generation to generation, they had created a bond of strength and tradition that was their legacy to the women of their family.

Now it was Julia's turn. Standing at the window, she whispered a soft thank-you to her grandmother, and resolved to visit Sara the coming day. But first—

The night beckoned, as it had ever since she was a child— as it had, too, for Amelia and Deanna, who had walked their own land, unafraid beneath the moon, seeking the healing plants they knew so well.

On an impulse, Julia slipped from her room. She paused only long enough to slide on a pair of sensible shoes that she kept in the closet beside the back door. That done, she was gone, a white shadow flitting down the path walked by so many generations of women before her.

It led to the beach. She kicked off her shoes and went on. The sand was cool beneath her feet. Her toes curled into it. The breeze lifted her auburn hair and flattened the shawl against her body.

A small, playful wave washed over her feet. She laughed and lifted the hem of her nightgown higher. On such nights, she had been known to shed her clothes and revel in greater freedom than surely any proper woman knew, then dive into the welcoming water.

But on this night she judged it just a little too cold for that. If she swam now, she would regret it later. Her leg would throb and she would be forced to spend a considerable time trying to massage the pain out. In the end, she would pay dearly for a brief frolic.

A few years before, that wouldn't have stopped her. But at twenty-three, she had acquired a maturity not always found in a woman of her background and age. With a sigh, she stepped away from the water and continued on down the beach.

Despite the hour, she didn't feel tired. Indeed, energy flowed through her. She kept going, heedless of the distance. She barely noticed when she passed beyond her own land.

Not that it mattered. The land west of hers was uninhabited, and had been since the last family gave up farming it almost a century before.

Julia was accustomed to walking along the beach there, and thought nothing of it. In all the years that she had done so, she had never encountered another living soul. Which perhaps explained why she didn't at first realize what she was looking at. Ahead, perhaps forty yards down the beach, was a sight she could hardly credit.

A man—tall, heavily muscled, bathed in moonlight—and naked. Most definitely naked.

Her breath caught. It had to be an illusion. There could not possibly be such a thing on her beach—all right, not hers, next to hers—such proud and powerful masculinity, unrestrained by the slightest veneer of civilization.

She was dreaming, that was it. Indeed, she might very well be back in her bedroom in Amelia's house, having never even gone out. This might all be happening in her imagination.

But if that was the case, then she had a far more vivid, not to say shameless, imagination than she had ever realized.

The man dived into the water. He swam out with smooth, swift strokes until he was no more than a head bobbing on the water, then turned and headed back.

Julia took a quick glance over her shoulder. She could not possibly stay where she was. Decency demanded that she withdraw at once. But if she went back down the beach, he might very well see her.

The thought of being discovered under such circumstances made her acutely uncomfortable. With only a slight hesitation, she darted into the bushes along the far side of the sand.

She was barely in time. Even as she reminded herself to close her eyes, or at least turn her head away, the man emerged from the water.

She really must not look. It was shameless, totally improper, completely out of keeping with her upbringing. And yet the temptation was irresistible. Curiosity overcame her. She looked, blinked hard, looked again. Her breath caught.

He was magnificent standing there in the moonlight, water sluicing off the long, hard length of him. Every muscle appeared perfectly articulated, each limb perfectly formed, the whole of him superbly constructed to what was surely the highest standard of the male ideal.

Her chest hurt. Julia realized she wasn't breathing and drew in air raggedly. She might have grown up in a sheltered environment, but she hadn't considered herself to be completely ignorant.

Her mother, far more enlightened than many women of her class, had taken each of her daughters aside as they came of age and explained, gently but sensibly, the differences between a man and a woman, and what resulted from their joining.

Yet none of that had prepared Julia for the impact of seeing a man's naked body. Deep inside her there was a stirring she had never felt before.

A sound came from the back of her throat. Faint as it was, it was enough to pierce the shock and fascination that held her.

Terrified that she might have been heard, she turned away and headed deeper into the bushes. They pulled at her skirt, thorns scratching her legs and brambles tearing at her feet. Still she went on, until finally she judged it safe enough to return to the beach.

Once there, she kept going until she was safely on her own land. Pausing only long enough to pick up her shoes, she took the path back to the house, reaching there out of breath, tattered and bleeding.

When the door was at last securely closed behind her, she leaned her back against it and squeezed her eyes shut. Her whole body hurt, but she hardly noticed. The vision she had seen and the stunning way she had reacted wiped out all other thought.

Only gradually did she become aware of her discomfort. Glancing down, she flinched. Red, shining droplets of blood were collecting on the finely polished floors of her house.

Limping, she walked slowly into the kitchen and set a kettle to heat on the new coal stove installed only a few weeks before. In her room she found a soothing unguent she had used on others many times but had never before needed herself.

When the water was heated, she bathed her injured feet, grimacing at how they stung, then dried them and applied the unguent. It helped, but not entirely. Her feet still throbbed as she tidied up and climbed the stairs to her bedroom.

By the time she had changed out of her tattered nightgown into a fresh one and slipped beneath the sheet, the unguent was taking effect.

A blessed numbness settled over her injured flesh. But there was no such remedy to banish the deep pool of yearning that seemed to have opened within her.

She twisted restlessly in the bed, watching the moon flow past her windows. When at last she slept, it was to dream of silver on water, and a man she already feared she would never be able to forget.

Chapter One

Belle Haven, Connecticut, 1895

The women had their heads together, bonnet brims touching, when Julia entered Goody's Notions. She thought nothing of it, until the quick flitting of eyes in her direction and the sudden silence made her aware that she had been the subject of their conversation.

Her face tightened, but so fleetingly that only one who knew her well could possibly have discerned her reaction. In an instant, all emotion was suppressed. She smiled coolly.

"Good morning, Mrs. Lester, Mrs. Blake. I trust you are both well?"

Even as she spoke, her azure gaze settled on the ribbons set out on the counter, making it clear that she was interested in things other than their response. Yet she wasn't rude—never that. She was simply very cautious, long accustomed to protecting herself from the comments, well-intentioned and otherwise, of others.

The women, both in their fifties, nodded. They were substantial matrons, dressed in white summer cotton and lace. They looked startled and a bit abashed, but eagerly attentive.

Why? Julia wondered as she fingered a length of turquoise satin she thought might be suitable for her sister Daphne's new ball gown. Surely she had done nothing recently to merit such interest. She had moved to Amelia's house six months ago, hardly recently enough to make good gossip.

What, then? The women exchanged a glance. Mrs. Lester spoke. "Quite well, dear, and you?"

"Fine, thank you." Surely that took care of the pleasantries. Her manner made it clear that she did not wish to chat, and any semblance of courtesy required them to respect that.

But it seemed as though this morning courtesy had been overcome by curiosity.

"We were just saying, dear," Mrs. Blake chimed in, "what a shame it is, the changes we are seeing."

Julia suppressed a sigh. This was an old topic, trotted out so often that it creaked. Yes, Belle Haven was changing. The quiet backwater had been discovered by the nouveau riche of New York City, only a few miles away. Houses were being built, businesses started.

There were drawbacks to be sure—greatly increased traffic, noise along the main street near the new train station, rising prices. But there were also far more jobs, and there was a sense of vitality and prosperity that Julia found quite pleasing.

"Change is inevitable," she said, "don't you think?"

Again the women exchanged a glance. Her response seemed to egg them on, although she couldn't imagine why.

"Perhaps it's just as well you think so," Mrs. Lester said.

Julia's frown deepened. "I don't understand—"

"Although," Mrs. Blake interjected, "I personally don't believe it's as bad as people are saying. Why, the rumors about him might not be true at all."

"Rumors?" Julia had no idea what the older woman meant, but she had a sinking feeling that she was about to find out, and that she wouldn't be happy about it.

"The land, dear," Mrs. Lester said, "the land next to yours on Daniels' Neck. Surely, you've heard?"

A chill ran down Julia's back. She had a sudden, guilty memory of what she had done—and seen—in the silent hours of the night. Surely, no one could possibly know.

Reason reasserted itself even as panic threatened. Of course no one knew. Her secret was safe. Whatever the women were talking about, it wasn't that.

"It's been sold," Mrs. Blake said, pausing before adding portentously, "to a gentleman from New York."

Mrs. Lester tittered. "Really, dear, don't you think that's going a bit far? He's hardly what *I* would describe as a gentleman."

Julia barely heard her. Waking from dreams she blushed to remember, she had tried to convince herself that the man had been an illusion born of moonlight and too much imagination. She had almost managed it, reassured by the certain knowledge that she was the only one who ventured onto that stretch of beach.

Now, without warning, came the possibility that her moon-washed vision might actually exist, not simply in the world of hidden yearnings, but in hard, cold reality.

"But he is rich," Mrs. Blake said flatly. "Rich as Croesus, people are saying." She rolled her eyes heavenward. "Who knows what he's planning. Probably one of those horrible great mansions they're building in Newport."

Julia's stomach clenched. They had to be wrong. But even if someone had bought the land, there was no reason to believe that that was who she had seen, if indeed she had truly seen anything.

"We'd love to chat," Mrs. Lester said, "but I promised my William I wouldn't be gone long."

"And if I don't keep after my laundry girl," Mrs. Blake put in, "she'll make a hash of everything. Do have a good day, dear."

"Yes, do," Mrs. Lester added.

They departed in a swirl of billowing summer gowns and knowing smiles, well pleased with their morning's work.

"Old biddies," said Charlotte Hemper, the proprietress of Goody's Notions. She had been standing quietly behind the counter listening to the whole exchange. Now she looked at Julia worriedly. "Don't take it to heart. They may very well be wrong."

Julia nodded, but without conviction. Charlotte was the only true friend she had outside her own family. They came from very different backgrounds, Julia having grown up in the bosom of a loving, prosperous and protective family, while Charlotte had struggled to find a place for herself among the hordes of immigrants thronging to the New World.

Despite all that, they had understood and liked each other from the first moment of their acquaintance. Julia had great respect for Charlotte's initiative and courage, while Charlotte had often expressed her admiration for Julia's intelligence and compassion. Each felt herself at odds with much of the world and found refuge in their friendship.

Yet the world inevitably intruded. "They sounded so sure," Julia said. Her face was white. She felt almost ill.

Charlotte hesitated. Julia could tell there was something her friend was having difficulty saying. "What is it?" she asked.

"I heard it, too," the young woman said finally. "This morning, when I was at the market. It seems everyone is talking about it."

"I see," Julia said slowly, although in fact she did not. "Who is this dubious gentleman from New York?"

"Brand Delaney," Charlotte said, then waited for Julia's inevitable reaction.

It came instantly. Julia's mouth dropped open. She shut it with a snap, and took a deep breath. "Brand Delaney?"

"I'm afraid so. At least that's the name that's being given about."

"But that's impossible. He's...he's the absolutely worst sort of man. His reputation..."

"Is horrible, I know. About the kindest thing I've ever heard him called is a robber baron."

The young women looked at each other. Charlotte's eyes were filled with sympathy, but Julia's sparked with a far different emotion.

Granted, the land wasn't hers. If it had been, there'd be no question of it ever ending up in the possession of someone like Brand Delaney!

Despite the lack of ownership, she felt a tremendous protectiveness toward the unspoiled stretch of wilderness next to hers, and she heartily disliked the notion that any financial pirate could do as he wished with it.

"There has to be a way to stop him," she said.

Charlotte shook her head. "I can't imagine how." Brightening, she added, "But if anyone can do it, you can, I'm sure. However..."

"What?"

"You might consider that the rumors aren't necessarily true."

Julia looked at her skeptically. "He is said to have come from nowhere, and in a few short years transformed himself into one of the wealthiest men in the country. Do you imagine he did that by being kind to widows and orphans?"

"No," Charlotte admitted. "But I also know that newcomers of any kind tend to be treated harshly when we attempt to rise above what polite society thinks of as our proper place."

Although Charlotte spoke without rancor, Julia was embarrassed. She wasn't usually so insensitive. "I'm sorry, that was stupid of me. It's just that the thought of that land being ruined is horrifying."

"Is that all it is?" Charlotte asked. She looked at her friend astutely. "There's nothing else upsetting you?"

"No, of course not. What else could there be?"

"I don't know. It's just that you seem different somehow..."

"It's the land," Julia insisted, "nothing else." She managed a smile. "Well, perhaps that and having to deal with two of the town's best gossips on an empty stomach."

Charlotte laughed. She looked relieved, but not entirely convinced. Still, she let the subject go. They went on to talk of Daphne's ball gown, and other more enjoyable matters.

Julia lingered a half hour or so before taking her leave. She always felt better after talking with Charlotte, who was more firmly rooted in what really mattered.

But scarcely had she stepped outside the door before the problem of the land—and the man she had seen—settled over her again. She told herself it was a coincidence. Brand Delaney was undoubtedly back in New York, wheeling and dealing, as robber barons did. The man she had seen—whoever he was—must be long gone.

She had to forget him and turn her mind to what to do about Delaney. But try as she might, the vision of moonlight and maleness continued to intrude. By the time she reached home, she was hot, tired and flustered.

Leaving her purchases on the kitchen table, she went out to the paddock. Mirage had only to see her to come running. The mare whinnied softly and butted Julia with her head.

"Is it only sugar you want," Julia asked playfully, "or do you want to go for a ride?"

Mirage tossed her mane and pawed the ground.

Julia laughed. "You know, I feel exactly the same way. I'll be right back."

Minutes later, she returned, having exchanged the simple cotton dress she had been wearing for sensible breeches and a shirt. With her hair tucked up under a battered old straw hat and her feet in scuffed boots that had belonged to one of her brothers, she led Mirage out of the paddock and saddled her quickly.

The mare stood patiently as Julia mounted. To be able to get into the saddle on her own—even with the help of a mounting block—was a triumph. Not too long ago, the doctors had said she would never be able to ride again.

But then, they had also doubted that she would walk. Day by day, struggle by struggle, she had proven them wrong.

The cost in pain and tears had been high, but she counted it all worthwhile. Independence and freedom meant everything to her. Without them, she might as well be dead.

Casting off such thoughts, she turned the mare toward the old shore road and pressed her heels lightly into the horse's sides. Mirage responded at once. They cantered past the ancient apple trees, which were filled with ripening fruit, and past the stone gateposts.

The road Julia took had been blazed along an old hunting track when Amelia's house was being built. While many of the other roads in Belle Haven had been widened and even lined with cobblestones, this road remained as it had always been, a narrow, packed-dirt lane bordered on both sides by blackberry bushes.

The summer day was bright without being hot. Julia rode along contentedly, determined to push her worries aside, at least for the moment. But that proved impossible to do. Thoughts of the land—and of Brand Delaney—kept intruding.

What could she do? Who should she speak with? Was there truly any way to stop him?

Preoccupied, she lost track of her surroundings. Mirage knew the road as well as she did, so there was no reason not to trust the horse.

But Mirage also knew—and feared—the meaning of the sudden flash of copper, and the hiss and swirl of the serpent's tail. The copperhead, jarred from its sunlit slumber in the underbrush, lifted its head to strike.

Mirage reared, screaming. Julia gasped and grabbed hold of the reins, struggling to hold on.

She was a fraction too late. Even as the snake slithered away into the bushes, Julia lost her balance. She cried out, grabbing air, and flew off the mare's back, landing hard on the dirt road.

Brand Delaney lifted his head from the plans he was studying and looked toward the wood beyond the shore. What was that he'd heard? It had sounded like a scream— but animal or human? Either? Both? Frowning, he set the plans down on the flat rock that was serving as a makeshift table.

"Did you hear that?"

The man beside him broke off his busy calculations. "Hear what?"

"That sound. I thought it was a scream."

Charles Hewlitt frowned. The tall, slender young man lifted his head and looked in the direction Brand was gazing.

"I didn't hear anything." The corners of his mouth lifted. "But then, I don't have your hearing. Remember that time when we were in the Wyoming Territory, and—"

Charles broke off. His friend wasn't listening. Brand was getting to his feet, uncoiling his full six-foot-plus length, and moving swiftly toward the fringe of trees beyond the shore.

There had been no further screams, but Brand was certain that he could hear something, some sound of move-

ment, of life, just up ahead, beyond the turn in the road
that ran beside his property. He slowed slightly and moved
more cautiously until he could see what lay ahead.

Immediately he stopped, his hands on his lean hips, and
stared. A young boy, not more than thirteen or fourteen, by
the look of him, was attempting to mount a horse.

Although the animal was patient and did not shy away,
the boy couldn't manage it. There seemed to be a weakness in one of his legs that prevented him from reaching the
saddle.

Not wanting to startle the lad, Brand called a greeting.
The boy whirled around and stared at him.

Brand stared back. He saw a heart-shaped face dusted
with freckles, large, thickly fringed eyes, so blue they
seemed to have been torn from the sky, and a full mouth
parted in surprise.

A boy?

He spared a quick glance for the slender figure, camou-
flaged in pants and a shirt, and grinned. No boy this.

"Your pardon," he said, more gently, "I didn't mean to
surprise you, but I thought I heard a scream."

Looking at him, she paled and took a quick step backward. Brand frowned. Her discomfort seemed not in keeping with the situation—unless she was embarrassed by her
garb, or simply unaccustomed to meeting a man in unexpected places.

He stopped where he was and held himself very still, exactly as he would if he had come across a doe or some other
gentle but wild animal. "Are you hurt?" he asked softly.

Paleness was replaced by fierce color. Her cheeks flamed.
She shook her head. In a choked voice, she said, "I'm
fine."

"Were you thrown?" The dirt on the back of her pants
seemed to indicate that.

He tried to concentrate on the fact that she'd been thrown, rather than on the enticing curve of her bottom. She appeared to have had the pants for some time, and to have almost outgrown them.

She nodded reluctantly. "Mirage shied at a snake." The words were spoken grudgingly. She was clearly waiting for him to depart.

Brand had no intention of doing so. Beyond a certain natural curiosity, he couldn't remember the last time a female had responded to him the way this one did.

Far from wanting to see the back of him, most women tended to cling, drawn by the irresistible flame of his money, and perhaps, also his reputation for danger.

Not this one, though. The look she shot him, and the haughty tilt of her head, made it clear she did not care to enlarge upon their acquaintance.

For a moment, he thought she might be truly young, but the swell of her breasts visible under the shirt and the curve of her hips in the snug pants quickly disabused him of that notion. This was no child but a woman full grown, and a curiously enticing one at that. Not beautiful, certainly, or at least not in any conventional way, but different enough to stir his admittedly jaded senses and make him want to know her better.

"You appear to be having some difficulty," he said, and moved toward her again.

His intention was simply to give her a leg up, there being no convenient stone or log to help her mount. But the moment he approached, she stiffened and tried again to climb into the saddle alone.

Again she failed.

A look of such unutterable misery flashed across her features that for an instant he thought she might cry. The look was gone as quickly as it had come, suppressed by a will he realized must be formidable.

"I don't need any help," she said. "If you will excuse me." She moved to the mare's head, took the reins and began walking with her down the road.

Brand hesitated. Good manners demanded that he respect her wishes.

A gentleman did not inflict his company on any woman, regardless of her age or class. He knew that, the same way he knew which fork to use and which wine to order.

He simply didn't care. Nothing in his life had come to him by his being concerned with the niceties of society. He had fought, struggled, and ultimately taken what suited him.

Yet at the same time, he knew his conscience to be clear in a way many men would never be able to claim. Put plainly, he had never hurt anyone who didn't well deserve it.

He didn't mean to start now, but neither was he willing to let her walk away. Not this creature of the woods he had stumbled on in dappled sunlight by the eternal sea.

Sweet heaven, he was thinking like a poet. She was only a woman, raggedly dressed, blatantly unfriendly, and not especially good with horses.

Or was she? Now that he had a chance to observe her more closely, she appeared to be limping. Moreover, it did not seem to be a new injury.

She compensated for the weakness in her left leg by putting more of her weight on the right side. So adept was she at it that she almost managed to mask the problem, yet it was there all the same. No wonder she hadn't been able to mount alone. Nor would she be able to, unless she found something to stand on farther down the road.

He sighed, and with quick strides closed the distance separating them. With deliberate casualness, he began to walk along beside her. "How far are you going?" he asked.

She cast him a quick glance from the corner of her eye, but otherwise did not look at him. "Not far, and I'm perfectly capable of doing it alone."

He hid a wry grin. That was certainly pointed. If nothing else, the encounter should have a humbling effect on his ego.

"Wouldn't it be simpler," he asked, "if you let me help you mount?"

"I prefer to walk."

That was so patently silly that he laughed. She stopped abruptly and glared at him. He couldn't tell if the color staining her cheeks was from anger or embarrassment, or both.

"You're Brand Delaney, aren't you?" she demanded.

"Have we met?" Surely he would have remembered.

She shook her head. "I just knew it."

There was no mistaking her disgust. Brand's face tightened. He was well accustomed to people thinking the worst of him. It generally bothered him no more than a breath of wind.

But this was different. He was standing on his own land, damn it, in the place where he meant to put down roots, and he was being confronted by a grubby female in boy's clothes who actually seemed to have worse manners than he did.

For once, he wasn't going to ignore it.

"Is there something wrong with me being who I am?" he demanded.

She sighed, as though the answer should be obvious. "You don't belong here."

His temper, which he usually kept so strictly in check, surged suddenly. Who was this brat to say such a thing? Stiffly, he said, "On the contrary, Miss... Just who are you, anyway?"

She hesitated, and for a moment he thought she meant to refuse him her name. Then, grudgingly, she said, "Julia Nash."

"Miss Nash, you're the one who's trespassing."

She stopped dead in her tracks and, for the first time, looked at him directly. Her eyes were wide, fathomless pools. He had an odd sense that he might somehow fall into them and never get out.

The sensation vanished as quickly as it had come. Coldly she said, "I'm trespassing? I'll have you know my family has lived here for two and a half centuries. In all that time, we've cared for this land, fought for it and protected it. If anyone has the the right to be here, it's me."

She spoke with such simple pride that he couldn't help but admire her for it. Still, she had stung him, and that demanded recompense.

He stared down at her from his considerably greater height. The wind blew a lock of black hair into his eyes. He brushed it aside. "That may be, but you don't own it. I do. Tell me, Miss Nash, are all of Belle Haven's residents this rude?"

She winced, but did not look away. Instead, she straightened her shoulders yet farther, took a firmer grip on Mirage's reins, and said, "I am not rude, Mr. Delaney. I am merely unfriendly. There is a difference."

"I fail to perceive it."

"That is your deficiency, not mine." Before he could comment further, she added, "However, you are right. Technically, this is your land, and I am trespassing. Therefore, I will remove myself. Goodbye, Mr. Delaney."

Head high, she continued on down the road, walking beside the horse. Brand stared after her bemusedly. He knew that he ought to be angry, and a part of him was. But he simply had no idea what to make of the proud, prickly— and definitely unfriendly—Julia Nash.

On an impulse, he called after her. "Am I to understand that we are neighbors?"

Without a backward glance, she answered him. "Only until I can find a way to remedy the situation, Mr. Delaney. Only until then."

He was left staring at dappled sunlight and the ripple of leaves rustling in a wind that was suddenly chill.

Chapter Two

Julia found a tree stump farther down the road, where she was at last able to mount. But even astride Mirage, she continued to tremble and her heart beat unnaturally fast.

How could she possibly have been like that? Brand Delaney had been kind when he merely called her rude. Never in her life had she behaved in such a way. He would have been within his rights to thrash her.

Truth forced her to admit the cause. She had been so stunned to see the vision of the previous night standing before her—albeit decently clad this time—that she had reacted in the worst possible way.

What must he think of her? Not that she cared, of course, or at least not any more than she would care for any person's opinion. All the same, her cheeks flamed, and she spent a few useless moments wishing that the earth might conveniently swallow her.

By the time she reached the house, unsaddled and brushed down Mirage, Julia was exhausted. There was no good reason for that, save the unpleasant memory of her encounter.

She tried to rouse herself with a glass of cool peppermint tea. When that failed, she went upstairs to the bathroom she had recently had installed and ran a tubful of cool water.

Soaking in it helped at least a little to ease the prickliness that seemed to have descended over her. But the bath did nothing for her leg. It still ached when she got out at last, wrapped herself in a thick towel and limped back into the bedroom.

Sitting on the edge of her bed, she massaged the calf of her leg slowly but firmly, as she had learned to do in the six years since her accident. It helped, but only gradually.

Patience had been the key to her recovery, and patience still had to be her partner every hour of every day. She would do well to remember that in her dealings with Brand Delaney.

The fact that there would have to be such dealings made her sigh deeply. She would have liked nothing better than to never have to face him again.

However, unless he was discouraged a good deal more easily than he was reputed to be, that wasn't going to happen. He was there, he was real, and if she didn't act swiftly, he would be staying.

Rather than dwell on that possibility, she busied herself dressing. Her hair was its usual tangle of auburn curls that refused to be tamed. She brushed it ruthlessly but to little effect, and finally did as she always did, securing it in a bun on top of her head. Sitting on the bed, she donned muslin drawers, a camisole and stockings. From the closet, she chose a plain blue serge skirt and white high-necked blouse in keeping with the style set by the ever-popular Gibson Girl.

Julia found them comfortable so long as she went without the harsh corseting necessary to attain a fashionable wasp waist. Her objection to such "figure improvers," as they were called, was simple—when she wore one, she couldn't breathe. Which also meant that she couldn't ride, cycle, or simply move about, without having to pause at frequent intervals.

In her opinion, it was simply ridiculous. But then, she thought "ridiculous" an apt description of most of what passed for fashion. Her mother and sisters were a good deal more modish and, truth be told, Julia had been, too, before the accident that had almost crippled her.

Having to deal with learning to walk again had robbed her of the usual interests of young women. She told herself she had no regrets about that but, looking at her defiantly unfashionable image in the full-length mirror in her bedroom, she felt a tiny twinge of regret. Swiftly repressing it, she pulled on high-buttoned boots and set a sensible straw hat on her head before going back downstairs.

Her bicycle was kept in a shed near the house. A gift from her brother, Patrick, on her most recent birthday, it delighted her. She was getting quite good at maneuvering it along the shore road, avoiding the worst of the inevitable ruts and making good time getting into town.

Once there, she hesitated. The train had just arrived from New York, and passengers were spilling out into the road beyond the station.

Most had come for a long weekend. They carried portmanteaus and looked about eagerly. Julia caught snatches of conversation about how fresh the air smelled and how good it was to be out of the city.

Carriages—and a few cars—waited to ferry the visitors to the inns that seemed to be opening everywhere. The residents of Belle Haven were rushing to accept paying guests or even rent out their houses entirely to those who wished to stay longer.

As a result, Julia saw few familiar faces as she walked her bicycle along the main street. The storefronts were also changing, old grain stores and harness makers giving way to more fashionable haberdasheries and eateries.

Still, there were things that didn't change, including the reassuringly solid presence of the Sanders building, halfway up Main Street. Built forty years before, it housed the law firm of Sanders and Sons.

Julia left her bicycle outside. She hesitated briefly, wondering if she perhaps should have called on the telephone before coming. Like the electric lights that were springing up all over town, the telephone had caught on rapidly.

She had used it herself on several occasions, and thought it marvelous. But the lines did not extend as far as Daniels' Neck, and were unlikely to do so anytime soon. Besides, Byram Sanders had known her all her life, and wouldn't expect her to stand on ceremony. She climbed the narrow staircase to the upstairs offices as the sounds of the busy street faded behind her.

A narrow-faced young man sat at a desk, guarding the entrance. He frowned as she entered, but quickly altered his expression when he realized who she was.

"Good morning, Miss Nash," he said, rising. "May I help you?"

"I would like to see Mr. Sanders," she told the secretary. "Is he in?"

"I regret that he isn't." He scrunched up his face in a show of concern. "But Mr. Sanders, Jr. is here. Will he do?"

Julia hid a smile at the thought of Wilbur Sanders merely "doing."

"That would be fine, thank you."

She was ushered with due solemnity into the smaller of the two offices overlooking the street. Wilbur hastened to his feet. A broad smile wreathed his fleshy face, but his eyes were cautious.

"Julia, dear, how nice to see you. Please sit down." He hastened to pull out a chair and shepherd her into it, then hovered until he was certain she was settled.

Undoubtedly she was being too sensitive, but Wilbur always seemed to make a great show of concern for her, much as he would if she were an invalid. But she most emphatically was not that, and it hurt her to be treated as such.

"To what shall I credit this visit?" he asked as he sat down again behind his desk.

"I need some advice."

"Why, of course, always happy to oblige. If it regards that house your grandmother's given you, the market is excellent right now. You could do very well."

"I have no intention of selling Amelia's house."

"Amelia? I thought . . . your grandmother . . . Oh, yes, I see, I have heard it called that. Daphne mentioned something about an ancestress, Amelia someone or other."

Julia suppressed a sigh. Wilbur was no worse than most of his ilk, and a good deal better than some. But his ignorance, and the cavalier assumption that she would be interested only in profit, would have been difficult to take on a day when her mood was sunny. Today, it was anything but.

Coldly, she said, "You are speaking of Amelia Daniels, who founded this town, and who named Daniels' Neck in honor of her father. However, I suppose such ancient business has no place here. It is not Amelia's house that concerns me. My worry is what's going to happen to the land next to it."

"That's been sold."

Julia closed her eyes for a moment, summoning patience. "I know that. To Brand Delaney. Surely I am not the only person in this town who finds that outrageous."

"Outrageous?" Wilbur looked genuinely perplexed, but he seemed to realize that his reaction wasn't appropriate. With a manful effort, he put his concerned face on again.

"Yes, of course, outrageous. I quite understand."

"Do you? The man has the worst possible reputation. It's reasonable to expect him to thoroughly despoil a stretch of property that is pristine wilderness. Do you have any idea just how many birds alone live along that stretch of the shore and in the adjacent woods? I've counted dozens of species, and I'm sure there are some I've missed."

"Birds? I see.... Lovely things, birds."

"Not to mention all the other wildlife."

"No, not to mention. Self-evident, as it were. Obvious to anyone... A great deal of animals, would you say?"

"And plants. Vast amounts of plants."

"Tremendous. But then, I suppose much the same stuff is on your property, isn't it?"

"That isn't the point. Plants and animals can't be confined to a few enclaves. They need room to spread or they could be in danger of dying out."

Wilbur laughed. He seemed to find the idea amusing. "Good heavens, I can't see that happening. There are just so many of them, after all. Why look at what goes on out West. People shoot buffalo by the thousand, but there are always more of them. Why, when I made my trip west..."

Julia shut out most of what followed. Along with everyone else in Belle Haven, she had already heard several times about Wilbur's great adventure in the wild West.

Of course, each time it was retold it seemed to gain in scope and drama. In the earlier versions, Wilbur had observed a buffalo hunt from the safety of a train. In subsequent retellings, he had participated, accounting for variously one, ten, and a hundred of the beasts.

"So you see," he concluded, "there's really no need for you to be concerned."

"But I am. Belle Haven is at a significant turning point in its history. With so many new people coming in, we must take steps to protect our natural resources and the special character of this place."

Wilbur sighed. He stroked his handlebar mustache thoughtfully. "As to that, progress marches on. It's unstoppable, don't you know? The forward advance of mankind, and all that. I really can't see what might be done."

"If a committee of the town residents was organized to bid against Mr. Delaney for the land..."

"Won't work," Wilbur said flatly. "Sale has already gone through. Signed and sealed, as it were."

"Then an effort must be made to influence what he does with the property."

"Can't see how. Man has a right to do what he wants with his own land."

"Do you mean to tell me," Julia demanded, "that if Mr. Delaney decided to build a slaughterhouse on the property, no one would object?"

"'Course they would... stink the whole place up. Good God, you can't mean that's what he intends? I thought he planned to live there."

"And how exactly would you know that, Mr. Sanders?"

Wilbur flushed. He was caught neatly enough, and he lacked the wit to find a way out.

"All right," he said reluctantly, "it's true that this firm handled the sale." Defiantly he added, "And we were proud to do so. His money's as good as anyone's."

"Would you feel that way if he was going to be living next door to you?"

"I don't live way out on the edge of town, Julia. North Street is turning into a very nice stretch of quite attractive homes, if I do say so myself. Naturally, we would object to any questionable influence being asserted there."

"But it's all right for it to happen where I live?" Angry, Julia got to her feet. "There seems to be a double standard at work here, Mr. Sanders. This town's citizens seem willing to protect their own neighborhoods and throw the rest of us to the wolves."

"Progress, Julia," Wilbur said as he, too, rose. "I've told you, it can't be stopped. At best, it can only be managed."

"You earned a significant commission for the sale."

"Not as significant as it might have—" He broke off, realizing he was saying more than was wise. "Let's just say that Mr. Delaney is a shrewd businessman, and leave it at that."

Julia thought of the man she had met on the road. He had seemed a good deal more than shrewd—tough, self-possessed, and compelling in ways she did not care to examine.

"He is not going to harm Daniels' Neck," she insisted.

Wilbur shrugged. "I really don't see how you're going to stop him."

And that was apparently supposed to be the end of the discussion.

With all the dignity she could muster—which was considerable, under the circumstances—Julia took her leave. She walked out of the office and down the steps with her shoulders straight and her head held high.

Only when she stood once again outside, on the bustling street, did she allow herself to consider the challenge she was taking on. Brand Delaney was rich, powerful, ruthless, and apparently very well accustomed to getting his own way. She came from a prosperous family, and might claim some influence within it, but she could not possibly hope to be anywhere near his level.

But then, she didn't want to be. She had her own values and her own objectives, chief among them the preservation of Daniels' Neck and the lands adjoining it.

Brand Delaney might think that the town of Belle Haven was happy to accommodate him in any way he saw fit. He might even be right. But Julia Nash was an exception.

Win or lose, she was going to make him rue the day he'd barged into her life and threatened all the peace and security she held dear. For the sake of the land, of course. Only for that. Her feelings about him had nothing to do with anything else. Nothing at all.

Years ago, her father had taught her to play chess. She had gotten rather good at it, and she still enjoyed the game. Among other things, it had taught her that in any conflict she needed a strategy.

Standing on the street in the late-afternoon sun, she thought hard about what she might do. Her options were severely limited. But there was one possibility she could not dismiss, no matter how much she wished to.

In all fairness, she should begin by discussing Mr. Delaney's plans with him.

But that meant confronting him face-to-face. She took a deep breath and tried to think of an alternative. None presented itself. Like it or not, she had to talk with him, and the sooner the better. Surely tomorrow would be soon enough. A good night's rest, a sensible breakfast, time to think over exactly what she wanted to say, and she would be ready to confront him.

As plans went, it wasn't bad. The only problem was that tomorrow didn't seem content to wait. Even as she stared in dawning dismay, a powerful black stallion came up the street and stopped almost directly in front of the Sanders offices.

Brand Delaney dismounted, fastened the reins to a nearby post and glanced around. Julia fought the temptation to try to sink into the masonry. It wouldn't have worked, anyway. He spotted her immediately.

Frowning, he walked toward her.

"It's you," Brand said. He stopped right in front of Julia and stared at her. "The badly behaved urchin."

Her cheeks flamed. She silently cursed her inability to conceal her emotions. Instinct told her to walk away. But intelligence said otherwise. Sooner or later, she had to face him. It might as well be now.

"My name is Julia Nash, Mr. Delaney, as you know," she said. "I am neither an urchin nor badly behaved. You caught me at something of a disadvantage this morning, but that is no longer the case."

In her sensible blue serge skirt and her prim white blouse, she felt armored against him. If the look on his face was anything to go by, he was unsure what to make of her. Julia took a certain grim pleasure in that. He was undoubtedly accustomed to women who were both beautiful and deferential. She was neither.

"I apologize, Miss Nash," he said gravely. "But I assure you my concern was sincere. As you appear to be unharmed, perhaps we could talk."

He was making it almost too easy for her. Julia smiled. "An excellent idea, Mr. Delaney. " She paused, struck by a problem she hadn't anticipated. Talk where?

Despite her appearance of being unharmed, her leg continued to ache. If she continued to stand much longer, it would worsen quickly. And if she tried to walk any distance, she would begin to limp.

She needed to sit down but there were few places a man and woman could go together without offending propriety or inviting speculation. Julia didn't care about either for her own sake, but she was considerate of her family's feelings.

The three boisterous saloons along Main Street were out of the question. Mrs. Carmichael's Tea Room was a possibility, but its proprietress was one of the biggest gossips in town. Julia was stymied until she glanced up the street and saw the solution to her difficulty.

"Have you seen our lovely church yet, Mr. Delaney?"

He shook his head. "I haven't."

"Then perhaps you would like to do so now." When he hesitated, she added, "It will be empty at this hour. We can talk undisturbed."

Understanding flitted across his chiseled features. He nodded. "Lead on, Miss Nash."

She was glad that he made no attempt to take her arm. Were he to touch her, she had no idea of how she would react. Better not to test the matter. So long as he kept his distance, she could maintain her cool, aloof pose.

They reached the church and went inside. It was a typical New England place of worship, elegantly simple in design, faced in white clapboard repainted each year by the congregation, and topped by a single steeple equipped with three magnificent bells to sing the faithful to services.

But, being typical, it was also reached by a flight of outside steps. Julia climbed them holding on to the railing. By the time she reached the top, she knew she'd been right not to try to walk any greater distance. Her leg hurt enough that she had to resist the urge to rub it.

Instead, she led the way inside. Sunlight filtered through the high windows, falling over neat rows of pews and a simple altar. The air was warm and smelled of beeswax and lemon oil. She breathed it in with pleasure, taking comfort in the familiar scent.

"Nice place," Brand said casually.

The church was not small; it served a growing, prosperous community. But his presence seemed to make it shrink. Julia was suddenly, vividly, aware of his size and nearness. Big men were not strangers to her. All the Nash men tended to be large, her father and brothers alike.

But Brand Delaney was somehow different. Perhaps it was as simple as his not being related to her, but more likely it had to do with the strange, disturbing feelings he had unleashed.

She sat down quickly in a back pew and stared straight ahead at the altar. Brand slid in beside her. She scooted far enough over that there was several feet of space between them.

Silence reigned. He showed no sign of ending it. Indeed, if the quick glance she dared was anything to go by, he seemed content to sit there all day. The church seemed to interest him. He appeared particularly drawn to the beams below the clock tower.

"They're very old," Julia said finally. She felt as though she were somehow losing by being the one to speak. But the silence was stretching out too long. She wanted this over and done with.

"How old?" he asked, turning to look at her. The expression in his dark eyes was unreadable.

"Almost two and a half centuries. This building was the first put up in Belle Haven. It served as the common hall, and was used as a fort during an Indian raid. Later, the tower was added and it became a church."

"There's an old house out on the point near the land I bought. Is that yours?"

She nodded. "My grandmother gave it to me. It was built for my ancestress, the woman who founded Belle Haven."

His slashing brows rose. "A woman?"

"That's right. She led the settlers. Her signature is on the founding documents. Belle Haven was her vision, and she made it a reality."

"I see," he said slowly. "Are you very like her?"

Julia almost laughed out loud at the notion. "Me? Not at all. Well, perhaps in one way. Amelia Daniels liked to collect plants, and so do I." She saw no reason to mention that Amelia had been a healer, as she was herself. "Other than that, we're very different."

"How so?"

He was persistent, wasn't he? Fine, if he wanted to know, she would tell him. But after that they would talk about the land.

"Amelia was very beautiful," she said. "Her husband was a sea captain who had no interest in a life on land until meeting her changed his mind."

Brand grinned. "Just like that?"

"Well, no, it took a while, but—"

"So she had to convince him?"

"She didn't even try. He came to it on his own. Anyway, that is hardly relevant now." She took a deep breath and steeled herself. "I would like to know what you plan to do with the land you have bought."

He stretched out as far as he could in the narrow pew and folded his hands across his broad chest. "For starters, I thought I'd chop down all the trees, slaughter any animals I can get my hands on, and burn out the underbrush."

Julia gasped. She turned on him in horror. "I knew it! I absolutely knew it! I tried to tell Sanders, but he wouldn't listen. Well, if you think for one moment that I'll let you get away with such a vile course of action, you—"

Without moving, still seemingly at his ease, Brand asked, "How did you know?"

"What do you mean?"

"Just what I asked. How did you know what I intended?"

"Because of who you are, that's how. Your reputation precedes you, Mr. Delaney. And believe me, it's nothing to be proud of!"

He turned then, suddenly, closing the small distance between them until she was squeezed against the divider between their pew and the next. His face was dark, and his eyes, a deep shade of green lit by shards of amber, gleamed ominously.

"Which reputation, Miss Nash? The one that says I'm an arrogant Irishman who won't bow to his betters? Or the one that has me a renegade Indian lusting after scalps? Or perhaps you prefer the version that calls me a half-breed, with the worst parts of Irish and Cherokee both? That, at least, has the virtue of being partly true."

Julia gasped. He spoke quietly, never raising his voice in the slightest, but the rage in him was unmistakable. So, too, was the pain.

"I didn't—"

"Of course you did," he said. "Your kind always does. Somehow the fact that your people got here first, and killed and pillaged to get anything they wanted, makes you better than everyone else. But it doesn't, Miss Nash, not by a long shot. Sooner or later, you're going to have to deal with my kind."

"And just what kind is that, Mr. Delaney?" she demanded. "Presumptuous men who presume the worst of others? For your information, I was referring to your reputation as a robber baron. If you're part Irish and part Cherokee, good for you. It sounds fascinating. But that doesn't give you the right to kill a piece of land and pillage it for whatever you happen to want. At least my ancestors knew better than to do that. They cared for this place."

He stared at her for a long moment. Though she quailed inwardly, Julia refused to look away. Now that she was aware of his dual heritage, she could see it stamped on his proud features. Sweet Lord, he was a handsome man, as well as a fiercely determined one. No wonder he was so accustomed to getting his own way. Who would have the nerve to deny him?

Julia Nash, that was who.

"If you try to do what you said," she informed him, "I will rally this town against you." Nothing in her tone even hinted at her fear that she wouldn't be able to make good on that threat. Boldly she said, "You'll be stopped, I promise."

To her surprise, not to say shock, he laughed. "I hate to disappoint you, Miss Nash, but what I intend to do is build a house. A rather nice one, actually, or at least it will be if the architect I've engaged has anything to say about it."

He looked at her wryly. "Charles reminds me a bit of you. He's also rather fanatical on the subject of not harming the land. Rest assured, he has nothing terrible in mind, and neither do I."

"Oh." She was taken aback, unsure of whether or not to believe him and embarrassed by her earlier outburst. He was right up to a point—she had made assumptions about him that weren't necessarily fair. Was it possible he truly meant no harm?

Quietly, he said, "Sooner or later, someone is going to make use of that property. You have to accept that. But the house I build will sit lightly on the land."

His smile deepened. It was really the most attractive smile she could remember ever seeing, and it made him look far more approachable. "You might say it's a family tradition. My Cherokee grandmother believed that people should move so lightly over the land as to leave no mark of their passing. I can't do quite that, but I won't despoil it, either."

"I'm sorry," Julia said softly. "It seems as though I have misjudged you." A great weight seemed to lift from her. Wisely or not, she was drawn to trust him.

He looked surprised. "Do you mean that?"

She nodded. "I could hardly say otherwise. It seems I needed a reminder that it is never wise to listen to rumors. But tell me, what made you decide on Belle Haven? I would think the city more to your liking."

He hesitated. She wondered if she had been too forward in asking. But at length he said, "I would appreciate your discretion, Miss Nash."

The fact that he thought her capable of such warmed Julia. "Of course," she assured him.

"I have decided that it is time for me to settle down."

"Settle—"

"There comes a point in a man's life when he realizes that all he has achieved and acquired amounts to nothing if he has no one to carry on after him."

"I see. . . ."

"Put simply, I intend to marry for the purpose of having children. However, as I said, I would appreciate it if you keep that to yourself."

Julia's stomach plummeted. She felt washed by alternating waves of hot and cold. With all the dignity she could muster, she said, "I assure you, Mr. Delaney, I won't breathe of word of it."

"Excellent." He stood and held out a hand to her. "I count you as a friend, Miss Nash."

Julia had no choice but to rise and take his hand. It was firm and hard, completely encompassing hers. An electric shock seemed to race up her arm. It took all she could not to yank her hand away.

"Friends," she said, and wondered how she would be able to bear it.

Chapter Three

"**Y**ou're jesting," John Nash said. He set down his evening newspaper to look at his wife. "Invite Brand Delaney? Why?"

"Well, for one thing," Heather Nash replied, "he's going to be a neighbor. He's buying the land next to Julia's."

John was genuinely surprised—testimony to the fact that he never listened to gossip. "He's what?"

"The land next to Daniels' Neck. He's buying it. He intends to build a house."

Her father glanced quickly in Julia's direction. They were all sitting in the parlor of the elder Nashes' country house, a pleasant, high-ceilinged room elegantly furnished with a collection of fine pieces, many of which had been in the family for generations.

It was the day after Julia's encounter with Brand. She had not mentioned it to anyone, and was grateful that her parents apparently knew nothing of it.

All the same, her mother was well-informed. As usual, Heather Nash had her finger on the pulse of everything that happened in Belle Haven. Yet Julia had never heard her say an unkind word about anyone, or known her to tolerate such talk in her presence. She was an unfailingly gentle and loving woman. Julia adored her sweet-tempered mother, even as she despaired of ever being like her.

"How do you feel about this?" her father asked.

"I wasn't very happy at first," Julia admitted, "but now I'm reconciled to it."

He looked surprised, but he said nothing.

"There you are," Heather said. "Julia has no objection. Simple good manners say he should be invited."

"I don't know about that," Julia's oldest brother, Peter, interjected. "The man's a brigand."

Before she could stop herself, Julia asked, "How do you know that?"

Peter shrugged. Like his father, he was long of limb and broad of shoulder, with hair almost as auburn as Julia's, but without the wayward curl. "Everyone knows it."

When she continued to look skeptical, he said, "You have only to ask any man on Wall Street. They will all tell you that his methods are the most ruthless."

"And the most effective, I gather," Julia said. A small voice in the back of her mind told her she should be silent, but she couldn't seem to heed it.

"Well, yes, I suppose there is that," Peter acknowledged.

"Is it possible that he may simply be smarter and more hardworking than the average investor?"

Peter's eyes narrowed. He studied his sister. "It sounds as though Brand Delaney has acquired a champion."

"Not at all," she said hastily. Heaven forbid that they believe that. "But I admit that I thought the worst of him at first, for no good reason. I simply wonder if others are doing the same."

"I don't know...." Peter said slowly. "It's true that I've never actually heard of him being linked to anything illegal."

"There you are, then."

"But that doesn't mean that he's one of nature's noblemen. He came up from nowhere to achieve a great deal very quickly. You don't do that by playing by the rules."

"Perhaps not all the rules are fair," Heather said quietly. "Besides, I'm merely suggesting that we include him in a party where there are going to be a good many other guests. Once you've said hello, you needn't have anything more to do with him if you don't wish to."

Peter grunted. Their father looked unconvinced, but he wasn't about to gainsay his wife. To the best of Julia's knowledge, John Nash had never knowingly denied Heather anything.

"Oh, very well," he said, "if you think it's proper."

Heather nodded and went back to her embroidery.

"Of course," Peter said, "he may decline to come."

Small chance of that, Julia thought. A man shopping for a wife—for the purpose of having children, no less—was hardly likely to refuse an invitation to what promised to be one of the most popular social events in Belle Haven. Brand Delaney would be there. And so would she.

Her stomach tightened. Above all, she would not make a fool of herself. She was a plain, prickly woman who preferred her independence. He was a handsome, virile man in search of, quite literally, a mate. So long as he did nothing to harm the land he was buying, she had no interest in him. Or he in her. They would go their separate ways.

But only figuratively. Circumstances would throw them together again and again. She had better get used to it, and what better place to start than her family's party?

Julia reached for her teacup. Her hand shook. She glanced around quickly to see if anyone had noticed. No one appeared to have.

Her mother was talking about who else to invite. Although the subject did not interest her at all, Julia did her best to listen.

"Tess Withers told me there's the most interesting young man in town," Heather said. "His name is Charles Hewlitt, and he's an architect."

"We could use one of them around here," John grumbled, "considering some of the monstrosities that are going up."

"Now, dear, don't be mean. There are those afflicted with more enthusiasm than taste."

"By all means invite this Hewlitt person," John said, discerning what his wife intended. "Perhaps he'll be a good influence."

"If the invitation list is still open," Julia said, "I'd like to suggest someone."

"Who?" Peter asked.

"Charlotte Hemper."

There was silence as her parents looked at one another. They both knew of Julia's friendship with the young shop clerk. While not disapproving of it, they would have preferred for her to spend more time with girls of her own background.

Still, they were glad to see her coming out of the shell she had kept pulled around her in the years since the accident. If she preferred Charlotte Hemper's company over that of others, they weren't going to complain.

"We'd be happy to invite Miss Hemper," Heather said. "If you're sure she wouldn't be uncomfortable."

"I don't see why she should be. She knows everyone."

Julia knew perfectly well that was a foolish remark. The fact that Charlotte knew everyone—or at least all the women—from having waited on them in Goody's Notions did not put her on the same social plane with them.

It was just that all such posturings seemed so inane, so foolish, and often simply cruel. Charlotte had worked desperately hard all her life. She deserved a chance to stop and enjoy more of the rewards.

"I'll see to it that she feels at ease," Julia promised.

Her mother hesitated a moment longer before she nodded. Heather Nash had never been a snob, but Julia knew she was the exception, not the rule. Others were far less generous.

She felt a momentary twinge of guilt, wondering if Charlotte would appreciate her presumption. But it was too late to worry. The deed was done. Besides, if she was honest, she would admit that she wanted Charlotte to come in part because she needed an ally.

Only in part, though, as she was at pains to make clear when she stopped by Goody's later that day to tell Charlotte about the party.

"Me," her friend said incredulously, "at a posh Nash bash? For heaven's sake, girl, what were you thinking of?"

"Myself," Julia admitted, "but only a little. I really think you'd enjoy it."

Charlotte looked at her in frank disbelief. "What could possibly have given you that idea?"

"Why not? You're certainly presentable enough, and you can't tell me that you wouldn't like to get out and meet more people."

Charlotte hesitated. A look of wistfulness flashed across her strong, clear features. "I'd like to be able to fly, too, but the real world doesn't work that way. I'm a shop girl, and, to most folks around here, a foreigner. They won't be lining up to socialize with me."

"Then that's their loss." Julia smiled. Shamelessly she bid what she knew to be her trump card. "Peter will be there."

Charlotte's milk white skin flamed. Her wide chocolate brown eyes flashed. "And what's that supposed to mean to me?"

"Why nothing, of course. I just thought you liked Peter... a little."

"I hardly know him." Peter, dutiful brother that he was, had stopped in at Goody's once or twice to pick up orders for his sisters.

Charlotte had spoken of him, in the careful way a young woman will when she doesn't want anyone to know the extent of her interest. Julia sympathized with her, all the more so now that she had some personal insight into the problem. But, unlike her, Charlotte was genuinely pretty. And she had a good heart to match her good sense. Peter could do a whole lot worse.

He probably would, too, Julia thought, if the few comments she'd overheard him make about women were anything to go by. He seemed to have the usual infatuation with fluffy blond helplessness.

How that was supposed to tally with a woman being a helpmate and a mother, Julia had never managed to figure out. Nor was she about to ask. She would put Charlotte and Peter together in the same place at the same time. Nature could then take its course, or not, as fate decreed.

"You'll have a good time," Julia promised gently.

Charlotte looked doubtful, but willing to be persuaded. "I haven't got anything to wear."

"Yes, you do. I've got a dozen dresses that don't suit me at all but would suit you perfectly. Most of them have never even been worn. You can take your pick."

Charlotte blinked hard. "You're a good one, Julia Nash."

"Come on by when the shop closes. We'll pick something out."

Julia went on her way a short time later, convinced that she had done the right thing. Charlotte would shine at the party, and perhaps, just perhaps, Peter would have his eyes opened. Or perhaps—

She froze at the sudden thought that it might not be her brother who found the pretty, resolute young woman appealing. Brand Delaney just might decide she was exactly what he was looking for.

Well, too bad for him if he did. Charlotte would never be so foolish as to involve herself with a man who was interested in her solely as a brood mare.

Would she?

Julia refused to think about that. She bicycled home, going slowly of necessity, and got busy going through her closets to find the perfect dress for Charlotte. Doing something for someone else made her feel obscurely better about herself.

But as the day faded and twilight settled over the house, she wandered over to the window and looked out in the direction of Brand Delaney's land.

Brand Delaney's land. She had to start thinking of it that way. If he was true to his word, Delaney roots were going to sink deep. Her gaze wandered down the beach. Was he out there, surveying his domain and making his plans? Or perhaps he was swimming, as he had been when she first saw him.

The thought made muscles deep within her tighten. She groaned and turned away from the window, back into the safety of Amelia's house.

Brand stared at the invitation in his hand. It was penned in graceful calligraphy on a heavy cream-colored paper.

"The pleasure of your company...an evening musicale... The Nashes, Greenstead."

Where was Greenstead? Somewhere in backcountry Belle Haven no doubt, one of those sprawling places with a big house and lots of horses. He'd be able to find out easily enough.

A more interesting question was why the Nashes had decided that his company would be a pleasure.

If he read the situation correctly, and he was certain that he did, they were as old-line Belle Haven as old-line could be. His experience with such people in New York did not indicate an eagerness for his company for its own sake.

His social calendar in the city was as full as he cared to make it, but only because polite society there could no longer afford to ignore him. He simply had become too wealthy and powerful to exclude.

He presumed it was the same in Belle Haven, and was only mildly surprised that word had gotten around so soon. Briefly he considered the possibility that Julia—no, not Julia, Miss Nash—had put her parents up to inviting him.

But he dismissed that possibility as firmly as he reminded himself not to think of her by her first name. She was—and had made it clear that she intended to remain— Miss Nash.

Fingering the invitation, Brand considered whether or not to refuse. Ordinarily he found such events tedious, and avoided them as much as he could. But he had resolved to find a wife, and that goal would not be served by his becoming a hermit.

He scrawled a quick acceptance and set it aside with the rest of the day's outgoing mail, then turned his attention back to the accounts that required his study.

It was more difficult doing business while away from the city, but he found that he could manage. Correspondence was messengered up to him twice a day, and taken back the same way. And, of course, there was the telephone. Many men in his position refused to use it, delegating that task to secretaries. But Brand liked being able to speak directly with anyone he chose, or at least anyone who was also connected to the new but rapidly growing system.

Having concluded his business for the moment, he took a quick glance at the stock ticker he'd had installed. The companies whose stock he currently held all appeared to be doing well.

He noted without surprise that a firm he had pulled out of the week before was on a steep downslide. Initially he'd believed the company's outlook was strong and invested heavily. But the previous week, he had come into possession of information that caused him to change his mind.

With his usual decisiveness, he had sold all his shares. Belatedly, others were following, but most were too late to avoid being caught as the stock plummeted. He spared a brief thought for those who might be taking serious losses, then turned his mind elsewhere.

Wall Street seemed refreshingly far away when he finished and wandered out onto the porch for a breath of fresh air. Charles Hewlitt was coming up the walk toward the house Brand was renting while his own was built. He waved a roll of papers triumphantly.

"We've been approved," he said as he bounded onto the porch. At twenty-five, he was ten years younger than Brand. He was fresh-faced and eager to be at work on his first truly significant commission. Brand had chosen Charles after he was fired from the prestigious New York architectural firm where his father had gotten him work.

It seemed that young Hewlitt had radical notions about houses that were less ostentatious showcases for their owners and more harmonious additions to the landscape. Tossed out in disgrace and despairing of ever making a place for himself in his chosen profession, Charles had chosen to drown his sorrows at a popular watering hole.

Brand smiled as he remembered that the young man had proven as inept at the consumption of spirits as he had at behaving deferentially with stick-in-the-mud senior partners. Involved in not one but two fistfights, he had staggered straight into Brand, knocking his drink directly into his face.

That had been enough to bring a near-reverential hush over the bar. Such was Brand's reputation that the patrons had presumed they were about to see the hapless Hewlitt vanish in a flash of brimstone.

Charles must have caught a whiff of the same. Bruised, battered, and in a thoroughly bad mood, he'd put up his fists and advanced on Brand with a combination of resignation and bulldog determination.

Brand still remembered his astonishment. He hadn't been able to decide whether the furious young man was crazy with drink or inordinately brave.

Drink had had the edge. Brand had waited until Hewlitt was almost upon him, and then he'd sidestepped, leaving the younger man to crash into the side of the bar.

Charles had given one long groan and collapsed. Brand had glanced around at the bar crowd and sighed. Then he'd hoisted the hapless Hewlitt up by his belt and carted him out of the place.

That had been the beginning of an unlikely friendship. The rebellious scion of a wealthy family and the hardscrabble survivor turned ruthless financier had found their common ground in the vision of a house rising beside the shore, at one with the sea and the land.

Charles slapped the plans down on the porch table and grinned hugely. "No changes at all. The town council took it exactly as is."

"That's fine, then," Brand said. He didn't add that the council had a powerful incentive for not making trouble. Or they did if they wanted the new hospital he'd developed a sudden yen to build. There was nothing to say it had to go up in Belle Haven, only that it would if Brand found the community congenial. So far he had to admit that he did.

"When are you thinking to begin?" he asked as he and Charles sat down in the high-backed wicker chairs on the porch.

"Immediately. I've spoken with several builders in the area, and I think I've identified the best. If you're agreeable, we can go out for bids tomorrow."

Brand nodded. He was not inclined to delay. The sooner his house was built, the sooner he'd have a place to put those children he intended to sire. He had a sudden, startling image of them running, brown-legged and laughing, along the beach by Daniels' Neck. The vision was so real that his breath caught. He shook his head hard to clear it.

"Something wrong?" Charles asked.

"Not at all. Set a deadline for the bids, a week from tomorrow."

"That's scant time."

"Enough for a builder who really knows what he's doing."

Charles nodded. "Fair enough." He hesitated a moment before asking, "Will you be staying on?"

"I hadn't intended to," Brand admitted. He had envisioned using the house on weekends and remaining in the city the rest of the time, but now he was reconsidering. It was very pleasant here and, besides, he liked the idea of being able to keep a closer eye on the work once it began.

"I'll be back and forth," he said finally. "Have you found lodging?"

"An excellent inn, belongs to a family named Fletcher. By the way, they've been telling me some fascinating things."

"Such as?"

"That house down the beach from you—did you know it belonged to a witch?"

Brand's head shot up. Charles was grinning. "What are you talking about?" Brand demanded.

"Her name was Amelia Daniels Marlowe. She founded Belle Haven. No mean feat in itself, but I gather she also had something of a reputation for wading in where others feared to dip a toe. She was renowned as a healer and general wisewoman. The Fletchers still speak quite proudly of her."

Brand relaxed slightly. It wasn't Julia—Miss Nash—he was speaking of, but then, how could he possibly be? The word *witch,* so laden with superstition and agony, was seldom even mentioned in this more enlightened age. It was regarded as no more than an amusing relic of a benighted time.

"Fascinating," he muttered.

"Oh, that's not all. Her descendants, especially the female ones, seem to be distinguished by fiery independence and a habit of getting into trouble of all sorts. I gather they've kept Belle Haven enlivened for generations."

"And do they still?" Brand asked, trying not to sound as interested as he felt.

"That's hard to say. The current line rests with the Nashes. By the way, are you going to their musicale?"

"I suppose."

"Excellent. So am I. Now, as I was saying, the Nashes have three daughters, Daphne, Gloria, and Julia. The first two are apparently models of good behavior, but Miss Julia's a different story."

He could shrug and change the subject, Brand thought. Or he could give in to his curiosity.

He gave in. "How so?"

"She was always the high-spirited one who was forever getting into mischief, alternating delighting her parents or driving them to despair. But she's changed."

"Why do you say that?"

"I don't. The Fletchers do."

Brand closed his eyes. He was going to be patient. "Why do the Fletchers say that?"

"She had a rather bad accident six years ago. Took a terrible fall while riding. The horse had to be put down, and the young woman herself was never expected to walk again. She proved the doctors wrong, but her spirit was never the same. The Fletchers seem resigned to there being no worthy descendant of the marvelous Amelia in this generation."

"I wouldn't be too sure about that," Brand murmured, thinking of the hoyden he had seen on the road, bravely denying the need for help, and the young woman who, with equal courage, had confronted him about his plans for the land. Julia Nash might seem to have been subdued by her trials, but he suspected her strength had simply been channeled in different directions.

A servant appeared at the door to inquire whether the gentlemen would like refreshment. Charles bounded up. "I hope you don't think me rude, but I'm anxious to get started."

Brand laughed. He appreciated the younger man's enthusiasm, and told him so.

"I've never had a commission like this," Charles said. "Heck, you already know that, but it's just beginning to really dawn on me." Almost shyly, he added, "This is really a special place, isn't it?"

Brand shrugged. "It's a place. There are many as beautiful."

"I suppose." Charles appeared unconvinced. He went on his way a few moments later.

Brand was left to wonder why he had lied about his own reaction to Belle Haven. Like it or not, he, too, was becoming convinced that it was somehow unusual.

It was only an impression, elusive, teasing, and in all likelihood wrong. Yet it continued to drift lightly through his mind as he sat on the porch, enjoying a rare interlude of relaxation, and watched the setting sun turn the sky to fire.

Chapter Four

"I don't understand you," Daphne said in exasperation. "You've got lots of pretty clothes. Why won't you wear them?"

"Because I don't feel like it," Julia said. They had been arguing for a quarter of an hour, ever since her sisters had walked into Julia's old bedroom in their parents' house and seen what she had put on for the party.

Daphne was in white, the perfect foil for her rich russet hair and angelic features. Gloria, the middle sister, was in peach, perfectly suited to her more refined and elegant beauty. They both looked like what their father always called them—his flowers.

John Nash was always careful to include Julia in that, and she appreciated it. But his loving kindness didn't make any difference. If Daphne and Gloria were the flowers, she was a straggly weed.

Julia grimaced. Her thought was perilously close to self-pity, something she absolutely could not bear. But the disagreement with her sisters was straining her nerves and making her respond more sharply than she would have ordinarily.

"What I wear is my business," she said, "not yours." At their quick look of dismay, she was immediately contrite.

Daphne and Gloria were the best of sisters, loving, considerate, a pleasure to be with it. She loved them dearly, but she was not like them, and no amount of wishing would change that.

Gloria studied the pale gray dress Julia was wearing and sighed. "It's not the dress that's so bad. It's too old for you, but aside from that, it's rather elegant. Or it would be, if the color weren't so drab."

"I prefer to think that the color is also elegant."

"Come on, Daph," Gloria said. "What Julia wants is for us to get out of her hair." She gave Julia an apologetic smile. "We'll see you downstairs."

Julia nodded. She felt bad about rejecting her sisters' help, but she was also grateful to Gloria for her understanding. This evening would be difficult enough for her. She had to face it in her own way.

A short time later, Julia left the room and went down the curving wooden staircase to the main floor. The house was alight from one end to the other.

More and more of the prosperous families of Belle Haven were installing electricity, proud of the fact that their community was one of the first to acquire this most modern convenience. Julia had to admit that it made an astounding difference, virtually banishing night.

But she felt a lingering fondness for the soft glow of the oil lamps that still lit Amelia's house. Perhaps it, too, would someday be electrified. The thought amused her. She was smiling as she crossed the entry hall to join her parents and the rest of the family.

Pride warmed her. They were an impressive group, her father and Peter tall and strong, her mother and sisters beautiful and graceful. To her delight, even her grandmother Sara was there, looking lovely in a gown of pale mauve. She held out a hand to Julia as she approached.

"There you are, dear. What a delightful evening we're going to have."

Julia covered the elderly woman's gnarled hand with her own and smiled. Sara was sitting down, of course, and would continue to do as the guests were received. But she was looking much better than she had recently, with color in her cheeks and a bright light in her wise eyes. Julia wished she shared her grandmother's confidence about the evening but she wouldn't have dreamed of saying so. Instead, she said, "I'm sure we will, Gramma."

The hour that followed passed largely in a blur as the guests arrived in a steady stream. Julia was determined to remain standing throughout. It was a point of pride to her to make it seem as though she were completely recovered. In fact, she was not, and inevitably her leg began to hurt. She ignored it and kept smiling.

Most of the people arriving were well-known to her, but there were also unfamiliar faces, reflective of the many new arrivals coming into the community. One of these belonged to a cheerful young man who introduced himself as Charles Hewlitt, architect.

"Very kind of you to invite me," he told the elder Nashes.

"Not at all," John Nash replied. "I believe you know my cousin Daniel's boy, William."

"Why, I do. We were at school together."

"There you are, I thought so. Let me get done with this and we'll have a drink together."

Charles nodded pleasantly, offered his greetings to the younger Nashes and went on eagerly into the ballroom. Charlotte arrived not long after that. She was wearing the rich blue dress Julia had pressed on her, and her hair was upswept in curls not unlike Daphne's. But she was pale and looked very anxious.

Julia squeezed her hand reassuringly. "You look beautiful," she said, and meant it. There was something different about Charlotte now that she was free of her drab, sensible clothes and her workaday existence. She moved with grace and dignity, and when she spoke her voice was soft and melodic.

"I'm scared to death," she whispered, gripping Julia's hands.

"Nonsense," Julia said firmly. No woman so beautiful and so gifted could possibly be scared. Turning to her brother, she said clearly, "Peter, dear, you remember Miss Charlotte Hemper."

Peter started to nod politely, then stopped. He stared at Charlotte as though he had never seen her before. "I think I do...."

"Good," Julia said. "As most of the guests have arrived, I wonder if you would be so kind as to take Miss Hemper in. She hasn't been here before, and I would hate for her to lose her way."

This was patently absurd, as no one could possibly miss the ballroom. But Peter seemed to take the risk seriously.

"Of course I will." He offered his arm.

Charlotte looked torn between dismay and delight. She shot Julia a glance that promised there would be more said about this later, and carefully laid her hand on Peter's arm. He smiled at her. Tentatively she smiled back.

Julia felt her evening had been well spent. She could happily have withdrawn right then, curled up with a good book, and not thought she had missed anything. But in the next moment she realized she would have.

There was a flutter near the door, and several heads turned. Instinctively the people standing in the entry hall parted, clearing the way for a man who stood tall, powerful and elegantly garbed, his chiseled features composed but a slightly sardonic smile playing across his hard mouth.

Brand Delaney stepped forward. He moved with lithe ease and offered his hand to John Nash. The two men regarded each other silently for a moment. They were of a height, and similar in build, but the elder Nash clearly wore the mark of a civilized man, whereas on Brand the veneer of civilization touched only lightly.

"Mr. Delaney," John Nash said. "You are welcome."

A brief look of surprise flitted behind Brand's eyes. Julia had the impression that he was not necessarily accustomed to such graciousness. "Thank you," he said gravely, and shifted his attention to his hostess. They exchanged a few words. Brand's smile softened. He laughed gently.

For Grandmother Nash, he bent and again offered his hand, cradling hers gently. They, too, spoke briefly. Again he smiled.

Daphne nudged Gloria. They tilted their heads together and shared a quick whisper.

"Welcome," Gloria said, echoing their father.

"Most welcome," Daphne corrected.

"Ladies," he said, and turned to Julia.

"Miss Nash."

"Mr. Delaney."

Why didn't he move on, instead of standing there looking at her? If he must look, shouldn't it be at Daphne or Gloria, both of whom had managed to make it clear that they wouldn't mind?

Indeed, Julia couldn't remember her sisters ever being quite so bold. But perhaps she simply hadn't been paying attention. They had both been growing up while she struggled to overcome the effects of her accident. Although she still tended to think of them as little girls, they were anything but.

"I hope you will have a pleasant evening," she said at length.

"I'm sure I will." Finally, just when she thought she could bear it no longer, he inclined his head again and turned toward the ballroom. Several more guests arrived after that, but Julia scarcely noticed them. She could think of nothing except Brand Delaney, and her almost desperate wish that the evening would soon be over.

* * *

He was dancing again, but who with this time? Oh, yes, Genevieve Halsted. Julia remembered her as a particularly obnoxious little creature when they were both attending the Belle Haven Academy for Young Women, and she didn't seem to have changed. She was positively simpering, and looked as though at any moment she would throw back her head and crow.

All because the most handsome—except, of course, for Julia's brother, Peter—the most compelling, and quite possibly the most dangerous, man in the room was dancing with her. Not only that, he was being unbearably gracious, almost like a great wild beast that had somehow been tamed.

Julia shut her eyes to the spectacle, thoroughly disgusted. When she opened them again a moment later, she forced herself to admit that Brand really didn't look all that happy. His brows were knit, and he appeared to be keeping his temper firmly in check.

Surely Genevieve could see that, or at least sense it? Didn't she realize she was trying the man's patience to death with her incessant chatter? No, apparently she didn't, for she was off again, giggling and batting her eyes at him to boot.

"Plus ça change," Gramma Sara murmured.

"What?" Julia asked.

"Only that the more things change, the more they seem to remain the same," her gramma explained. "Young women, for example. They haven't changed at all since my day, for all this talk lately of emancipation and so on."

"Emancipation is a fine idea," Julia said. "The sooner the better."

"Undoubtedly, but the point stands. Nothing changes."

"Genevieve Halsted is an idiot."

"No, she isn't," Sara said. "She is simply insensitive. She thinks he likes her, because she desperately wants him to and because he's being polite. But she's wrong. She is boring him to extraction."

"Why should she care?" Julia demanded. From where she sat beside her grandmother, they both had a clear view of the ballroom.

The supper repast had been served, and the dancing was well under way. The evening was going swimmingly, with all the guests seeming to have a wonderful time for themselves, especially those young women who had partnered Brand Delaney.

"Because of who he is, of course," Sara said. "There have always been women who regard wealthy, powerful men as a trophy worth the winning. Genevieve is no exception."

"He's a person, not a trophy."

"You know that, and presumably he does, as well. But it has escaped dear Miss Halsted. Oh, look, he's taking her back."

"Thank God," Julia muttered. She was being unreasonable and knew it, but couldn't seem to help herself. The spectacle of Brand dancing with one woman after another had done nothing for her spirits.

At least Peter and Charlotte seemed to have hit it off. They had danced together several times—not so much as to arouse comment, but enough to make it clear that they preferred each other's company.

Charlotte had also danced with several other young men while Peter stood on the sidelines, glaring at them. She had a dazed, delighted look on her face, and she took every opportunity to smile in Julia's direction.

Her friend's happiness eased her own discontent, but couldn't completely erase it. She was so out of sorts that she barely noticed the aching in her leg.

"Oh, look," Sara murmured. "Daphne doesn't seem to know what to make of it all."

Julia looked in the direction her grandmother was gazing and saw her youngest sister dancing with Brand. Daphne was an excellent dancer, and she liked nothing better than to dance. But she appeared somewhat intimidated by the big, dark man, whose broad shoulders and massive chest made her seem as fragile as a china doll.

Not that she didn't seem to like him; she did. But it was the liking she would have had for a majestic stallion or a great, soaring eagle, a magnificent work of nature she would have preferred to observe from a distance, Julia thought.

"Twit," Julia muttered.

"She's your sister," Sara said reproachfully.

"I know, I'm sorry." Indeed, she was horrified by what she had said. Daphne was the furthest thing from a twit, and it was horribly unfair to her to suggest otherwise.

"She seems to be relaxing a little," Sara commented.

So she did, but only because Brand was obviously doing his level best to win her over. In a moment, he had her smiling and quickly, after that, laughing.

Julia sighed. Was there a woman he couldn't charm—besides herself, of course? Evidently not.

The ladies of Belle Haven seemed to be bending over backward to impress Mr. Brand Delaney. Even the worst snobs, who might have been expected to look down their noses at him, had clearly decided that his riches excused any deficiencies in his bloodline.

Not that any such deficiencies were evident. He was very much in his element, completely in command, exactly as though he had been born to such events and had attended them all his life.

Or at least long enough to have become thoroughly bored with them, for, try though he did, Brand could not hide the fact that the occasion was wearing on him.

At least he couldn't hide it from Julia. She continued to observe him surreptitiously while chatting with her grandmother and others. So cleverly did she go about it that she was quite confident he did not have any idea she was watching him.

On that score, at least, she was quite wrong. But she was right about the rest. Brand smiled yet again, and told himself this was all in a good cause. Men of position and wealth went through this sort of thing all the time in order to find appropriate wives.

Ruefully Brand thought how much more practical it would be if he could simply buy one. Society, in its infinite wisdom, decreed that impossible. Until it decided otherwise, he was left with little choice. But, sweet Lord, did every woman he encountered have to be so tiresome? Not the Nash girls, he amended. Daphne was a sweet thing, and Gloria actually had an engaging wit. His host and hostess themselves were genuinely pleasant, for all that John Nash remained understandably cautious. But as for the rest—

She was watching him again, exactly as she had been all evening. He didn't know whether to be amused or annoyed. Judging by her expression, she thought she was being clever about it.

But he was acutely conscious of Julia Nash at all times. Every flick of her head, every soft laugh or fragment of overheard conversation, drew him. He had thought several times about asking her to dance, but Charles's information about the injury she had suffered, and her seeming disinclination to join in, stopped him. Above all, he didn't want to do anything to embarrass or hurt her.

That was unusual for him. He didn't generally spend a great deal of time thinking about the feelings of others. Life worked out far better for him when he simply did as he wished.

But not this time. Tempted though he was, he was also quite certain that she would refuse. The elusive Miss Nash was standoffish enough, without his giving her even more reason to be that way.

With a sigh, he resigned himself to yet another turn around the floor with a proper young woman. Sweet Lord, but they were boring. He'd had little time for women in his life, beyond the obvious physical need, but he'd always thought of them as at least vaguely interesting. In particular, he admired the way they faced life in a world that kept them at a perpetual disadvantage.

These women were different, sweetly simpering beings who, with few exceptions, seemed without a thought in their perfectly coiffed heads.

Could he tolerate marriage to one of these...these mannequins? For the first time, it occurred to Brand that his grand plan might have a few holes in it, chiefly his own inability to tolerate the woman he expected to give him children.

Still, what was the alternative? He was determined that his own offspring would grow up in an environment totally different from that which he had known, not spoiled, but with all the material benefits he could reasonably give them. Above all, they would never be cold or hungry or afraid. He would make absolutely sure of that.

Once he found the right woman. She needed to be attractive, cultured, demure, devoted to home and hearth, and content to dwell in the domestic realm while he went out into the larger world.

All things considered, he didn't think that was asking too much. In return, she would have security, wealth, position, and the pleasure of his own company—when he could spare it.

All in all, he thought, any sensible woman would be happy to accept such an arrangement. As long as he could steel himself to the inevitable tedium of it, he ought to be able to wrap up this marriage business promptly. By the time his house was ready, he fully intended to have an occupant for its nursery on the way.

He was a man of action who was well accustomed to accomplishing anything he set out to do. Not for a moment did it occur to him that wooing and winning a woman would be any different. Indeed, wooing never entered into his thoughts. Marriage, so far as he was concerned, was just one more form of business arrangement. There was no need to surround it with all the mystique and foolishness some seemed to think appropriate.

Still, all this being polite to boring women was taking a toll on him. He needed a respite.

Slipping into the garden, Brand walked a short distance from the house. He leaned back comfortably against an old oak tree and lit a cheroot.

The sky above was clear. He could make out Orion, the hunter chasing his prey across the endless fields of heaven, and there the mother bear and her cub prowling the night.

When he was a child, the stars had often been his refuge. He had woven his own stories to match the shapes he found in them, only much later discovering that others who had gone before him had done the same.

Behind him, the party went on. He knew he should return, out of courtesy to his host and for the sake of his search. But he could not quite bring himself to leave the fresh, sea-scented quiet of the garden. The cheroot glowed red in the night as he resolved to stay just a little while more.

Chapter Five

Sara had grown weary. Julia saw her upstairs to her room and helped her to remove her gown. When her grandmother was comfortably abed, they chatted for a few minutes before the elderly woman drifted off to sleep.

Slowly Julia left the room and went downstairs again. She was not eager to return to the party, but neither did she wish any longer to retire.

Her thoughts were in turmoil, and her emotions didn't seem to be very far behind. If she tried to read, she doubted she would be able to make sense of the words on the page. As for sleep, she did not feel at all tired, and she dreaded tossing and turning without relief.

That left the garden. She had practically grown up in it, seeking its wonders in every season and at all hours of the day and night. It was there that she had planted her first herbs and tended them. And there she had always gone when she needed to find a special kind of peace.

These days she found peace even more at Amelia's house, but that was miles distant. She wouldn't return there until the following morning. Meanwhile, the garden beckoned.

It was very peaceful. She could hear the sounds of the party drifting out through the high French windows beside the stone terrace. But they faded as she walked a short distance along one of the many gravel paths.

The night wrapped around her. Immediately she felt more relaxed. Breathing in the cool air cleared her head. Her leg no longer hurt, and her spirits lifted.

Up ahead was a small grotto, home to pale birch trees and wild rosebushes. It had always been one of her favorite parts of the garden. Immediately before it was a large oak tree, centuries old, where she had climbed as a child to survey her world.

Something flared beside the tree, a spark. She stopped, unsure of what she had seen. A shadow moved, coming away from the broad trunk. Soft as the velvet night itself, a deep voice said, "Hello, Julia."

She froze, straining her eyes into the darkness, yet already knowing who she would see. Brand. Here, in her garden, shattering the solitude she had counted on to protect her.

Julia took a quick step backward. Just as quickly, he stepped forward. Moonlight fell across his hard features.

"Don't go."

Instinctively she stopped. Not for a moment could she have said why. Indeed, the action was completely contradictory to her nature. But with this man, all habit and custom seemed no longer to exist.

"Are you enjoying the party?" he asked.

Was she? No, in truth she was not. But here in the garden, with him, she felt a sudden, tingling burst of pleasure that amazed her. "Well enough," she said, not even sure what words she spoke. "And you?"

He smiled. "Well enough. Still, I prefer being here."

"So do I," Julia admitted. "Not that the party isn't very nice," she added hastily. "It's only that the best of such events can wear after a while."

"Exactly. You know, I realized standing here that I know nothing at all about gardens, but this one seems unusually appealing. Would you care to show me around it?"

Julia hesitated. Reason told her that absolutely the last thing she should be doing was wandering around a garden at night with Brand Delaney. On the other hand, she had never had the opportunity to do anything of that sort with any man, much less one who drew her as he did.

Immediately she pushed such a foolish thought aside. It was the garden that interested him, nothing more. Perhaps he was thinking of what he would have done around his house.

As a neighbor, she could hardly refuse her help.

"I would be glad to," she said very properly.

They began in the Dutch garden, where thousands of tulips dozed, their petals closed until morning. "I'm not sure who planted the first of them," Julia said, "but every year when I was growing up we planted more. I still remember the excitement when the bulbs arrived from Holland every fall. We would race to plant them before it became too cold and dreary to work, then all winter and spring we would wait for them to bloom."

She pointed to a pie-shaped bed that even in the moonlight shone with the hues of yellow and gold. "This is Gloria's. In daylight, you can see how the different shades flow into one another. It's really quite beautiful."

"Lovely. What about this one over here?"

Julia laughed as she saw where he was pointing. That bed was a riot of reds and pinks, planted in no particular order, but appealing all the same. "That's Daphne's. Mother tried to talk her into doing something a bit more formal, but she wouldn't hear of it."

"Good for Daphne. What about yours?"

"Mine? Oh, I just helped the others."

"You didn't want your own?"

Julia shook her head. "I was more interested in herbs."

"What for?"

She hesitated, reluctant to say too much. There were those who even in this day and age had unfortunate ideas about such things. "Cooking," she said finally, "soaps, creams, a few other uses." Only thousands of them, but she was not inclined to go into that just now.

"Perhaps I should plant a few around Summercove."

"Where?"

He smiled, a little self-consciously. "That's what I mean to call the house."

"Summercove," Julia repeated. "That's lovely."

"I don't mean to only use it in the summer, of course. But this is when I first saw the land, and I suspect it will always make me think of this season."

He had poetry in him, this hard man who had climbed his way up from nothing. There might even be a romantic streak he would no doubt do his utmost to conceal. Or she might simply be imagining it all. There was nothing unusual about naming a house, and people were always full of suggestions about how to do it. Charles Hewlitt might have come up with the name, or someone else she didn't know about.

"Is there a herb garden here?" he asked.

She allowed as how there was. They walked a short distance along the path, past a fountain that gurgled softly in the night.

"When I was a child," Julia said quietly, "I imagined this was an enchanted place populated by fairies and elves. I was convinced that if only I looked hard enough, I would see them."

"It's more of a pookah sort of place."

"A what?"

"Pookah. You've never heard of them?" He sounded surprised, as though he wouldn't have suspected her of such a vocabulary deficiency.

"I'm afraid not," Julia said, a smile in her voice. "What are they?"

"Oh, they can be many things. Mainly they're invisible."

"Convenient."

"Not always. It can make it hard for them to communicate when they want to."

"How big are they?"

"It varies—an inch or so, or ten feet, depending on the pookah."

"Are they dangerous?" she asked with mock seriousness. This was a side of him she would never have suspected—fey, even a little silly. Beguiling.

"Only if you aren't friendly," he replied. "But you are, aren't you?"

"I shall make it a particular point to be friendly to all pookahs I encounter."

"That's probably the best course."

"Do you think there will be pookahs at Summercove?"

He considered that. "I'd like to think so. Is this the herb garden?"

She nodded. They had come upon the part of the garden she had cared for. Since leaving her parents' house, she had been relieved to see that several of the older servants had taken over caring for the plants. There was an extensive selection, many brought as seedlings from Europe, others nurtured through generations in Belle Haven.

Julia pointed to a bed of chamomile. "These are the descendants of plants grown from seeds brought by the first settlers in these parts. Many of the other specimens are the same. I've taken cuttings from most of them to plant around Amelia's house."

She was restoring the old herb garden there, the one Amelia herself had begun but Sara had, sadly, had to let go somewhat. In another season or two, it would be fully renewed.

"I can't imagine what it's like to have such a sense of heritage," Brand said. He stared at the rows of plants disappearing off into the darkness. The night air was alive with tantalizing scents—thyme and sage, feverwort and comfrey.

"I can't imagine what it's like to be without it," Julia replied gently. Daring greatly, she asked, "Did you know your parents?"

He cast her a quick, hard look. She thought he wouldn't answer, and was about to apologize for being so presumptuous when he said, "I knew my mother. My father died before I was born."

"How dreadful." Her dismay was sincere. "What happened?"

"Several men with guns," Brand said dryly. "They disliked the notion of a Cherokee marrying a white woman, and killed him for it. Never mind that once they had widowed her, my mother's well-being concerned them no longer. She was left to survive as best she could, as was I."

No wonder he was so hard, Julia thought. Any person born under such circumstances would be either hardened by them or destroyed.

"What did your mother do?" she asked, knowing she probably shouldn't, but unable to stop herself. She wanted to know all about him, to understand him as completely as she possibly could.

Brand dropped what was left of the cheroot on the gravel path and crushed it under his boot. Without expression, he said, "She whored."

Julia gasped. She thought at first that he was making a dreadful joke, but one look at his face was enough to tell her he was not.

There was nothing she could say, absolutely no response she could make. But he was waiting, daring her to make some polite reply.

So be it. If he expected her to utter some conventional platitude, he was going to be disappointed.

"Very wise of her. Things being as they are, there are few other ways for a woman to earn an adequate living when she has a child to support. I presume this arrangement allowed her to care for you during the day?''

Brand stared at her bemusedly. "As a matter of fact, it did.''

"And to keep a roof over your head, food on the table?''

"That, too. She even managed to send me to school."

"As I said, very wise. Infuriating, of course, for no woman should be forced to make such a choice. Someday the world will be different, when we can vote and run our own businesses, earn a fair income for our labors. But that's a ways off yet, I fear.''

"Odd that you should say that.''

"Why?''

"My mother says the same.''

"She's still alive, then?'' Julia was relieved to hear it. She hated to think of him being completely alone.

"Very much so.''

"What does she think of your moving here?''

"She doesn't know yet.''

"Undoubtedly she will approve.''

"Hmm . . . we'll see.'' He sounded as though he did not share Julia's conviction. Quietly, into the darkness, he said, "You are a surprisingly easy woman to talk with.''

"Do you really think so? Most people would disagree.''

"Why?''

"I suppose they regard me as different . . . and therefore difficult.''

He laughed, as though that amused him greatly. "I know what that's like. Tell me . . .''

She held her breath, suddenly aware that he was much nearer than he had been. He hesitated, clearly undecided. But then his hands brushed her shoulders.

"Do you like being different, Julia? Does it frighten you?''

"Sometimes," she whispered. For instance, it frightened her now. A proper, sensible young woman would never have allowed herself to become involved in such a situation. Oh, it would be different if she were pretty, like Daphne, or elegant, like Gloria. If she had the confidence of knowing that men desired her. But she had no such thing, only the certain knowledge that if she wasn't very careful she was going to make a terrible fool of herself.

She had to step away, take her leave, go back to the party and the safety in numbers. But her feet seemed rooted to the ground. And all around her the garden was stirring in the night breeze.

"It shouldn't," Brand murmured. "I saw tonight how boring it can be when everyone is the same."

"I thought you were enjoying yourself," Julia said tremulously. His fingers were firm on her shoulders. She could feel each and every one of them, even though his touch remained light.

She could remove herself at any moment. All she had to do was make up her mind to walk away.

"No, you didn't."

She could hardly deny it. He had looked out of sorts to her. But why should he be? Surely those women in there were what he wanted—one of them, at least, to take her place beside him and produce the children he wanted.

Brand was staring at her. He seemed about to speak again, but evidently thought better of it. His gaze drifted to her lips, which were slightly parted in surprise. His head bent. For just a moment, she had the astounding thought that he was about to kiss her.

He straightened suddenly. A dull flush suffused his cheeks. Dropping his hands, he turned away slightly. "I'm sorry, I forgot myself."

Julia's eyes stung. She put a hand to her lips, trying to still their trembling. Embarrassment flowed through her, but she fought it down. As always, she found her refuge in pride. Quietly, her voice rock-steady, she said, "I suggest we return to the house."

Brand nodded. He walked beside her down the gravel path, but he did not speak. Nor did he make any attempt to touch her again.

"Are you sure you won't stay longer?" Heather Nash asked her daughter. It was the day after the party. The family was gathered over breakfast in the sunny morning parlor at the back of the house.

Julia shook her head. She understood her mother's concern. Heather had never really reconciled herself to Julia's living on her own. But the sooner she was back under her own roof, the better off she would be.

The strain of keeping up appearances, of pretending that nothing was wrong, was becoming too much for her. She wanted only to creep off by herself to hide the pain that during the night had only grown worse. She wished that Brand Delaney had never come to Belle Haven. Before his coming, she at least had been able to pretend that her life suited her.

Now that was no longer possible. She had stood too close to him, heard his laughter and his dreams, been touched by him. She would never be able to pretend again.

Heather looked at her eldest daughter with concern, but said nothing more. Breakfast ended in happy reminiscences about the previous evening.

Daphne, in particular, seemed delighted. "He's terribly well educated," she was saying, "and so well-read. He spent a year in Europe, touring all the great museums and sketching everything that took his fancy."

She sighed. "Not only that, but his eyes are the most remarkable shade of blue I've ever seen."

John Nash laughed. "Now if that isn't a recommendation for a man, what is?"

"Oh, Daddy," Daphne said, "you know perfectly well that you liked Mr. Hewlitt, too. That was obvious."

"He seems a good enough sort," the elder Nash allowed. Daphne nodded happily, oblivious of the bemused look her parents exchanged. Sweet as she was, the baby of the Nash family was not precisely known for her interest in the arts and literature.

Perhaps that would change now, Julia thought wryly. She was glad for her sister, but the dull throb in her own heart stole all the pleasure she ordinarily would have felt.

At length, the family parted to go their separate ways. Julia was seen off at the door with as much ceremony as if she were departing on an extended voyage.

She supposed eventually that ceremony would stop, but in the meantime she had to admit that she had never appreciated her family's love and concern more than now.

Just as she was about to get into the small landau she drove for herself, her grandmother stepped from the shade of the porch. She had a package in her hand, carefully wrapped in brown paper.

"This is for you," Sara said. A smile creased her face, beautiful with the wisdom and grace of her years. "I've been keeping it in reserve, but I think this might be a good time for you to become acquainted with it."

"What is it?" Julia asked as she reached down to take the package. It was about the size and weight of a small book, and her fingers, touching the edge of it, seemed to detect binding.

Sara smiled. "That's for you to discover. Promise me this, that you won't open it until you are under your own roof."

Julia promised. Not for a moment would she ever consider breaking her word to her grandmother.

The ride to Amelia's house took almost an hour. She glanced at the package beside her from time to time, but did not touch it. Not until she had unhitched the horses, wa-

tered them and set them to graze, then carried her port-
manteau inside and stoked up the fire in the coal stove, did
she at last turn her attention to Sara's gift.

Sitting on the small front porch, she carefully removed
the paper wrapping. Inside, there was a book, bound in
leather that was dried and cracked. Curiously, there was no
title on the spine, nor on the cover. Slowly Julia opened the
book. Such was the quality of the paper that it still shone
white, despite what she guessed was a considerable age.

On the very first page, neatly penned in letters different
from those she was familiar with but still readable, were the
words:

> For my beloved daughter, Amelia. Her book.
> 4th of June, 1648.
> In the knowledge of self lies the wisdom of God.
> Jonathan Daniels.

Julia's breath caught. Was it possible? Over the years,
she had heard mentions of a journal kept by Amelia Daniels, but she had presumed it lost. Now here it was, in her
very hands, back in the house where it must have been kept
so long ago.

With reverence, she turned the page and continued to
read. At first the going was difficult. Despite its age, the ink
had not faded, but the style of writing was as on the first
page, although in a different hand. She had to read slowly,
picking out each letter. But before long the words began to
flow more smoothly.

Amelia had begun the journal during her voyage to the
New World, and the first entries were sparse. Her father
had been ill and she had been desperately worried about
him. Finally, a few days out of Boston, in November 1649,
he had died.

Julia's throat tightened as she considered what that must
have meant. A young woman suddenly alone in an un-

known land, without friends or relatives. But with people more than happy to exploit a wealthy heiress, apparently.

She had been taken in by a family called Barton, who were paid in coin and labor for their "hospitality." But it hadn't been enough. They had wished to marry her off to a Puritan elder, a violent, crude man she had rightly despised.

And then, there on the page before Julia, the first mention of Amelia's great dream, the seed of the idea of founding her own colony—a colony free of the restrictions and oppression of the Puritans.

It had been a truly revolutionary thought, and she might have been pardoned for dismissing it as mad. But Amelia had been made of tougher stuff. She had determined to persevere.

Julia read on. The light faded. Hardly realizing that she did so, she moved inside and sat down at the kitchen table. There, by the glow of an oil lamp, she continued to listen as Amelia Daniels' voice came alive within her.

January, 1650. The Pequot are here in Boston seeking settlers for their lands west of the Connecticut River. They wish for allies in the struggle against their enemies, the Mohawks. Land for the giving, it seems, but how to get there?

February, 1650. There are others like myself, similarly discontent but afraid to speak out for fear of punishment. We are meeting in secret. The trek through the wilderness to the Pequot lands would be long and dangerous. But with a ship, we could go quickly and bring all needed with us. No Puritan captain would take us but there are others.

And then, on the page dated March 3, 1650, his name at last, writ bold.

Surely, Captain Garrick Marlowe is the most insufferable man to walk God's earth. He has refused to help us, even mocked the idea, but I will not yield. He is our only hope. Also, to his credit, the Puritans despise him.

A few days later, the writing tightened, growing cramped, as though with shock and sorrow.

A terrible tragedy. Captain Marlowe's fine ship has been burned and his first mate terribly hurt. May the Almighty forgive me, but there is hope in this. The captain can no longer afford to dismiss us.

Julia rubbed the back of her neck, vaguely aware that it hurt. She had completely lost track of the time. A glance out the kitchen windows showed that it was fully night. She should retire and leave the rest of the journal for tomorrow.

But she could not. It held her enthralled, as though she had discovered not only a way into the past, but also into herself, and the forces that had made her.

Garrick Marlowe had continued to resist Amelia's efforts, but in the end her persistence and his need had won out. Her inheritance had purchased another ship and equipped it for the great effort.

Their understanding had been that he and his crew would transport the settlers and stay with them through the first winter. Then Garrick Marlowe would become master of the vessel and be free to go on his way.

The early months had been hard. Amelia wrote frequently of fear that the crops would fail or the Pequots change their minds and attack. Such an attack had finally come, led by the chieftain's renegade son, but had been thwarted by the courage of Amelia and Garrick both.

And somewhere in those days of desperate struggle and great effort they had become lovers.

Amelia wrote frankly of her feelings for this man, which had led her to violate every moral teaching she had ever known. Julia understood them completely. With Amelia, she counted out the days through the winter to the coming of spring, when Garrick would be free to leave.

Days, too, that had marked new life stirring within her, and a new struggle to save Belle Haven from the punishment of vengeful Puritans who would use her, a fallen woman, as their excuse to take over the settlement.

When Julia read the entry that described Amelia's decision to leave Belle Haven in order to protect it, she gasped. This was something she had never heard about.

So caught up was she in the story that Julia almost forgot she already knew its outcome. She breathed a sigh of relief when Garrick returned, freely deciding that his dream of the sea could not prevail over the love he had for Amelia Daniels and her own dream of Belle Haven.

Over the years that followed, Amelia noted important events in the remaining pages of the journal—the birth of their children, the growth and strengthening of Belle Haven.

But, apart from that, her tale ended with Garrick's return. There was no more sign of fear, only of great love and happiness.

Slowly Julia put the book down. It was very late. The house lay wreathed in silence. Her eyes ached, and she realized suddenly that she had eaten nothing.

She found bread from the previous day and cheese in the cupboard and nibbled on both as she thought over what she had learned. Much of it agreed with all the stories she had heard over the years about Amelia, her great vision and courage, her refusal to give up even when faced with enormous obstacles.

But there had been a discovery in the pages of Amelia's book that Julia would never have expected. It was fear, so often and openly expressed.

Amelia had frequently been afraid, even close to despair on occasion. She had worried that her efforts at Belle Haven would come to nothing and that she might be leading trusting people to their deaths.

But she had also feared tremendously that Garrick would leave her. That the love she had for him, and the passion they shared, would in the end bring only pain.

Even more striking to Julia was that Amelia had accepted not merely the possibility of that, but what must surely have seemed to be its inevitability. She had taken tremendous risks, and done it knowingly.

Wearily Julia put the remains of the food away and took the oil lamp in her hand. Carrying the book, she went upstairs to her room. She undressed, washed and dropped a thin nightgown over her head before getting into bed. Turning onto her side, she lowered the oil lamp to a gentle glow, then lay on her back, looking up at the ceiling.

So much had changed in Amelia's house since her ancestress had lived there. It had grown to accommodate an ever-expanding family, and had acquired the conveniences and comforts of each passing age. But the essence of it remained unaltered.

Listening very hard, Julia could almost hear the murmur of lost voices—Amelia's laughter, and Garrick's murmured reply. Although she had always imagined that she knew them, she realized now that she had not.

Amelia's journal had given her an entirely different impression of her famous ancestress and the man with whom she had made her life. It had made them both far more real—Amelia, especially—she was no longer the paragon of virtue triumphing effortlessly over every obstacle. Instead, she was a flesh-and-blood woman, filled with yearnings. And with fears.

Amelia kept coming back to that in her writings. She had been afraid—of failing, of being hurt, of living with regret and pain. But she had taken the risks anyway. She had refused to accept life on its own terms, but instead had reshaped it to hers.

Julia smiled in the darkness. She had no doubts as to why Gramma Sara had chosen to give her the journal now. Her grandmother was far too wise and perceptive not to realize that Julia was deeply unhappy.

But was what Sara was trying to tell her correct? Was she truly a prisoner only of her own fears, or of a harsh reality she could not change?

There was only one way to find out.

The night passed slowly. Julia didn't truly sleep, only dozed from time to time. Before the birds had awakened, she was out of bed and sitting at her dressing table.

In the privacy of her own house, unobserved by anyone, Julia took a long, hard look at herself. Honesty forced her to admit that her face really wasn't bad. She didn't have Daphne's bandbox looks or Gloria's refinement, but her features were regular, her smile was pleasant, and her eyes were actually rather nice.

What about the rest of her?

She rose and went to stand in front of the mahogany-framed full-length mirror that was set near one window. The mirror had belonged to Amelia Daniels' great-granddaughter Deanna Marlowe Nash. It had been given to Julia on her eighteenth birthday, a tribute to her status as the eldest daughter of the house and her well-known interest in the family's history.

Gazing into the mirror, Julia slowly raised her arms and pulled the nightgown over her head, letting it fall to the ground. She shut her eyes for a moment, then looked at herself.

Julia was not a prude. She had been raised to believe that the human body was one of God's greatest creations and should be treated as such. But she hadn't really looked at herself in a long time, not since the accident that had crippled her. Hesitantly she ran her eyes down herself. Seen from this different perspective, her breasts were surprisingly high and full. She caught herself wondering what Brand would think of them, and flushed deeply.

That was ridiculous. If she was contemplating any change in herself, it was not for his sake, but strictly for her own. Never mind that he was the most handsome and compelling man she had ever encountered. He meant to marry and, worse yet, to do it strictly to have children. She was in no hurry to tie herself to anyone, let alone a man who saw a woman strictly as a brood mare.

Remonstrating with herself to be more sensible, she continued to look. Her waist was slender, her hips were slim, her legs were well shaped and tapered. All except her left leg below the knee, which remained smaller than the other and slightly twisted.

Julia stared at it for several minutes. There was no escaping that it looked different, but it wasn't anywhere as bad as she had somehow presumed. Seen dispassionately and in relation to the rest of her body, it was noticeable, but not shocking. It also did not look particularly weak. And why should it? She walked, rode, worked in the garden, swam. There was no reason to think that her injured leg would look useless when it certainly wasn't. Yes, it hurt from time to time, often when she was tired or anxious. But it also functioned when the doctors had said it would not, and for that she was intensely grateful.

Still naked, Julia walked over to her wardrobe and opened it. She pushed past the clothes she usually wore to find the dresses hanging toward the back.

When she was helping Charlotte find a gown, she had noticed a day dress her mother had bought for her the previous year that she had never worn. It was in a particular shade of dark rose that she loved, without any hint of the brashness of red, but deep and rich.

She found it and, with an effort, pulled it free of the others. Among other things, she seemed to have lost track of how many clothes she had.

It was ridiculous for any one person to have so much. She would have to see what else she could get Charlotte to take. Holding the dress in front of herself, she looked in the mirror. The woman who stared back was wide-eyed and uncertain.

Julia grimaced. "Courage," she murmured, and studied the dress again.

It had a high neck banded in velvet, ruching down the bodice, puffed sleeves that narrowed to fit snugly from elbow to wrist, and a gored skirt. Although she had paid little attention to fashion in recent years, Julia knew it was in the latest style. She was relieved that the cumbersome bustles had gone away finally. The dress looked discreetly lovely—not in the least ostentatious, but feminine and graceful.

Finding a camisole, drawers and stockings, she put them on, then reached for the dress. Before she could think better of it, she stepped into it.

Chapter Six

Brand stared at the column of figures on the paper he held, without truly seeing it. For more than an hour, he had been making a determined effort to work. But his mind kept wandering, and finally he gave up. Frustrated, he tossed the paper aside and stood up.

It was a perfect summer day—bright, beckoning, beguiling. But his mood was as dark as night. He had been trying to remember the last time he had felt ashamed of himself. It was a singularly unpleasant exercise.

He did not think of himself as a gentle man, or a kind one, but honor lived deep within him, the honor of a people too often driven from their land and even from their lives, who kept certain principles inviolate all the same.

Honor was the steel in him. He was tough, even ruthless, but he was never deliberately cruel. Unlike others, who indulged in cruelty as a way of feeling and demonstrating their own power, Brand shunned it.

His strength spoke in the results he got, the wealth not merely accumulated but used to build jobs and hopes, and the confidence with which he moved through a world in which many would gladly have tried to destroy him if they possessed the nerve.

In all the years of his relentless climb to wealth and success, he had known fear and doubt, relief and pleasure. But he could not remember ever being embarrassed.

He was now, acutely. The mere memory of his behavior with Julia made him wish he could leave his own skin, if only for a short time, and no longer be himself.

It was a novel and unsettling sensation, but in all honesty he thought it well deserved. He had behaved very badly. And yet, there was something about her that confused—yes, that was the word—something that confused him. Over the years, he had been attracted to a wide variety of women, but not ever to a Julia Nash, a plain-looking, plainspoken woman who did not exert the slightest effort to make herself pleasant. Never before had he felt the slightest stirring of interest in such a woman.

Until now. Perhaps it was her quiet pride in her heritage and her determination to protect it, or her willingness to accept his word when he promised he would not despoil the land, or simply the courage and intelligence he sensed in her. Whatever it was, he could not get Julia Nash out of his mind.

But there in the moonlit garden he had come perilously close to exploiting her innocence and naiveté. It was completely unlike him. He could apologize, of course, but he suspected that would only make it worse. Probably his wisest course would be to do nothing. He would go on about his business, and she would tend to hers.

Brand nodded to himself. That was best. Yet, even as he made up his mind, he remembered how calmly she had taken what he'd said about his mother. Not only that, her response had been completely sincere, of that he was certain.

She'd been wrong about one thing though, his mother was not at all pleased by his decision to settle in Belle Haven. It wasn't the town itself she minded, she'd never actually been here. But she'd gotten wind of his plans, and was appalled by them.

His mother—who was as tough and determined as he could ever claim to be and who had overcome obstacles beyond his imagining—had informed him that the only reason to marry was for love.

He'd thought she was kidding, but she'd quickly made it clear that she was not. She thought him a fool, plain and simple, and she hadn't hesitated to say so.

There was even a possibility she was right.

Now where had that thought come from? His course was set, and he saw no reason to change it. A few more excursions into Belle Haven society and he'd find a wife.

If that failed, he could always pick one from the variety of suitable candidates in New York. He merely thought a local girl would be more comfortable remaining close to her family, especially since he reasonably had to expect to be away a great deal.

Family. The Nashes were his idea of what a family should be. Briefly he thought of Daphne and Gloria. They were as unlike Julia, and as unlike each other, as it was possible to be. He enjoyed them both, but not for a moment could he imagine fitting either of them into his plans.

Then there was that other young woman, what was her name? Oh, yes, Genevieve Halsted. He'd thought at first he'd met her before, but then he'd realized that was only because he'd met a dozen and more young women exactly like her in New York. She undoubtedly would fall in with his scheme without the slightest hesitation. The only problem was that he would rather share a bed with a boa constrictor.

Never mind, it was only the first try. But he had to admit to being mildly discouraged, especially when he saw Charles bounding up the street and guessed immediately what was on his mind.

"I would have been earlier," he said apologetically, "but I stopped at the bookstore. Miss Nash was there." He might as well have announced the presence of an angel.

"Miss Daphne Nash?" Brand asked. It was an easy guess. He and probably everyone else at the party had observed Charles's unbridled interest in the youngest Nash daughter. Moreover, it had been returned.

"Yes," Charles said reverently. "She is fascinated with literature, and is very knowledgeable."

Brand hid a smile. He felt a certain wry affection for Charles, even if the younger man was unfailingly naive. It was refreshing to realize that someone with Charles's soft heart could survive in the world. Or at least he could with some help from his considerably tougher and more hard-headed employer.

"There's a band concert on the green tomorrow evening," Charles said. "Miss Nash mentioned it."

"Did she? Feel free to attend, if you would like."

"Actually, I thought you might want to go along as well. It's a regular event in summer, and very popular."

"I'll consider it," Brand allowed, and turned his attention to the plans Charles had brought.

In fact, he did not—consider it, that is. A telegram arrived early the following morning to inform him of a major development in a business arrangement he had been closely following.

Brand was on the phone much of the remainder of the day, as with cutting speed he placed several million dollars at risk and then, just as the market was closing, recouped it three times over.

He smiled, imagining the reaction as the closing bells rang on the floor of the New York Stock Exchange and the magnitude of his win became clear. If he was in town, men would be finding excuses to drop in on him at his office, his club, and any social event he happened to attend, simply to say that they had spoken with him.

But, given his absence from the city, they would have to contend themselves with yet more gossip about his methods, his seemingly intuitive grasp of when to take risks and when not to, and the breathtaking gambles that always seemed to pay off for him.

They would not speak of the long months of tedious, painstaking work, the thought and analysis, the unrelenting effort, that had gone into the day's results. But then, they didn't care to know anything about that. It was so much easier for them to believe that he had some trick, some deceit or as a few said, some "devil's luck," that always brought him out on top.

Absently he rubbed the back of his neck. After the long day, it ached slightly. As was his habit, he took a final glance at the stock ticker. It confirmed the extent of his coup. In passing, he also noticed that the stock he had sold off was doing even worse than he'd expected. Anyone foolish enough to have held on to it would be in real danger of being wiped out.

As evening fell, Brand belatedly remembered the band concert. It seemed a tame way to celebrate a memorable victory, but nothing more interesting presented itself.

He hesitated. There was still a late train he could catch into the city. He would be at his apartment by 9:00 p.m. From there, virtually any amusement he might wish would be within easy reach.

The thought had its attractions. He felt a certain need to break out, throw off the shackles of respectability and have a rip-roaring good time, preferably in the company of at least one young woman who knew her business as well as he knew his.

But that wouldn't get him any closer to his goal. With a sigh, just beginning to consider the full magnitude of the task he had set for himself, Brand rolled down his sleeves, reached for his jacket and headed for the green.

* * *

Julia stepped from her carriage and glanced around. People were streaming toward the green, on foot and in a variety of conveyances, from the most elaborate broughams to simple wagons. They carried wicker picnic baskets, and blankets to sit on. The children romped ahead, playing tag and spinning hoops. Everyone was in good cheer, looking forward to the evening's entertainment.

She fastened the reins to a stone post topped by a lion's head with a ring through its nose and carefully smoothed her skirt. Self-consciousness assailed her, but she did her utmost to ignore it. She was wearing the dark rose dress she had picked out the previous day. It was perfectly suited to the event, being neither too casual nor too formal.

Julia knew that, but she was still uncharacteristically anxious. Slowly, her own basket in hand, she made her way toward the spot on the green from which her family had always enjoyed the summer concerts. Her mother was already there, spreading out a blanket and peering inside the basket as she always did for a last-minute check.

"I'm sure you've got everything, Mother," Julia said softly.

Heather glanced up, started to speak, and abruptly fell silent. She stared at her eldest daughter. "Why, Julia," she said quietly, "don't you look lovely."

"It's not too much?"

"Not at all," Heather said firmly. She patted the blanket beside her and smiled at her daughter. But she also sensibly changed the subject.

"Daphne is reading *Uncle Tom's Cabin*."

Julia's eyes widened. She could not remember the last time she had seen her sister read anything other than a ladies' magazine, let alone a novel that actually required some concentration.

"Are you sure?"

"Quite," Heather said. "Indeed, she was so absorbed that she skipped lunch."

"Good heavens, this sounds serious. She isn't ill, is she?"

"A bit heartsick, perhaps, but only in the nicest way. This is apparently Mr. Charles Hewlitt's influence."

Julia settled more comfortably on the grass. She tried to imagine her giddy young sister reading for love. It was an engaging thought. "He's the architect, isn't he?"

"That's right. He's doing Mr. Delaney's house. Speaking of whom..." Heather stared over her daughter's shoulder.

Instinctively Julia turned. She expected to see Charles Hewlitt, and indeed she did vaguely notice him arriving at the same time. But it was Brand who caught her gaze and held it as he strolled across the green toward them.

Julia took a quick breath, fighting for calm. She had not seen him since those moments in the garden, but he had been in her thoughts constantly. Much as she hated to admit it, she had half hoped, half dreaded that he would be at the concert.

Having convinced herself that he would not, she was momentarily at a loss. But a previously unsuspected talent for acting was beginning to make itself evident. She stood, preferring not to meet him while reclining, and nodded coolly.

"Good evening, Mr. Delaney."

Heather echoed the greeting and offered her hand. Brand bent over it, but his attention was on Julia. His dark green eyes flashed as they swept over her.

A slow smile curved his mouth. "Mrs. Nash... Miss Nash... May I thank you again for your hospitality?"

"How very gracious of you," Heather said. "I am expecting Mr. Nash and Peter at any moment. Do join us."

Julia waited, hardly breathing. She thought for sure he would refuse. But he merely hesitated before agreeing. "I would like that, thank you."

When John Nash returned from speaking with a few of the other men, he found Brand seated with his wife and daughter, engaged in animated conversation. Or at least Heather was. Julia and Brand were mainly silent; she staring straight ahead, he glancing at her from time to time, as though unsure of what he saw.

Brand rose as the elder Nash arrived. The two men shook hands, studying each other as they had before. But there was an added element in John's scrutiny.

"Congratulations," he said. "It's the talk of the town."

Brand shrugged. "That won't last."

"Perhaps not," John said as they both sat down. "But it was an impressive coup."

"What was?" Julia asked, unable to stop herself.

"A rather brilliant maneuver on the market today," her father said. "Mr. Delaney outdid himself."

He looked at their guest with an air of dawning discovery. "That didn't happen by accident."

"I'd been keeping an eye on the issues for a while," Brand acknowledged.

"I thought as much. People love to think that sort of thing happens through luck, but it almost never does. I've tried to impress on all my children the need for hard, intelligent work." He glanced at Julia as though to confirm this, only to notice her dress belatedly.

"Is that new?" he asked.

A lightning glance passed between Julia and her mother. If Brand hadn't been watching Julia so closely, he wouldn't have noticed it. She shook her head. "Not at all, Father."

"Oh, well, it's pretty all the same. You ought to wear that color more often. Now, where were we? Oh, yes, hard work. It can't be beat. Don't you agree, Mr. Delaney?"

Brand did. He also seemed to approve of—and share— the elder Nash's views on urban development, fly-fishing, Tammany Hall politics and the gold standard. By the time the concert began with a rousing rendition of Mr. John

Philip Sousa's new march "The Stars and Stripes Forever," the two men were getting along famously.

And Julia was baffled. She loved her father dearly, but even she didn't get along with him as well as Brand appeared to. Indeed, they seemed in full accord on virtually everything.

Not only that, but it was clear that John Nash was enjoying being seen with the man of the hour, as Julia actually heard a nearby couple murmur without rancor. Brand was the center of a great deal of attention, none of which he appeared to notice. Indeed, he seemed completely content with the company of the Nashes, Daphne and Gloria included.

Gloria was all courtesy and relaxed friendliness, for which Julia envied her enormously. Her own acting talents did not extend to such easy banter. Fortunately, the steady flow of mainly boisterous music kept conversation to a minimum. When it was possible, the others more than took up any slack.

Charles Hewlitt joined them. He hardly managed to take his eyes off Daphne, and she seemed to have a similar difficulty with him. But she did manage to take solemn note of his recommendations for more books she might like to read.

Peter, on the other hand, seemed distracted. He kept glancing around as though looking for someone. Finally, just as the intermission was beginning, he leaned over to Julia and asked, "Is she here?"

"She who?"

"Miss Hemper. I thought she might attend."

Julia had no idea whether Charlotte planned to be at the concert or not. But she was delighted by Peter's interest, enough to be distracted from the discomfort of her own situation.

"Charlotte loves music," she offered. "She plays the piano beautifully, even though she has scant opportunity to practice."

"I've been thinking about that. It doesn't seem right that a person of her qualities should be denied so much of what we take for granted."

As Julia heartily approved of this observation, she nodded encouragingly. "I imagine if you looked around you might find her."

"I'll do that," Peter said, and rose, taking leave of his family and Brand.

As was the custom, intermission was the time when a refreshment table was set out to augment whatever people had brought with them. The town's renowned concert punch was served, as well as an assortment of biscuits and cheeses made in local homes.

It was an excuse to rise and stretch muscles that had become cramped from sitting, to stroll around and greet neighbors and generally to be seen.

"May I?" Charles asked as he stood and offered his hand to Daphne. She accepted with alacrity.

Heather directed a glance at her husband.

John Nash had not been married for twenty-five years for nothing. He didn't entirely understand her meaning, but that made no difference. Enough of it was clear. "My dear," he said, rising, "shall we?"

"By all means. Gloria, dear, isn't that your friend, Melanie?"

Whether it was or not, Gloria stood smoothly, smiled, and vanished as promptly as her sister had. The elder Nashes did the same. Brand and Julia were left alone.

"Would you like to try the punch?" Julia asked, mainly because she could think of nothing else to say and she didn't relish the thought of remaining seated, almost in the center of the green, where everyone could take note of them together.

It was an entirely misleading picture, given that they had absolutely no interest in one another. All the same, he was new to the town, and the least she could do was introduce him to some of the customs.

Brand agreed, and they set out together. By simply pretending not to see the hand he offered, Julia managed to avoid touching him. Not that there was any reason she should not. She simply wished to avoid any misunderstandings.

They joined the line for punch, and were soon at the front. Brand accepted two cups, handing one to Julia. He took a sip. "Not bad. What's in it?"

"That's a closely guarded secret."

He took another taste, thought for a moment, and said, "Mango juice."

She looked at him in astonishment. Years ago, when her father took his turn on the men's committee responsible for assembling the punch, she had accidentally gotten a glimpse of the ingredients. Mango juice was indeed among them, but to the best of her knowledge, no one had ever guessed it before.

"How did you know that?"

"I spent some time in Jamaica. More to the point, how does it get up here?"

"A family in town ships it up once a year, specifically for the punch." Hastily she added, "But there's a good deal more to it than that."

"Brown sugar, honey, ginger, lemon and, oddly but not unpleasantly, a hint of saffron."

Her mouth dropped open. She couldn't help it. Quickly she glanced around to make sure no one had overheard. Fortunately, everyone appeared just far enough away to have missed it.

"How in heaven's name did you do that?"

"One of my first businesses was a spice importing company. I went back and forth to the West Indies several times a year, mostly in ships where the smell of the cargo had seeped into the wood."

"That must have been wonderful." Indeed, she could think of few things better. "How could you bear to give it up?"

"I didn't, entirely. I still own the company, and I have a house in Jamaica. I visit there every winter."

"You might be wise to continue doing so. Winter can be harsh here."

Deliberately she turned the talk to less personal topics. But the image of a great vessel at anchor on a moonlit Caribbean night stayed with her. Did he swim from its deck as he had from the beach near his land?

Appalled at the unruly direction of her thoughts, she was greatly relieved to hear the music beginning again. When she and Brand returned, her mother had opened the baskets.

They enjoyed an al fresco supper to the sounds of Mozart and the younger Bach. A rousing rendition of the national anthem closed out the evening.

Brand escorted Julia back to her carriage. He did not ask her permission, but simply accompanied her, carrying the basket before she could demur.

As he handed her up, a courtesy she did not try to refuse this time, he said, "I wonder if I could ask a favor?"

Long ago, Julia had noticed that the world could be divided into two kinds of people depending on the answer to that single question. There were the cautious and sensible who answered, "What is it?" And then there were the more openhearted, who simply said, "Of course."

She was an "of course" person, always had been, and she suspected that it was much too late to try to do anything about it. "Of course," she said, and waited to hear what he would ask.

Chapter Seven

"**I**'m not really all that knowledgeable about horses," Julia said. "You might have done better to ask someone else."

"I would have, if there were anyone I counted on to give me as sensible advice as you," Brand said. It was early morning, two days after the town concert.

They were standing on the edge of an open field to the north of Belle Haven proper. For almost two hundred years, it had been the gathering place every summer for those who wished to buy and sell horses, as well as those who merely liked to admire them.

Brand had come to buy. He had in mind a stallion and several mares, the beginnings of a breeding operation.

The day was damp. They were both sensibly dressed, he in old cotton trousers, a shirt left open at the neck and a tweed jacket. She was in a dark brown skirt that came to midcalf, boots, and a bulky sweater that had long been one of her favorites. Anyone seeing them might mistake them for a couple fresh from the country.

"Are you sure you want to do this?" Julia asked.

"I have given it some thought," he assured her.

"Still, you may not have considered the full cost. To be blunt, breeding horses produces manure and bills in about equal amounts."

Brand laughed. He shot her an appreciative glance. Julia smiled in turn. She had considered the wisdom of tempering her usually frank speech, but had decided against it.

After all, it wasn't as though they were anything more than neighbors. Happily, he didn't seem at all put off.

"I'll keep the financial aspects in mind," Brand assured her. "If you find me going overboard, feel free to speak up."

Julia assured him that she would, even though she had the feeling he was teasing her. He clearly thought her capable of speaking her mind without prior permission.

They walked on in companionable silence. A temporary paddock had been put up in the center of the field. Several horses were being shown on lead lines. Others were clustered outside, grazing placidly while their owners extolled their virtues.

"Finest hack horse you'll find," a burly man assured Brand as they passed. "Pull the lady's carriage, and nary give her a moment of trouble."

"Shallow in the chest," Julia murmured.

They walked on. Most of the horses being offered were hacks, but there was also a group of jumpers. One was a high-spirited chestnut mare Brand admired.

"I know her," Julia said. "She's out of Fairfield, good lines. Would you like to speak with the owner?"

He would. The man was young, slender, and sharp-eyed. Either he didn't use the usual sales talk or he had dropped it in deference to Julia. She did not introduce Brand, but gave the man's name as Sean O'Neill. He told them the mare was three years old, had made a name for herself on the two-year-old circuit, and held the promise of better yet to come.

Brand was inclined to agree. He knew a thing or two about horses himself, although he lacked the experience of actually caring for them that Julia had. But he liked the looks of the chestnut mare.

Moreover, she seemed to like him. She came at Sean O'Neill's whistle and nuzzled both Julia and Brand.

"Gently reared," Julia said. She smiled at the younger man. "I don't believe Sean's ever put a whip to a horse. Isn't that right?"

"It is," he agreed. "Which makes as good a time as any to say my piece. I'd like to sell Maeve here well enough, for there's another baby coming and the money's needed. But I'd need to know something about where she's going to." He looked at Julia. "Is she for you then, miss?"

Julia shook her head. "For the gentleman."

"Well, then, sir, if you don't mind my asking, what would you be planning for her?"

"I'm thinking of starting a breeding operation."

"Do you know much about that sort of thing?"

"Not a great deal," Brand acknowledged. He was surprised at being questioned, but not put out by it.

"There's a great deal to know," Sean said. "Also, to be frank, it costs the earth." He looked Brand up and down openly, as though to say he might well be the salt of the earth, but that didn't mean he had the means to make his intentions real.

"You manage," Brand pointed out. To Julia's relief, he was smiling.

"Aye, but I was lucky. I inherited a bit of land, and my wife's father was in the business. He got me started."

"Good point. Aside from Miss Nash's kind help, I'm on my own."

"There you are, then. Far be it from me to discourage you, but you've got to know what you're getting into."

Again Sean studied him. He seemed to come to a decision. "You look like a regular enough sort, and if Miss Nash is helping you, then you're all right. Tell you what, I'll give you a good price on the mare. I'll expect half now and half when she foals for you. That way, you won't have to come up with it all at once."

"What would you call a good price?" Brand asked.

Sean quoted a price. Brand hesitated. Against his better judgment, he said, "That sounds low."

"Depends. Where have you bought before?"

"New York."

Sean laughed. "There you are, then. In the city, they ask anything they think they can get, and with all the nobs running around there, often as not someone pays."

Brand's grin was rueful. "I always thought I drove a fairly hard bargain."

"And maybe you did. It's all relative. Anyway, if you want to pay more, feel free."

Brand laughed and shook his head. "I'll meet your price, but you'll have it all now. If the mare's as good as she looks, how would you like the job of finding a few more to go with her?"

Sean cast a quick glance at Julia. She remained impassive. "Well, now, as to that, sir..."

"You don't have to call me sir. The name's Delaney. Brand Delaney." He held out his hand.

Sean paled slightly. There was no question that he recognized what that name meant, the sheer weight of the wealth and power that lay behind it.

He looked shocked for a moment, but recovered quickly. Ruefully he said, "Well, now, I guess it's true—you can't tell a book by its cover. I would have taken you for an ordinary gent."

"Thank you," Brand said gravely. They shook hands, eyeing each other with care.

As she had with her father, Julia had the sense of a private male communication passing between them, something to do with issues of strength and honor. Whatever they shared, they seemed satisfied.

"So you'll be setting up your stable," Sean said.

Brand nodded. "I'm building a house. The same architect has designed the stables to adjoin it. He's a good man, but his experience is buildings, more than horses. I wonder if you'd be interested in reviewing the plans for me?''

Sean looked delighted by the prospect. Clearly he assumed Brand had both the money and the will to build the ideal stables, the same kind he would build for himself he could. To have a hand in such an endeavor was plainly more than he'd ever expected.

''I'd be glad to do that.''

''Fine, we'll be in touch to discuss your fee.''

Sean looked startled. Julia hid a smile, for she knew he would have done the service as a kindness. Moreover, she suspected Brand knew that, too.

''For the baby that's coming,'' Brand explained.

When it was put that way, Sean could hardly refuse. He accepted solemnly, pledging Brand to give his best advice on the stables and the acquisition of more horses for it.

They parted a short while later. The horse show was far from over, but Sean would be heading home early, to tell his wife of their good fortune.

Julia knew what a struggle it had been for the O'Neills. She had dealt with them for several years. They were a proud, honest and hardworking couple who, aside from the land Sean had inherited, had nothing they hadn't struggled to attain. Now, suddenly, a whole new world of possibilities was opening up for them, and just when they could most benefit from it.

She stole a glance at Brand, wondering what it was like to have such an impact on people's lives, to be able almost with a wave of his hand to fulfill dreams, change futures, banish worry. For the first time, she considered what it really meant to have such power.

''Do you do that sort of thing often?'' she asked.

''What, buy a horse?''

''No, change someone's life.''

He looked surprised. ''Is that what I did?''

"You must know it is. Sean's not a poor man, but there's never been any extra, either. There isn't for most people. The chance to work for you, to help design a stable and pick out horses, and get paid for it to boot, that's extraordinary. He's probably feeling ten feet high right about now. He'll rush home to Maire, his wife, and they'll celebrate. Whatever happens from this point on, they'll remember this day all their lives."

"I think you're exaggerating."

Julia stopped walking. She turned and looked straight into his eyes. How could she have thought them impenetrable? They were the windows to his soul—dark as night, yet alive with all the strength and energy of his compelling spirit.

"No," she said softly, "you know exactly what you did."

For a moment, she thought he would deny it again. Instead, he laughed wryly and resumed walking. "Don't spread it around, all right? I've got a reputation to protect."

"The terror of Wall Street?"

"Something like that."

"It doesn't seem fair."

"Fair? I'll have you know I worked hard to strike fear into the hearts of the top financiers in this country—assuming they have any. That didn't come overnight, let me tell you."

Julia laughed. She could feel herself stepping over a line. This was not the conversation of mere neighbors. It was more that of friends.

She had never had a male friend. The thought was disconcerting, but not impossible. Indeed, it had definite attractions. He was fun to be with, had a fascinating background and made her feel a new sense of confidence in herself. Best of all, there was no possibility that they could fall prey to the sort of confusion that so often seemed to plague men and women. She knew what he wanted—a

brood mare in human form—and she would never remotely be tempted to such a fate herself.

That was fortunate. It left her free to enjoy Brand as both
neighbor and friend.

She was actually enjoying a certain pleasant compla-
cency as they strolled back toward the paddock. It was the
last such she would feel for a very long time.

"Ladies and gentlemen," the auctioneer intoned. "Today's prize offering, a five-year-old stallion out of Newfield Stables, nicknamed Damien. A truly magnificent
animal, winner of more than a dozen major stakes
throughout the capitals of Europe. An exceptional offering on these shores. Bidding will begin at five thousand
dollars."

Julia and Brand had reached the paddock. Along with
almost everyone else attending the show, they watched the
animal now being led in. He truly was magnificent, standing almost twenty hands high, with a silky roan coat and
superb musculature.

As the trainer led him forward, he balked slightly and
pawed the ground with his front hooves.

"Beautiful," Brand murmured.

Julia hesitated. She, too, thought the animal was impressive. But there was something about him that didn't
seem quite right.

"I've never heard of Newfield Stables," she said.

"Perhaps they're English. The auctioneer did say he'd
been racing in Europe."

"It's customary to enter a racer in stakes here before offering him for sale. Our meets may not have the status of
those in Europe, but they're valid contests all the same."

"You wouldn't hold the elitism of the owner against the
horse, would you?" Brand asked with a smile.

He looked again at the horse. He was pulling on the lead lines, his powerful muscles bunching. The trainer said something to him, but it seemed to have no effect.

"Needs training," Brand murmured, thinking that could be done readily enough. He'd yet to see an animal that didn't respond to a gentle hand and patient persistence.

"No," Julia murmured. She, too, was staring at the stallion. "There's something wrong."

Brand glanced down at her. Tall though she was for a woman, she came just to his shoulder. He could see the bright crown of her auburn hair gleaming in the sun. Not for the first time, he noticed that she did without a hat whenever she could. The sun had left a smattering of freckles across her upturned nose. There were ladies he knew—and some not such ladies—who would have had fits at such a seeming flaw. But Julia wore it well. The freckles suited her.

So, too, did the unfashionable clothes she wore. They spoke of days spent happily outside, work well done, and a strong sense of self, all qualities he didn't often find in women. There was a healthiness about her, a sense of strength and competency he found oddly engaging.

At the concert, he'd been surprised to find her far more fashionably dressed than he had seen her before. That had been a very different Julia from the hoyden on the road or the prim and prickly New England spinster of the church and the dance. This was yet another Julia, and he suspected the one closest to the truth.

Abruptly he realized that he was staring at her. And that she had spoken. "What did you say?"

"Something's wrong with that horse."

Together they looked at the stallion again. The trainer had gotten him to the center of the paddock.

He appeared to be standing quietly enough as the bidding began. It quickly moved upward, reaching nine thousand dollars within minutes and showing no sign of stopping.

An excited hush fell over the crowd. Most of the people at the show would never be able to spend a fraction of that amount, but there were enough others, men with significant money behind them and the yen for such a magnificent animal, that a real contest was promised.

"Ten thousand," the auctioneer called. "I have ten thousand. A pittance for this animal. Do I hear eleven?"

He did, and that was quickly bested. Swiftly it came down to four bidders. People craned their necks to get a better look at them. Or at least most did. Julia kept her attention on the stallion.

Just as Brand was thinking that he might be tempted to offer for the animal himself, she tugged at his sleeve and said, "Look at his eyes."

The whites of the stallion's eyes were showing as he rolled them frantically. He tossed his head, snorting hard, and reared.

The crowd cried out, more in excitement than in fear. More than a few in the audience were cheering him on, seeing his rebellion only as evidence of high spirits.

But the trainer didn't seem to agree. He cursed mightily and grabbed for the lead lines, trying to pull the horse back down.

He failed. The stallion reared again, slashing out with his hooves and coming perilously close to the trainer's head. In the next instant, the man dropped the lead and ran.

The crowd gasped, still not at the horse's behavior, but at the man's. They had all been around horses who reared, and didn't think over much of it. But for a trainer to bolt like that, leaving his charge alone in the paddock, that was a dereliction of duty that shocked them.

Brand caught a glimpse of the man's face as he hurdled the fence and kept going. He looked flat-out terrified. In another moment, Brand saw why.

Freed of all restraint, the stallion seemed to gather himself. He reared once more, ducked his head deeply against his chest and blew hard.

"He's going to run," Brand said, hardly aware that he spoke. Instinctively, he wrapped his arm around Julia. He pulled her close and turned away from the paddock.

The same thought seemed to occur to others in the crowd. For an animal of the stallion's size, the fence presented little obstacle.

He could probably have crashed through it, but instead he took it in a smooth leap that had the hunters and jumpers in the audience tempted to hold their ground, just in case he suddenly calmed. An animal like that was just too good to waste.

Brand sympathized with them, but he was standing close enough to see the crazed look in the stallion's eyes. Julia was right. The animal was simply wrong, in some deeply embedded way that could have been the result of breeding or training. There was a violence about him that was suddenly clear to all.

The crowd ran, breaking up in all directions as men and women alike rushed to get out of the stallion's path. In the process, they presented a far worse danger to each other. Several people were knocked down and at risk of being trampled, not by the mad horse, but by their fellow humans.

"Come on," Brand said, and with Julia tucked tight against him, plowed a way through what was now a mob. His only thought was to get her to safety.

The stallion charged into a cluster of people in front of them. There were screams, and the sound of bones crunching.

"He's got to be bridled," Julia cried out, "before he kills someone!"

Brand nodded. She was right, of course, but with the fire of panic ignited, reason seemed to vanish. People continued running in all directions, except for those who lay moaning on the ground.

About a hundred yards from the paddock was a line of horses staked to graze while their riders attended the show. Brand and Julia quickly found their own mounts.

Mirage whinnied nervously when she saw her mistress. Julia calmed her with a touch. She glanced back at the crowd, which was still running in all directions.

Her face went pale. "Oh, God, look."

A man stood on top of one of the wagons. He was a big, bearded fellow with untrimmed hair, a battered cavalry hat jammed on his head, and a rifle gripped in his hands. As Julia and Brand watched, he raised the rifle and prepared to shoot.

Brand cursed. "He'll kill half a dozen people before he ever wings that horse." He grabbed Julia's hand and drew her away from the horses to the shelter of a wagon.

"Get down," he said, and pressed her beneath him. For an instant he cupped her face in his hands and looked directly into her eyes.

"Stay here. Don't put your head up until it's over." He looked at her a moment longer before suddenly lowering his head. For a shattering fragment of time, his mouth touched hers.

Julia moaned. Instinctively she lifted her arms and twined them around his neck. The sweetness of her response almost overwhelmed Brand. He needed all his vast will to gently disentangle himself.

Standing, he looked down at the woman crouched at his feet. Her hair was in disarray, her eyes were wide and luminous, her lips were parted. Her skirt was caught under her, displaying the long, slender curves of her hip and thigh. He thought of how she had felt pressed against him and marveled that he had ever considered her plain.

Yet neither was she pretty. The clean, pure lines of her face, her spirit and strength, her pride and honesty, all made her beautiful.

And infinitely desirable.

He took a deep breath, summoning all his strength.

"Don't move," he said again, and was gone.

Chapter Eight

Brand was less than ten running strides from the wagon when Julia popped her head up. She gasped and bit down hard on her lower lip, drawing blood.

Without hesitation, he ran straight at the man with the gun, climbed to where he stood and tackled him hard, just as the man was about to begin firing. The rifle flew into the air as the two men hit the ground hard, rolling over and over.

A brief struggle followed. The would-be shooter was big, and clearly no stranger to violence. But he was no match for Brand's ruthless, no-holds-barred means of dealing with him. Within moments, he was gasping in the dirt, the fight gone out of him.

Without pause, Brand got to his feet and ran straight toward the charging stallion. Several people finally had the presence of mind to fetch bridles, but none had the nerve to try to use one. Julia cried out as she saw an ashen-faced man in a frock coat and top hat thrust one of the bridles into Brand's hands, then make a run for it.

He couldn't mean to try to stop the stallion by himself, she wondered. Ten men, all as strong and determined as Brand, might have a chance of doing it. One would not. He would only succeed in getting himself seriously injured.

Julia could wait no longer. She jumped up and ran after him, heedless of any risk to herself. It was an extraordinarily stupid thing to do, but she didn't think twice. All she could see was Brand rushing straight into danger. Her desperate rush to save him overrode all else.

But she was too late. Before she could reach him, the horse saw him. He stopped, staring at him. Brand slowed. He walked, bridle in his hand, almost casually, toward the stallion.

Julia froze. She was afraid to move. Her eyes widened as she stared incredulously at the scene in front of her. The crowd fell silent. A hush settled over the field, disturbed only by the murmur of the wind.

The stallion tossed his head. His hooves flashed. He snorted and let out a shrill cry, as though of warning.

A shiver ran through Julia. The animal was immense, pure muscle and fury, more than capable of killing a man.

Yet Brand didn't appear at all concerned. He kept walking, moving slightly to one side of the horse.

The stallion rolled his eyes. His mighty head flicked back and forth. He cried out again and prepared to charge.

Brand moved so suddenly that he seemed a blur. One moment he was walking toward the animal, and the next he had leaped onto his back, gripping his mane and quickly pulling the bridle over his head.

The horse screamed. He bucked furiously, determined to throw off the unwanted rider. But Brand remained, rocksteady, on his back. His thighs, bulging with muscle, fastened on the animal's sides and held firm, even as the animal reared again and again, frantically trying to dislodge him.

It became a question of whose strength and will would break first, Brand's or the stallion's.

Brand's won.

Slowly, the horse weakened, not calming but simply exhausting itself. There were a few last, defiant charges, but finally he stood, head drooping, breathing hard with Brand still firmly on its back.

The crowd cheered, but at least had enough sense not to surge forward. Brand was able to walk the horse slowly back to its trainer, who regarded it with acute distrust, but accepted the reins.

As the stallion was led away, people surged around Brand, all wanting to shake his hand or pound him on the back. It was some time before he was able to break free.

Julia stood off to the side, watching. Her heart was still racing, and she felt ill. Images of what could have happened to Brand kept flashing through her mind. But so did the vision of him astride the maddened horse, not hurting the animal in any way, but bending it to his will all the same.

At last Brand managed to free himself from his admirers. He looked around. When his gaze alit on her, he smiled. Was she mistaken in thinking that he walked toward her with the same purposeful stride with which he had approached the stallion?

Undoubtedly. She was overwrought, and her imagination was running away with her. The effect, no doubt, of that brief kiss they had shared. She absolutely wasn't going to think about that. It was an aberration, nothing more, and best swiftly forgotten.

Best or not, the memory of his mouth on hers lingered. She did not dare to look at him, keeping her eyes focused no higher than his chin.

He stopped directly in front of her. Unable to stop herself, she glanced up. The lines around his eyes deepened. "Let's go."

Julia was only too happy to do so. They found their horses, mounted and rode out. It wasn't until they were a quarter mile or so from the field that Julia realized something was wrong. Brand was sitting a little stiffly in the saddle.

"What's the matter?" she asked, forgetting her own self-consciousness.

They ducked their heads to pass beneath the arching branches of oak trees that fanned out over the road. As they straightened, he said, "Nothing."

She looked again. His mouth was tight. He definitely looked as though he were in pain.

"You got hurt." It came out almost as an accusation, which she certainly didn't mean.

He had acted with incredible courage, possibly saving who knew how many people from injury. But he had done it at some cost to himself.

Brand sighed. He looked abashed. "When I was sixteen, I spent a summer with my father's people, tracking wild horses and schooling them. I rode hard all day, slept well all night, and never thought twice about anything, except the fact that I was having a glorious time."

"How long ago was that?" she asked with a slight smile.

"Almost twenty years."

Julia cleared her throat. "Far be it from me to mention this, but have you considered that you aren't sixteen anymore?"

He shot her a hard look. She could well understand that people would quail before such a glance from Brand Delaney. But she did not. The memory of his mouth on hers still fresh in her mind, she lifted her head and met that look straight on.

"What's that supposed to mean?" he demanded.

"That you can do a great many things now that you couldn't do then, but riding a maddened stallion until he exhausts himself isn't going to leave you ready to do cartwheels."

"It's just a twinge," he insisted.

"Have it your way. What do you think will happen to the horse now?"

Brand hesitated, but only for an instant. "I'm going to buy him."

"You're what?"

"You heard. I had a quick word with the trainer. For a thousand dollars, his owner will be glad to see the back of him. Actually, if I wanted to, I could probably get the price down farther than that."

"After what he did today, they should pay you for taking him."

"Maybe," Brand admitted, "but I've got a feeling about him. Some horses are just plain wrong, it's a sickness in them. But he isn't like that. He's been hurt, I'm sure of it."

Julia flinched. She hated the idea of cruelty to animals and loathed people who indulged in it. "You may be right, but if you are, there's no saying he can be changed."

"I think he can. I've seen it done. With enough patience and gentleness, he'll be brought round. And when he is—" Brand's eyes gleamed. "He's magnificent, exactly what I'm looking for."

"You can't breed him until you're sure he's gentled. Aside from the fact that you might be wrong and his get could be as damaged as he is, he couldn't be let near a mare in his present condition."

Brand nodded. Once again, he didn't seem at all taken aback by her frank speech.

Very few women of her class would acknowledge having the slightest idea of what happened between a stallion and a mare. Even women who had borne a half-dozen children indulged in the absurd pretense that they had no notion how such a thing had happened to them.

Julia found that as much amusing as annoying. At her most polite—say, at a meeting of the ladies' garden club— she could never manage such hypocrisy.

But she had always presumed that most any man she met, save those in her own family, would expect her to do so. Brand seemed to be the exception.

"Good luck with him," she said softly. "I know Sean will have a thing or two to say about it, for he has a hard head even when it comes to animals. But he wouldn't want to see such a fine horse wasted, either."

"If I can't gentle him, I'll put him somewhere where he can't hurt himself or anyone else. But I won't destroy him. I just don't believe we've any right to do that."

Julia nodded. Silently she noted that this hard, ruthless man seemed to have no hesitation about revealing a gentler side of his nature with her. The edges of her lips curled up in a smile.

Slowly but surely, he was undermining her defenses, making her think in ways she knew she must not. If she had any sense—

"What's so funny?" Brand asked.

Belatedly she realized he'd been watching her. "Nothing. I was just thinking."

"About what?" he asked quietly, as though well aware that she might refuse to share her thoughts with him.

At almost any other time, she probably would have. But the kiss and all that had followed had shaken her so deeply that she wasn't thinking very clearly.

Or perhaps she was.

"About how things change. I read Amelia Daniels's journal the other night. I thought I knew all about her, but it turned out I knew almost nothing."

"How so?"

Julia smiled. "She's regarded as this paragon of womanhood, extraordinarily courageous, self-sacrificing, wise, and so on. Do you know there's a move under way in town to raise a statue to her?"

"What's wrong with that?"

"Nothing, except Amelia herself would laugh her head off. You see, she had a rather more controversial life than is generally known."

"Any woman who founded her own settlement would have to have been controversial, wouldn't she?"

"Definitely, but over the years people have lost track of that. She's Amelia Daniels, you see, founder of Belle Haven, so she has to be a model of rectitude and propriety."

"Whether or not she really was?"

"Exactly. She . . . she lived life on her own terms, more than most people do."

"Do you think she was wrong to do that?"

"No," Julia said hastily. "On the contrary, I think she was simply more honest than most people. She had her own sense of honor, and she followed it."

"I almost regret not knowing her."

"Almost?"

He looked at her and smiled. "I prefer being alive now."

"So do I," Julia said softly. "It's your shoulder, isn't it?"

He started to shake his head, then stopped. "It'll be fine."

She was sure that it would be, but knew he would suffer a good deal of discomfort in the meantime. "A hot bath would help," she suggested.

"Undoubtedly."

"But not much."

"It doesn't matter. I've been in far worse shape."

Julia decided she would just as soon not hear about that. The pain he was in right now hurt her enough as it was.

"There's an ointment," she said.

His nose wrinkled. "Not one of those horrible patent medicines?"

"No, I make it. Actually, it works rather well." Her family swore by it, and so did everyone else who had ever had occasion to use it. She was certain it would make him feel better.

"If you don't mind riding as far as the house, I can give you some. Or if you'd rather, I'll bring it into town."

He looked at her levelly. They were nearing the place where the road forked, west toward town, east toward the shore and Daniels' Neck.

It was getting on for midafternoon. Clouds were gathering out over the sea. The wind had picked up. It looked as if a storm might be approaching.

"There's no need for you to come into town," he said, and turned his mount alongside hers.

The ointment was kept in the stillroom, just off the kitchen. It was a cool, dry place, good for storing all sorts of herbs and medicines. Julia took a small pot down from a shelf and returned to the kitchen where Brand was waiting.

He was looking around with undisguised interest. "That's the original fireplace, isn't it?" he said, pointing to the large fieldstone mantel blackened by time. A beehive oven was built into the side of it, and various wrought-iron hooks jutted out at useful angles.

Julia nodded. "This was the first part of the house, built in 1650 by Garrick Marlowe."

"Who was he?"

"Amelia's... husband."

Brand cocked his head slightly to one side. "Why the hesitation? Who was he really?"

"Her husband, really, only he wasn't that yet when he started building this house."

"Was he trying to win her affections?"

"Oh, I think he'd already done that. I mean... that is to say..."

"Yes?" Brand drawled. He looked amused.

"It was a different time," Julia insisted.

"That's hard to argue with."

"People did things... Well, why not? They were out in the wilderness, not knowing if they would survive from one day to the next."

"Is it really so different now?" he asked. "None of us knows our fate."

That was true, Julia thought. He could have been killed trying to stop the stallion. She could have died years before, in the accident she'd had. Any one of them was vulnerable.

"I suppose," she said slowly. Clearing her throat, she added, "You can put this on now, if you'd like."

He nodded and took the small pot from her. Removing the lid, he sniffed cautiously. "Smells good."

"It feels even better." She turned away, intending to leave him to his privacy, but Brand stopped her.

"There's a problem."

"What's that?"

"Reluctant though I am to admit it, I don't think I can reach the spot that hurts." He tried, and promptly winced. "Of course, I can keep trying."

"No, that's all right. I can do it, but you'll have to—"

"Take off my shirt. I know. Would you mind—?"

Julia helped. He undid the remaining buttons at the top, then tugged the shirt out of his waistband. Together they managed to ease it off over his head.

Brand groaned slightly. He rubbed his shoulder. "Hurts more than I realized."

Julia nodded, although she hadn't entirely heard him. She was staring directly at his chest, a massive expanse of burnished skin, heavily muscled and lightly dusted with dark hair that looked feather-soft.

Her father and brother were well-built men, but she couldn't remember the last time she had seen either of them shirtless, and, besides, they would certainly not have had this effect on her.

Her stomach suddenly seemed full of butterflies—an expression she had never fully understood until just then—and there was a tightening deep inside her that was almost painful.

"Sit down," she said faintly.

He did. She took up the ointment, meaning to make short work of it, but the moment her fingers touched his skin, her resolve evaporated. She could think of nothing except how he felt beneath her touch. His skin was smooth as velvet pulled taut over solid rock. He was warm, alive, and infinitely male.

Her senses swam. She closed her eyes for a moment, fighting for control. When she opened them, Brand was looking at her. "That feels much better."

"Does it?"

He nodded and flexed his shoulder. "Much. If a man's going to be foolish enough to do what I did, he'd be wise to have you close by."

Julia thought she ought to have a tart reply to that, but she couldn't seem to come up with one. She couldn't think of much of anything—if *think* was the right word—except how he looked and felt, and, heaven help her, how he made her feel.

"You can put your shirt back on," she said, appalled at how weak her voice sounded.

"Doesn't it have to dry?"

He was right, it really should. She nodded, knowing she had to turn away, had to stop staring at him, had to find something—anything—to distract herself with.

"Are you hungry?"

His smile deepened. He stood up and flexed his shoulder again. "Not really." Glancing around the kitchen, he added, "I don't think I've ever been in a house this old."

It was an invitation she gratefully seized. "I'll be happy to show you around."

Surely he would put his shirt back on now. But either he felt the ointment wasn't dried yet or he simply didn't think of it. Bare-chested, he followed her into the small hall that connected the kitchen with the rest of the house.

For the next half hour, they explored the main floor. Julia pointed out the small birthing room in which generations of her family had first seen the light.

"Did Garrick Marlowe build this, too?"

"He did, and rather quickly, I gather. They had nine children, all born here. Rather remarkably for those times, they all grew to adulthood and had children of their own."

The house had grown apace, with each generation making its own contributions. There were gracious bow windows added to the front parlor shortly before the Revolution, marble mantels installed around every fireplace except the kitchen's at the time of the Civil War, and finally, most recently, indoor plumbing.

"I suppose I'll be the one to electrify," Julia mused as they stood in the front parlor. "Although I have to admit, I'm in no hurry."

"You plan to stay here, then?"

She was surprised by the question. "Of course, where else would I go?"

"You might marry someone who prefers to live elsewhere—or has to."

"Oh, no, I don't think so. I have no intention of ever marrying."

It was his turn to be startled. "Why not?"

"A woman gives up too much when she weds."

"What an extraordinary thought. I presumed all women wanted to marry."

"Only because they can't think of an alternative. I'm more fortunate." She gestured around the parlor. "I have a home of my own, for which I am beholden to no man. I can take care of myself, financially and in every other way. What possible reason would I have for marrying?"

"Companionship?" he suggested. "Children?"

"I like children," she acknowledged, "but I undoubtedly will have plenty of nieces and nephews to lavish affection on. As for companionship, I suspect a dog is more reliable."

He laughed. "I'm not sure, but I think you've just insulted my gender."

"Not really. My parents have a wonderful relationship, but it's rare. Besides, my mother is a much nicer and more agreeable sort of person than I. She's the sort of woman who's suited to be a wife. I'm not."

"So you intend to remain a spinster?"

Julia grimaced. She was amazed at how comfortable she felt talking with him about such matters, and in his present state of dishabille to boot.

But then, that undoubtedly only went to show how right she was. She simply wasn't like other young women, and couldn't expect to want what they wanted.

"I prefer to say that I intend to remain independent. You should understand that. Don't you yourself believe that marriage is no more than a business relationship in which a woman produces children in return for the protection and support of the man?"

The corners of his mouth quirked. "Did I really put it that bluntly?"

"Essentially, and I think in many cases you're right. People used to be much more honest about that. Nowadays they're all afire for romance and true love, but marriage hasn't truly changed."

Brand scratched his chest absently as he considered what she'd said. Julia followed him with her eyes and felt a shocking urge to stay his hand, to trace its course with her own, to give vent to the overwhelming curiosity she felt about this being who was so very different from herself.

And so very compelling.

"The ointment is surely dry," she said, looking away quickly.

"I suppose." Yet he made no move to return to the kitchen. Instead, he took a step closer to her, then another. "Julia..."

She stood, hardly breathing. He raised a hand and touched her hair. His smile was bemused. "The first time I saw you, I thought you were a boy."

"Understandably."

"Then I thought you plain."

Pain stabbed her deep inside, but she refused to show it.

"Prim and proper Miss Nash," Brand murmured. His hand moved deeper, cupping the back of her head. She was aware suddenly of the rapid rise and fall of his chest, so close to her.

He laughed. It was a thoroughly male sound that sent shivers through her. "There are people who would be delighted to know I could make such a misjudgment. You won't tell them, will you?"

Mutely Julia shook her head. She had to move away, had to stop this impropriety right now. But her body would not obey her mind. She remained where she was, beneath his hand.

His head bent, blotting out the light. As she had before, she felt the touch of his mouth. But this time it was different, less tentative, more insistent. His lips were hard, parting hers. The taste of him filled her. She trembled and instinctively reached out for him, the only solidness in a world suddenly quaking out of control.

Instinctively her lips parted. The slow thrust of his tongue shocked her, but that was quickly blotted out by overwhelming pleasure. She moaned and clung to him harder, desperate not to be separated from the source of such astounding sensation.

His arms closed around her, rock-hard, yet not at all hurtful. Again his tongue thrust slow and deep.

Hardly aware of what she was doing, Julia responded. Her hands stroked the granite length of his back, even as the tip of her tongue touched his.

A groan broke from him. Far in the back of her mind, she realized that some barrier had been crossed. His hands slid down, cupping her buttocks. He lifted her slightly, rubbing her against him.

She felt the hardness pressing against her and realized what it was. Embarrassment heated her cheeks, but she couldn't for the life of her make any effort to stop.

Her breasts suddenly felt swollen, the nipples hard and erect against her camisole. Moist heat gathered inside her. She cried out softly as she felt her legs give way.

Brand caught her easily. He pressed her back against the wall of the parlor and continued kissing her deeply. At the same time, he tugged her shirt loose and slid his hands beneath it, cupping her breasts.

The sensation was so exquisite that Julia seriously thought she might die from it. But it was followed quickly by pleasure even more enthralling as his thumbs rubbed slowly over her nipples.

The camisole was of plain cotton worn thin by many washings. It offered only the scantiest barrier. He pulled lightly on the erect tips of her breasts, moving them between his thumb and forefingers.

Raw, hot desire shot through Julia. She had to be closer to him, had to—

Her head fell back, exposing the vulnerable line of her neck. He raked his mouth down the slender length to the scented hollow between her collarbones, and farther, to the swell of her breasts. Instinctively she moved against him. Her fingers dug into his shoulders, feeling the skin hot beneath her touch, the tensile strength, the sheer, male power of him.

For a blinding instant, she understood—everything. The desperate, crazy things people did, the seemingly inexplicable choices they made, the moments they never forgot or yearned for.

And she understood herself—plain and proper Miss Nash—far better than she had ever thought she would, or would necessarily have chosen to.

In another moment—

Brand raised his head. His eyes blazed, and his breathing was ragged. Yet just enough reason remained to make him hesitate.

"Julia..."

His voice pierced the haze of passion. She shivered, as though awakening suddenly from a dream of such eroticism and power that she hardly believed herself capable of it.

But this was no dream. It was hard reality. She was stunningly close to an irrevocable step, one that went counter to all the teachings of her lifetime, yet one that she was still almost unbearably tempted to take.

Desperately she fought to regain what little self-control was left to her. Tears stung her eyes. Shorn of pride, with nothing remaining to her but sheer survival, she wrenched herself away from him and fled.

Chapter Nine

Julia did not come back downstairs until she was sure Brand had gone. Even then, she sat for a long time in the kitchen, huddled in one of the big old chairs beside the table.

Her knees were pulled to her chin, which rested on them. Her arms were wrapped around her legs. In that position, she at least seemed able to think, although not very well.

Confusion, embarrassment and regret all warred within her. It was a singularly uncomfortable sensation. Even worse, she felt like a stranger to herself.

Who was this woman of unbridled passion and, seemingly, no shame? This woman who would gladly have thrown away the strictures of a lifetime for a moment of pleasure?

She sighed. All right, more than a moment. And more than pleasure. Untried though she was, she was wise enough to recognize the dimensions of what she had felt with Brand. It would have been unforgettable.

And that was exactly the problem. If she forgot everything she had ever been taught about modesty, decorum, propriety and so on, and gave in to the devouring hunger he provoked, what would happen afterward? How would she be able to go on with her life as though nothing had happened?

There was no answer for that, or at least not one she wanted to hear.

Slowly she raised her head and looked out beyond the kitchen windows. Her brows drew together. It was still only late afternoon, yet the sky was darkening. Moreover, it had a grayish yellow tinge that made the hairs rise at the back of her neck.

As a child, she had been in a terrible storm that tore up out of the south and hit Belle Haven hard. It had raged for hours, taking the roofs of some houses, destroying a stable near the railroad station and generally wreaking havoc.

She, her sister Gloria and Peter had huddled together in a room at the center of their own house. They'd all been too little to help their father, who, with a few of the men servants, had fought the rising wind and driving rain to get the horses to shelter and secure the shutters over the windows.

Even then, they had still been able to hear the storm battering against the house, as though determined to get in. When it finally subsided the following day, they had all felt lucky to have escaped.

Was it going to happen again?

She walked over to the kitchen door, opened it and stepped outside. The sky definitely looked ominous, and there was a stillness in the air that she didn't like. Yet every summer brought storms. Generally, they were nothing to worry about. She'd take a few precautions, and everything would be fine.

Several hours later, the horses secure in the stable and the shutters closed over all the windows, Julia settled down to wait. Outside, the wind was rising. A sudden gust blew down the chimney, so hard that it sent ashes whirling around the kitchen.

She hurried to clean them up, and had barely finished when the rain began. Lighting several more oil lamps, she set them around the house to dispel the growing darkness.

The closed shutters muted the sound of the rain, but she was aware of it all the same. It was coming down harder by the moment.

As night fell, Julia put on the heavy canvas raincoat she kept for the bad weather and ran to the stables to check on the horses. They were glad to see her. Whinnying softly, they seemed fine.

The stables were in a sturdy, well-constructed building that was actually newer than any part of the house. She made sure there was adequate food and water, then carefully closed the doors behind her, sliding the bolt across to keep them shut against the wind.

Her lantern swung wildly as she hurried across the rain-slicked yard, back to the house. By the time she got inside, she was wet even through the canvas, and shivering, despite the fact that it was far from cold. There was a smell in the air, heavy, languorous, as though of the tropics.

She had rarely encountered it before, but knew that it did not bode well. If this storm had come so far north from tropical climes, it had to be bigger, stronger and uglier than most any other storm they'd ever had.

Hanging the coat to dry in the mudroom, she carefully closed all the chimney flues, then remembered her father saying that a window should always be left open just a crack. Having done that, she settled down to wait.

Brand sent his manservant to bed, assuring him that everything had been battened down to secure the house. There was nothing now except to wait and see how bad it would be.

Standing on the porch, his hands thrust deep in his pockets, he stood looking out at the night. The branches of the oak trees immediately beyond the house were beginning to bend. Loose leaves swirled in rising eddies. There was a smell to the air, heavy, fecund, tropical.

He'd been in some bad storms down in the Caribbean, including one he'd ridden out at sea and would never forget. But this was something different.

Something worse.

It was the smell, he decided, more than the wind, which was strong but not really threatening—yet. The rain was no worse than a bad nor'easter—yet. The smell was the key. It didn't belong here, not on this coast, not so far north. It hinted at a size and fury rarely seen in these parts.

Brand's slashing brows drew together. Unwillingly he thought of Julia, alone out on Daniels' Neck.

It wasn't really the storm that brought her to mind. She had been firmly lodged there ever since fleeing from him.

In the hours since, even as he returned home and made a valiant effort to distract himself, he could think of nothing but her and the effect she had on him.

He was not a man who lost control. His whole life was founded on that principle. And yet with her he seemed to have no control at all. Prim and proper Miss Nash—he smiled at the absurdity of that—turned him into a green boy at the mercy of hot blood and raging hunger.

But he had never been that boy. Never. He had grown up fast, and early on had become the man he was now. Or had been, until he set foot in fair Belle Haven and met a boyish hoyden turned schoolmarmish spinster turned seductress.

Was that fair? Surely she wouldn't agree. The mere suggestion that he was the seduced one would undoubtedly outrage her. And yet he had the disconcerting sense that that was exactly what was happening to him.

He couldn't let it. Honor and simple sense both demanded that he keep well away from her. She had no place in his life, and he had no place in hers. They'd made that more than clear to each other.

Was he merely being contrary, lusting after a woman who was totally unsuited to his purposes? Perhaps that was it.

Staring out into the night, he considered the possibility that he was deliberately sabotaging his search for a wife.

Try though he did, he couldn't get the idea to ring true. In his thirty-five years, he had lived more than most men of ninety could claim to have. He'd wandered the world, enjoyed his full share of women and then some, made a fortune and, most important of all, taken control of his own life.

He wanted to settle down, live in the same place, see the same people. And he wanted children. Was that so wrong?

Julia seemed to think so. She had made her disdain crystal-clear. No marriage for her, no children. She cherished independence above all.

Damn female. The wind suddenly surged, whipping around the house. For the first time, it spoke. Wind with a voice, not the soft murmur of a blowy day, but the keen howl of unleashed power.

It pushed against Brand as though trying to force him back into the house. He stood, hard and resilient as the oak, defying it.

And he thought of Julia. Alone.

She would be fine. She'd probably ridden out worse storms before, and she was certainly capable enough to do what was necessary. Except he doubted there'd been many storms worse than this one, and she wouldn't have been on Daniels' Neck during them. She would have been safe at home in her parents' house, where she damn well still belonged. Not living on her own in a crazy old house hard by the sea.

It could all blow over and amount to nothing. Even as he tried to convince himself of that, he lifted his head, inhaling that smell and feeling with every pore of his skin the heavy fury that was coming.

Abruptly Brand went back inside. He was out again within minutes, armored against the night in a heavy canvas coat he'd had for years and a slouch hat he'd bought somewhere out West on one of his expeditions.

At the stable, he debated which horse to take. His regular mount was a good-tempered gelding, but he was more schooled to hard, pounding rides over country lanes in good weather. Already the storm was spooking him. He tossed his head and whinnied urgently.

Brand patted him quickly and went on down the line. Toward the end, he spied the mare he'd bought that day. She was munching calmly at her oats, but raised her head when she saw him.

He put a hand to her side. She was rock-steady, without a tremor. Ordinarily Brand had the usual prejudice in favor of male horses. But he had a sense that on this night, in these circumstances, the mare might be the better choice.

Julia would undoubtedly think so.

He had to stop this. What she thought, felt, wanted... didn't want... was of no consequence to him. He was simply doing what any responsible neighbor would do, checking up on a woman living alone who might need help.

He would do it if she were eighty and bent-backed. That she was a fey sort of beauty who turned to fire in his arms made no difference.

Having made up his mind, he saddled the mare and led her outside. She hesitated for just a moment, then tossed her head and stepped forward eagerly.

Brand laughed, wondering if the woman who had picked the mare out for him was as pleased by the adventure this night was fast becoming. He hoped she, at least, had enough sense not to be, but he wouldn't have bet on it.

Mounting, he touched his heels to the horse's sides and cantered down the road in the direction of Daniels' Neck.

Julia was jolted awake by a sudden rending noise that pierced her sleep and sent her bolt upright. She was at the kitchen table, where she had dozed off a short time before.

The wind was screaming, tearing against the shutters like a thousand enraged hands trying to rip their way into the house.

She jumped up and ran to the windows, quickly checking to make sure that the shutters were holding. That done, she hurried through the house, trying to discover what had made the terrible sound.

A vase had fallen over in the front parlor, and fragments of china lay scattered on the rug. But she didn't think that could account for what she'd heard. The very walls seemed to be vibrating as the wind struck them again and again.

But the sound had come from outside. She was sure of that now. Was it the stables?

Quickly she ran to the mudroom and yanked the canvas coat on again. Taking the lantern from the kitchen table, she opened the door.

Or she tried to. It took all her weight hurled against it to open the door just far enough for her to slip out. Immediately she regretted it. The wind tore at her, almost wrenching the lantern from her hands.

She cried out fearfully, but the sound was lost in fury. Only concern for the horses kept her from fleeing back into the house. Instead, she plunged on, bent almost double.

Halfway across the yard, the wind drove her to her knees. It shrieked all around her so that she couldn't hear her own thoughts. Slowly she crawled to her feet and kept going.

At last, she reached the stable and managed to get inside. The moment she slammed the door behind her, the noise eased, at least a little. The sturdy walls and roof, all blessedly undamaged, stood firm, holding the storm at bay.

The horses were nervous all the same, and glad to see her. She reassured each and checked all along the length of the outside walls to make sure no cracks were showing.

Only when she was convinced that the animals were as safe as they could be did she steel herself to return to the house. Mercifully, the wind was in a slight lull. Though it still tore at her, she managed to cross the yard without falling and get the kitchen door open.

Slamming it behind her, she leaned against it and gasped for breath. She felt bruised and battered, as though she had been through a terrible struggle. And indeed, she had been.

Shakily she set the lantern down on the table and removed the coat. Her arms throbbed, and the sodden fabric felt almost too heavy to hold. But she got it off finally and hung it to dry in the mudroom.

That done, she looked around for some way to distract herself. A cup of tea seemed like a good idea. She had just put the kettle on to boil when another sound from outside drew her attention.

Julia muttered under her breath. She didn't want to go back out into that fury. Indeed, she doubted she could do so and get back inside. Besides, she'd probably just imagined it.

But the sound came again—a horse's frightened whinny. Grimacing, Julia reached for the door. This time, she didn't bother with the coat. It seemed to do her little good, anyway. Straining through the darkness, she looked toward the stable.

The sound came again, but from a different direction. Startled, she turned and gazed out toward the road. It couldn't be. She couldn't possibly be seeing what appeared to be a horse and rider fighting their way toward her through the shrieking wind.

Quickly she grabbed the lantern and ran outside. Holding it high, she cast a circle of light far into the night.

The rider was heading toward the stable. Could it be Peter or her father, foolishly out to help her?

But how could it be? They were miles away, far inland, and couldn't possibly reach Daniels' Neck. But then who?

She had the answer soon enough. The stable doors opened again, closed, and a dark shape strode toward her.

His head was down, but otherwise he made no concession to the storm. Far more quickly then she could have, he stepped into the circle of light.

"For God's sake," Brand said, "what are you doing out here?"

Julia could hardly believe her eyes or ears. He couldn't possibly be here, not this man from whom she had fled scant hours before. Her imagination was playing tricks on her, or she'd been hit in the head and hadn't realized it, or—

"Inside," he said, and, taking the lantern from her, shoved her through the door. Without any further ceremony, he slammed it shut behind him and glared at her.

He looked wildly rumpled and untamed, with a day's growth of beard shadowing his square jaw and a furious light in his eyes. He was a big, hard, cantankerous male, and he was right here, inches away from her, dripping water all over the kitchen floor.

Brand yanked the hat from his head and shook it. He ran a hand through his thick black hair and glared at her again. "I suppose it was too much to hope that you'd have had the sense to leave."

Julia straightened her shoulders, put her hands on her hips and glared back. She absolutely refused to be intimidated by him.

"Why should I? This is my home. At least I stayed put in it. Only a madman would venture out on such a night."

"Then I must be mad," he said grimly as he stomped over to the table and tossed his hat down. The lantern followed. He removed his coat and looked around for somewhere to hang it.

"I'll take that," Julia said quickly, motivated not so much by courtesy as the need to impose some sort of order on this raw, challenging presence who made the walls of her house suddenly seem to shrink.

But the moment she took the coat, she stumbled. It weighed far more than her own.

Brand shot her an I-could-have-told-you-so look and took the coat from her. She gestured toward the mud-room.

He returned moments later, looking in better humor than he had before. "You're right," he said. "I must be mad to venture out in this. I'd have been far smarter to leave you to yourself."

"You came because of me?" Julia asked, incredulously. Until that very moment, the possibility hadn't occurred to her. She had presumed he'd merely been foolish enough to venture out as people did sometimes when they imagined a storm was a spectacle for their enjoyment.

But she should have known better, for he surely did. He had lived in the Caribbean, and undoubtedly realized just how dangerous such storms could be. He would never have gone out for any casual reason.

But he had for her.

Her breath caught. "You shouldn't have done this," she said softly.

He shrugged, drawing her unwilling attention to the span of his shoulders. "Is everything secured here?"

She assured him that it was, but he remained unconvinced. He insisted on checking everything himself, upstairs, as well as down. Julia trailed after him. But when he entered her bedroom, she stopped just inside the door and waited.

He didn't so much as glance around, but headed straight for the windows, as he had in all the other rooms. Assured that the shutters were firmly bolted, he nodded and turned back to her. "It's a hell of a blow."

Julia swallowed hard, determined not to be at all discomposed by having him there, in her own bedroom, big, angry, and still dripping. "Perhaps you would like some tea."

He winced. "I'd rather have a whiskey, but I suppose it's smarter to keep a clear head. Tea it is."

"How is your shoulder?" she asked as they went back down the stairs. She really did want to know, but in addition she wanted to make it clear to him that she could mention the events of that afternoon without behaving like a stammering idiot. What had happened between them should not have. It was over and done with, forgotten. It would not happen again.

"Fine. The stable looks well built."

"It is."

"Still, we'll have to keep an eye on it. Everything else, too, for that matter."

"I had planned to sit up."

"I hadn't," he said bluntly, "at least not until this started. If you want to take the first watch, that's fine with me."

Truly, he was not at all hamstrung by the misguided notions of chivalry that dogged some men. Not at all. "How kind," she murmured, and went to check the kettle.

They drank tea, and ate stew for dinner, with fresh-baked bread. The stew was made from seafood brought to Julia the previous day by a nearby fisherman and stored in her icehouse, which was dug into the cellar of the house.

"There's no telling when we'll get more like this," she said as she forked out a mussel and popped it in her mouth.

"If it's as bad as it sounds, it'll be at least a fortnight before the fishing's back," Brand said. He glanced toward the kitchen windows, which were still firmly shuttered. They could hear the wind tearing against them. "I hope the boats got back in time."

"It came on slowly enough. There was warning."

"And this could be the worst of it. Who knows?"

There was no way of telling. The storm could blow itself out in another hour or two, doing only minor damage. Or it might worsen as only a few storms did in any lifetime, scything a path of terror and destruction for miles along the coast.

"I'll check on the horses," Brand said when they had finished eating. Julia was clearing up. He came back from the mudroom with his greatcoat and hat on and went to open the door. The moment he did so, the kitchen filled with the wind's scream. Behind the closed door and shutters, the storm had sounded bad enough. But now the full strength of it became evident.

Brand cursed under his breath. He slammed the full strength of his body into the wind. Over his shoulder, he yelled, "Help me close this."

Julia raced to obey. The door shut, if only barely. She stepped back, staring at it and wondering how much longer it would hold. Surely no house, no matter how well built, could withstand such a battering indefinitely.

Brand wasn't gone long, but while he was, she hardly breathed. Visions of something terrible happening to him kept darting through her mind.

What if a plank tore loose and hit him? What if a branch snapped? What if he lost his footing? What if . . . what if . . . what if?

By the time he shoved the door open again and stumbled into the kitchen, she was almost frantic with worry. Unthinking, she ran to him. "Are you all right?"

He stared down into her face. Slowly the tautness eased from his features. He touched the back of his hand to her cheek in a gesture of such tenderness that she blinked rapidly.

"I'm fine, and so are the horses. But it's getting worse out there. Forget what I said about you keeping watch. I'll do it."

"It doesn't seem fair, what with you coming all the way out here, and after all, I am capa—"

"Julia?"

"Yes."

"Shut up."

Perhaps he doubted she would obey. Or perhaps that had nothing to do with it all. In any case, Brand followed his directive with action. He took her into his arms and kissed her hard on the mouth.

Chapter Ten

An instant later, Brand released her. His heart was thudding against his ribs for reasons that had nothing to do with the fury of the storm. The taste of her lingered on his mouth.

It took every ounce of strength he possessed not to drag her back into his arms, carry her up the stairs and lay her down on the wide, welcoming bed he had glimpsed in her room. He had a sudden, searing image of her lying naked, her glorious auburn hair spread over the pillows, her arms raised to receive him.

The vision rocked him. He dragged in breath. His fists were clenched at his sides. The hardness in his loins was beyond any he had ever known.

Julia's face was flushed, and her eyes were wide and luminous. Wisps of hair trailed around her forehead. She looked disheveled, passionate, and altogether glorious. Prim and plain Miss Nash. He would have laughed if he didn't already hurt so much.

"The lanterns," he said.

She nodded and moved away. When she had her back to him, he was able to regain some semblance of control. But only some.

Not for a moment did he underestimate his state. Once again, he was perilously close to losing the control he had always counted on.

Maybe she was right. Maybe he shouldn't have come. But the moment he thought of that, he thought of her here alone and knew he had done the right thing. However hard it was for him—and he smiled ruefully at his choice of words—he needed to protect her.

Rather than let himself question why he should feel this way about a woman he had met only a few days before, he went upstairs again and found the narrow, winding staircase to the attic. Carrying a lantern, he climbed to the top and shone the light around.

With only the roof to separate him from the outside, he could hear the wind's keening more strongly than ever. But, to his relief, the attic was dry. The roof was holding, so far at least.

Back downstairs, he found Julia in the parlor. Her fingers trailed lightly over the keys of a piano set in one corner. The sound was barely audible over the wind.

"You should get some rest," he said.

His voice startled her. She jumped slightly and shut the piano cover. He felt some satisfaction in knowing that he wasn't the only one to find the situation extraordinarily stressful, but he didn't fool himself, either. Miss Julia Nash might be worried about the storm, nothing more. He had no reason to think she was as affected by him as he was by her.

No reason at all.

"I don't think I could sleep," she said.

"It's going to be a long night."

Barely had he spoken when the wind seemed to take on new fury, pounding against the house. Above it came the sound of rending wood.

"A shutter," Julia gasped.

"At least one."

They hurried to find it. Two shutters had been ripped loose in a small bedroom on the east side of the house. The glass panes had also broken. Water was pouring into the room, whipped by the wind.

Julia ran to get towels to mop it up while Brand found scrap wood, a hammer and nails in the basement. He closed off the windows and cleared away the glass.

"Those may only be the first," he said.

Julia nodded. "About ten years ago, we had a fall when one storm came through after another. None of them as bad as this, but bad enough. Gramma Sara had boards cut for all the windows."

"That must be what I saw downstairs. I'm going to start bringing them up."

"I'll help."

Together they brought the boards upstairs and figured out which windows they belonged to. Brand got busy covering over everything on the east side of the house, the side taking the greatest blast from the wind. Julia held the boards while he hammered.

Inevitably, their hands and arms brushed, and their bodies touched. Brand did his utmost to ignore the sensations this released in him. He had a job to do, damn it. There was no telling how bad this was going to be. He wasn't a sixteen-year-old, to forget everything but the driving hunger for a woman.

He was in control.

All the same, when the last board was up, he breathed a sigh of relief. Maybe now she'd go to sleep. If he didn't have to look at her, see the grace of her movements, smell the mingled perfume of soap, sun and pure woman, maybe then he would be all right.

And maybe not.

At any rate, Julia showed no inclination to sleep. He could hardly blame her.

The storm was increasing steadily in fury. Julia wrapped her arms around herself and glanced nervously toward the kitchen door. "The horses can only take so much."

Brand nodded. He had been thinking the same thing. Much as he wanted to believe that the storm couldn't possibly get any worse, he was beginning to think otherwise.

He had heard tales of storms that blew with such rage that they seemed capable of tearing apart the whole world. This might be one such. "Is there an outside entrance to the basement?" he asked.

Julia nodded. "Down a short ramp. My horses could make it. What about yours?"

He thought of the well-tempered mare. "It shouldn't be a problem."

But it would be, and they both knew it. No horses, no matter how obedient, would enter a basement in the midst of a raging storm without balking. Much as he wanted to, he couldn't get them in there alone.

"It's only going to get worse," Julia said, as though reading his thoughts.

"We can't be sure."

"I am." She was silent for a moment, concentrating. "It's the way the air feels, as though it's come alive. And it's so heavy. When I was watching you hammer the boards, I thought that that was what this is like, a great hammer of a storm that isn't going to stop any time soon."

Regretfully, he had to agree with her. The thought of her going out into the storm again made his stomach knot, but there was no alternative.

Huddled in their coats, they ran across the yard. Julia would have been knocked down by the wind if Brand hadn't kept an arm around her waist. Even so, they were both gasping for breath when they reached the stable.

Their instincts quickly proved right. Tearing fingers of wind had reached under the shingles at the far end of the roof and torn several off. A keen howling sound filled the building.

The horses were pawing the ground and ramming against the stall doors. In another few minutes, they would have begun to break loose. As it was, there was a real possibility they would injure themselves.

There were four in all, including the mare Brand had brought. Quickly they bridled them. Leading two each, they plunged out into the storm again.

Now came the sharpest test of the horses' schooling. If they bolted into the night, there would be no way to get them back. But, though they cried out in fear and tossed their heads, none tried to break loose. Mercifully, the wind decreased slightly. Brand was able to get the double doors to the basement open. He went first, urging the horses along.

For a horrible moment, it looked as though they would not follow. But trust and terror together won out. Slowly, then more quickly, the animals stepped down the ramp.

When all four were inside the basement and the doors shut again, Julia sagged against Mirage. Her face was ashen, and she was bleeding from a cut to her forehead.

"What happened?" Brand demanded.

She touched a finger to her head. "I don't know. Something must have hit me."

His face tightened. He made sure the horses were all right, then took her arm and headed for the stairs. When they reached the kitchen, he pushed her into a chair. "Where do you keep bandages?"

She started to rise. "It's nothing. I'll take care of it."

"Like hell." His hand was hard on her shoulder. He didn't mean to hurt her, hated even the thought of it, but he was exhausted, his patience was gone, and the wound on her forehead was still bleeding.

She took one look at his expression and quieted. "Over there, in the pantry."

He went in the direction she indicated, remembering after the fact that this was the room where she'd kept the ointment. It was a small, windowless space, fragrant with the scent of the dried herbs that hung in bunches from the exposed rafters. Old wooden shelves were crowded with tin boxes, jars, objects wrapped in cloth, and several books that looked ancient.

For an instant, he remembered what Julia had said about being interested in plants, the way Amelia Daniels had been. He flexed his shoulder, wondering what exactly was in that ointment she'd used.

The thought fled as quickly as it had come. He spied a basket filled with neatly rolled bandages, and next to it a regulation doctor's bag. Taking both, he returned to the kitchen. Julia was still sitting at the table. She hadn't yet removed her coat. For that matter, neither had he.

Removing his, he set the basket and bag on the table, then gently eased her coat off. Water-soaked, it felt as though it weighed ten pounds. He wondered how she had managed to remain upright long enough to get the horses across the yard and into the basement. By the looks of her, the effort had taken all her strength and then some.

"Hold still," he said gruffly as he bathed the wound. An ointment in the bag looked and smelled right. He applied a small amount and finished with a bandage.

By the time he was done, he thought she might be asleep, so very still did she seem. But as he fastened the bag, she murmured, "You did that very well."

"I've had some practice." Out West and in the Caribbean, he'd learned to bandage wounds, extract bullets and care for fevers.

Anyone who traveled in such places and wanted to stay alive did the same. But he'd never had to take care of any injury that disturbed him as much as Julia's did.

That was absurd. It was a small cut that, when healed, probably wouldn't leave the slightest scar. Still, the thought of her being hurt made him feel hollow inside. He was astonished to see that his hand trembled as he snapped the bag shut.

While he was caring for her, he hadn't been paying much attention to the storm. But as he returned from putting the supplies back, he realized that any lull in the wind was more than gone now. The storm seemed to howl with renewed fury.

There was a loud crack outside, followed quickly by another. Julia's head shot up. Her eyes widened to dark pools. "The trees."

"Most will come through fine," he said, though he had no way of knowing that. Just then, the wind seemed to redouble its fury. It attacked the house with such force that the very walls seemed to tremble. Quickly Brand helped Julia to her feet. "I think we'd better head for the center of the house."

She whitened even further, but made no objection. The sound of the storm had changed. It was like nothing either of them had ever heard before.

When Julia was safe in the stillroom, Brand made a final trip upstairs. He checked once more on the shuttered and boarded windows. In Julia's room, he paused, looking at the bed. With a muttered curse for the invincible waywardness of his thoughts, he stripped off the covers and pillows.

Back in the stillroom, Julia helped him spread the covers on the floor. They piled the pillows against the inner wall. With the door closed and a lantern for light, the small space was as comfortable and safe as they could make it.

Neither of them spoke. Brand sat upright against the pillows and drew Julia to him. She hesitated for a moment, but exhaustion washed away whatever resistance she might have felt. With a sigh, she rested her head against his chest.

He held her gently, breathing in the perfume of her skin. She felt slender and delicate in his arms, yet her strength was unmistakable.

Beyond the walls of the old house, the storm roared in fury. But inside there was only the soft beat of Julia's heart and the steady rise and fall of her breathing.

Brand knew the moment when she slipped into sleep. He didn't move, but continued to hold her. The glow of the lantern remained steady, illuminating the small room and the woman who slept so trustingly against him.

There was no longer any doubt in his mind that the storm was a full-fledged hurricane, and an immense one at that. He was caught smack in the middle of it, all the way out on a spit of land in a house that was over two centuries old. His body ached, his eyes burned, and his head felt as though it were going to explode.

Yet he was starkly, absurdly happy.

At another time, he would have questioned that. But at the moment it was enough that he knew it to be true.

There was another crash outside, this one almost on top of the house. Julia did not move. He smiled and drew the covers over them both.

Julia stirred slowly. She felt wrapped in contentment, more at peace than she could remember ever being, and supremely comfortable. Wakefulness beckoned, but she resisted it. Better to remain so blissfully asleep, caught in a dream the details of which she couldn't remember, but knew she did not want to leave.

Still, despite her best efforts, reality intruded. Her head was resting against something incongruously hard. Surely that wasn't her pillow?

As for the rest of her, it, too, did not seem to recognize the familiar contours of her bed. Also, she rarely slept with a light on, but there was one on now, very low and soft, but a light all the same.

Slowly she stretched out a hand. Her fingers encountered smooth, warm hardness, very pleasant to the touch. Very curious. Barely awake, half believing it was all a dream, she explored farther. She knew this, had felt it before, had wanted to—

She gasped and sat up, staring around her in disbelief. The stillroom, Brand, the storm... it all came back to her. She had been asleep in his arms, her head on his chest and one of his legs thrown over hers in a position that was shockingly intimate.

Really, shockingly. She ought to be horrified, embarrassed, dismayed, and so on. But all she felt was a delicious languor seeping over her, and a sense of rightness so profound she knew that it had to come from the very essence of her being.

But what of the storm? Listening, she could hear nothing. The wind was silent. Relief swept through her. She was tempted to rise immediately and check the house. But the moment she tried, even half heartedly, Brand murmured in his sleep and held her closer.

Sighing, she lay back. Whatever damage had been done would surely wait until morning. If she were wise, she would seize the chance for more rest. If previous storms were any indication, there would be days of cleaning ahead.

She closed her eyes and shifted slightly, seeking a more comfortable position. That was a mistake. It brought her into even closer contact with the lean, hard length of him. Julia murmured under her breath. She felt enveloped in his strength and heat, in the scent and touch of him. Moreover, there was no escape without waking him.

She could do that, of course. But she hesitated. He had to be at least as tired as she was and, besides, she wasn't at all sure what would happen if he woke now.

That admission, even made to herself, banished any hope that she would sleep. Instead, she lay, looking into the shadows that filled the stillroom. She had been in and out of this place much of her life, and particularly in recent months. But she had never really thought about how very old everything looked—the walls, the shelves, the rafters. This might well be the only part of the house that dated from Amelia Daniels's time, and had not been changed at all.

Despite herself, she smiled. What would Amelia say if she could suddenly come back through time and find her descendant lying here on the floor of the stillroom, in the arms of a man she hadn't even known scant days before?

Knowing Amelia as she did after having read her journal, Julia was sure of the answer. Amelia would laugh and wish her well. She might even have a thing or two more to say about the precariousness of life, and the rare opportunities it offered for true joy.

Julia bit her lower lip. She must be mad to even think along such lines. She was a woman of impeccable family and position. Honor was sacred to her.

But what was honor, exactly? The opinion of her community? Or that firm inner sense of rightness that seemed to be growing with every passing moment?

Not that it mattered. Brand was asleep. He was likely to remain that way for hours yet. Lifting her head slightly, she looked at him. In the shadows cast by the lantern, he appeared younger and more approachable, not the tough, ruthless man he seemed when awake, but someone far gentler—perhaps the person he would have been if his life had been different.

She thought of the care with which he had bandaged her forehead, and his insistence on protecting the stallion, who would otherwise have been destroyed.

A low sigh escaped her. Life was turning out to be far more complicated than she had ever imagined.

This night would end, and come morning they would once again be Miss Nash and Mr. Delaney, neighbors bound to be cordial to one another, but nothing more. They would go their separate ways. She would never again lie in his arms, so close to him, and enjoy the luxury of studying him so intimately.

Her throat tightened. For the first time, she noticed the small white scar on his chin. Without thinking, she traced it lightly with her fingertip. Were there other scars on his body, testament to struggles she knew nothing about? The thought was at once sad and exciting.

He had absurdly long lashes for a man, dark as his hair, a feathery fringe lying against his cheeks. Would they feel as soft as they looked?

And then there was his mouth, not so hard as it appeared by day, but perfectly shaped, the lips just slightly parted. She remembered how that mouth had felt against her own, how the thrust of his tongue had caused her body to respond in ways she blushed to remember.

Indeed, memory alone was enough to provoke much the same response. Her breasts felt uncomfortably full, the nipples taut. She stirred again, trying to slip loose.

His arm tightened. She thought it was mere reflex, but some instinct made her glance up. His eyes were open. He was looking directly at her.

"I thought..."

"Don't think," he said, and took her mouth with his.

At his first touch, something deep within Julia snapped. She moaned and kissed him back with unbridled hunger.

Far in the back of her mind, her behavior shocked her. But yearnings so long denied and only so recently admitted would no longer be suppressed.

In the hushed quiet of the tiny room, sealed away from all the rest of the world, she made a conscious choice to seize the moment. Later, in the harsh light of day, she might regret it. But if she turned away, rejected all that he was and all that they could be together, she knew she would never forgive herself.

For six years, ever since the riding accident, she had lived an unnatural life, cut off from the pleasures of a young woman, the excitement of courting and romance, first love and marriage. She had forged a far different course, becoming a woman of unusual strength and independence. A woman who had the courage to put aside the strictures of her world and reach for all life offered, no matter what the price might be.

The tip of her tongue touched his. Brand groaned. He turned suddenly, drawing her under him. Bracing his weight on his powerful arms, he gazed down at her.

"Sweet Lord," he said huskily, "you are so beautiful."

Astoundingly, she did feel beautiful, lying there under him with his taste still on her mouth and the warmth of his big, hard body enveloping her.

Very hard. Her hands traced the bunched muscles of his arms and back. The sense of such power so close to her made her tremble. Not with fear, for she trusted him absolutely, but with the knowledge of such strength and virility drawn to her even as she was to him.

Her touch, untutored as it was, seemed to shatter his control. He made a rough sound deep in his throat and tore his shirt loose, yanking it over his head and off. His fingers fumbled at the buttons of her blouse. He cursed, grasped both sides of the garment and tore.

"I'll buy you another," he rasped, "a hundred. But right now, I have to—" He broke off, sliding his hands beneath the thin camisole.

The touch of rough, callused palms against her skin made Julia cry out. Her back bowed.

She hardly knew when he pulled the camisole off. Leaning back, he stared at her breasts. Embarrassed and enthralled all at once, she followed the direction of his gaze and saw herself as he saw her.

Her breasts were high and full, the nipples a deep dusky rose. Staring at her, a pulse leaped in the hollow of his cheek.

"Perfect," he murmured. His head bent, and his tongue flicked over her again and again before he finally drew one taut nipple into his mouth and suckled her.

Her hands twisted in his thick hair. He released her, but only to kiss her again, his tongue plunging deep. At the same time, he moved against her. The touch of hard, hair-covered muscle rubbing over the tips of her breasts made her cry out.

He moved urgently, impatiently, fumbling with his clothes in his haste to strip them off. Hers followed, skirt and pantaloons joining the jumble on the floor beside them.

Naked, flesh to flesh, they clung. He rained kisses over the curve of her breasts, down her flat stomach to the soft triangle between her thighs.

When his fingers slid over her mound, parting the delicate folds, she tried to resist. But Brand would have none of that. He pressed her down into the covers, murmuring reassurances, all the while stroking her tenderly, repeatedly.

She melted beneath him, all thought of resistance vanishing. Sweet, hot pressure built. She moaned and clung to him, uncertain of what was happening. The storm seemed to have come inside her, whirling furiously. She had to... she needed—

He moved, a hair-roughed leg slipping between her thighs and parting them. His features were taut in the lantern light, his eyes smoldering. "Don't be afraid," he whispered.

But she was beyond fear, devoured by hunger, thinking only of him and the incandescent sensations he evoked. Something smooth and hot probed against her.

She drew back slightly. His hands grasped her hips, holding her for him. He moved again, penetrating her, then stopped, giving her time to adjust.

She wasn't sure that she could adjust. He was so long, so thick—how could she possibly accommodate him? For the first time, real doubt pierced the haze of pleasure. She stiffened, resisting.

Still holding her, he licked all around both nipples, then took one into his mouth. His thumbs rubbed over her abdomen, pressing lightly toward her mound. He moved slightly, thrusting deeper.

Pleasure turned suddenly to pain. Yet even then she truly did not want him to stop. Her hips rose, seeking him. He hesitated a scant instant, then took firmer hold of her and drove fully into her.

She felt ripped, her body torn. Pain filled her. But, incredibly, it vanished as quickly as it had come. Brand held himself still inside her, giving her time.

Sweat beaded his forehead, but he didn't move. Kissing her again and again, he whispered reassurances, apologies, comforting words.

Slowly, her body eased. The fullness of him became not an intrusion but a delight. Experimentally, she lifted her hips. Hot, pulsating pleasure swept over her. Her eyes opened wide in wonder. Her body tightened around him.

His control snapped. He thrust again and again, driving her to pleasure so exquisite that when it finally crested within her she thought she could not possibly survive. Yet she did, enough to know the moment when he surrendered in his turn, pouring himself into her.

Outside, the wind had begun to blow again as the storm whipped round and threw its full fury against Daniels' Neck once more. But inside, neither heard. They were lost in a world entirely their own.

Chapter Eleven

Sweet heaven, he hadn't had a dream like that since ...
since ever. A dream of such eroticism that he felt caught
between soul-shattering fulfillment and renewing arousal.

He smiled broadly. Hell, thirty-five wasn't so bad, if his
imagination could still work like that.

Where was he, anyway? Oh, yes, the stillroom in Julia's
house, where they had taken shelter from the storm. It must
be over. He'd get up, find her, start assessing the damage
and—

He was naked. Brand was almost on his feet before he
realized that. Half crouched, he froze.

Definitely naked. As a jaybird. As the day he was born...
Sans clothes, which were scattered on the floor. Moreover,
the satisfaction of his body was no dreamlike illusion. It
was real. Which could only mean that—

He pulled on his pants and boots, grabbed his shirt and
was tucking it into his waistband as he strode into the
kitchen. The shutters on the windows stood open. Sunlight flooded the room.

There was no sign of Julia. He checked the house, taking the steps to the upstairs two at a time. Nothing.

Outside, he stood on the porch, hands on his lean hips,
and looked around. A soft whistle escaped him. The yard

in front of the house was littered with tree branches, some of them very large.

In the distance, he could see the split trunk of what had been a mighty oak. Part of the stable roof was gone, but only at one end, and that looked readily repairable.

As for the house itself... He stepped off the porch and walked all the way around, checking carefully. The roof had held. Several shutters were gone but the inside boards he had put up had kept the rooms from being damaged. Again, there was nothing that couldn't be fixed quickly.

One of the paddocks had lost a chunk of its fencing, but the other was intact. The horses were there, grazing peacefully, as though the events of the previous day had never occurred.

A movement at the side of the stable caught his eye. He turned. Julia was there, wearing a plain cotton dress that hung loosely on her slender body. Her hair was caught up on the top of her head, but wisps had already worked their way loose. She was picking up fallen branches and loading them into a small wagon.

Straightening, she caught sight of him. He held his breath, wondering what she would say or do. Would she be horribly embarrassed or furious? She wouldn't faint, would she?

No, that didn't seem like his Julia. Besides, he was more than willing to calm and soothe her, give her every reassurance. In truth, he was looking forward to it.

Or at least he was until she spared him a scant glance before calmly returning to her task. Matter-of-factly she said, "There's coffee on the stove."

He'd had thoroughly professional whores react with more honest emotion than that. Anger rose in him.

But he reminded himself—with the wisdom of an experienced man—that she was only a green girl. She was bound to act a bit oddly.

"Julia..."

She dumped another load of branches into the wagon. "If you want to wait, I'll fix breakfast in a bit. I'd just like to get more of this done."

If he wanted to wait . . . If? Maybe he was being oversensitive this fine morning, but that sounded suspiciously like a dismissal.

Putting on a brave front to hide her feminine confusion was one thing. This was quite another. Without thinking, ruled solely by raw male impulse, he crossed the distance between them. She started, but did not retreat. Back straight, head up, she faced him squarely.

So be it. Brand took hold of her shoulders and dragged her against him. Before she could even begin to resist, he wrapped a steely arm around her waist and put a hand under her chin, tipping her head up.

His mouth claimed hers with ruthless strength, parting her lips for the thrust of his tongue. But what began as a demonstration of masculine power quickly changed.

The mere touch of her body all along his length, the taste and sun-dappled scent of her, were all enough to gentle him. This was Julia he held, proud and valiant, fire in his arms and incandescent loveliness. Julia of the storm, of sweet, hot passion and unforgettable memory.

His touch became tender, far more giving than taking. He felt the change in himself and was surprised by it, but nothing really mattered except the woman in his arms.

The resistance he had felt when he took hard hold of her vanished. She became as she had been the night before, the very embodiment of all that was woman.

Slowly he raised his head and gazed into her eyes. They were as slumbrous with passion as he knew his own to be. Triumph welled in him. Everything would be fine. They would work out the necessary arrangements, but first—

Julia gently disengaged herself and stepped back. She smoothed her hair in a gesture that was largely futile, then tucked her hands behind her back.

"Why don't I make breakfast now?"

The throbbing hardness of his body dictated a different activity, but Brand nodded anyway. She could have asked anything of him, and he undoubtedly would have moved heaven and earth to grant it. Besides, the notion of her fixing him breakfast had a certain appeal. His stomach rumbled.

Julia smiled tentatively. He thought her uncertainty was charming. Together they walked back to the kitchen.

"It looks as though we got off lightly," he said, hardly aware of his choice of words. It seemed only natural to think of himself and Julia as a "we." After what they had shared the night before, he doubted he could think any other way, even if he tried.

Everything was working out amazingly well. A man could spend years considering matrimony and not find a wife who suited him as perfectly as he had no doubt Julia would. Granted, she was also totally different from the woman he had set out to find. But in hindsight it seemed that was only to be expected.

He had no experience with this marriage business, after all. Naturally enough, he had started out with a few misconceptions. Still, his instincts were solid.

By allowing them free rein—and he'd certainly done that last night—he'd come to precisely where he wanted to be, in possession of a woman he was sure would be the ideal wife and mother. Feeling amazingly well satisfied—even rather smug—he sat down at the kitchen table and prepared to watch her cook for him.

She broke eggs in the most delightful way, whipping them to a creamy froth before pouring them into a skillet. Her every movement was both efficient and graceful. Even in the plain dress she wore, with her hair artlessly arranged, she was lovely.

The urge to draw her into his arms, let down her hair, strip off the dress and carry her up to the wide bed was almost more than he could resist. But he was a civilized man, after all. He could have breakfast first. And then . . .

He was smiling when she set the plate in front of him, then decorously sat down on the other side of the table. Brand noticed she wasn't eating, and frowned.

"Not hungry?"

She shook her head. "Not just now. We need to talk."

Just like a woman, he thought indulgently. He swallowed a forkful of what turned out to be a delicious omelet, took a sip of her excellent coffee, and nodded. Breakfast could wait.

"Of course," he said gently, "we'll talk." He reached across the table and took her hand.

At first, he was uncertain of what to say. He took a breath, surprised by how tense he was. Forcing himself to relax, he spoke simply and from the heart.

"Everything will be all right, Julia. I promise. There's nothing for you to worry about."

She blinked slowly. "That's very kind."

"I realize the situation is somewhat . . . unorthodox, but there's no need for you to be concerned. We can get a license in New York and be wed before the week is out. Several judges I know will be happy to perform the ceremony. Or if you absolutely feel a church wedding is necessary, that can also be arranged quickly."

Even as he spoke, he was mentally reviewing what would need to be done. It would be simplest if she didn't quibble over a civil ceremony.

The judges he had mentioned all had reason to be indebted to them. Any one of them would be delighted to oblige. Otherwise . . . Was she Protestant? Catholic? It didn't matter. He had excellent connections on all sides. The important thing was to get it done.

"No," Julia said. She thought a moment and added, "But thank you."

"No?" No what? What was she talking about?

"No," she said again. "As I believe I mentioned, I have no interest in marriage."

He must have heard her wrong. He could have sworn she'd said—

"You're not serious?"

"Completely. Now you should finish your breakfast before it gets cold." She rose and busied herself doing more of whatever it was women did in kitchens.

Brand stared at her in disbelief. This was the same woman who had lain in his arms the night before, who had welcomed him into her body with such unfeigned passion and delight. He could have sworn it. And yet, when he faced up to what he'd done and tried to make amends, she refused him.

Fine. If that was how she wanted it to be, she'd get no argument from him. Brand Delaney didn't propose to a woman a second time. He shoved his chair back from the table and stood. "I'll be on my way."

She glanced at him over her shoulder. For just an instant, he thought he saw a flicker of regret in her eyes. But it was gone before he could be sure.

Gently she said, "You may wish to reconsider."

"Why?" Let her give him one good reason. Only one. That was all it would take.

"We're cut off."

"Cut—"

"The storm seems to have cut a new inlet. Daniels' Neck has become an island." She shrugged apologetically. "Until the water recedes, or someone gets a boat over here, neither one of us is going anywhere."

The full impact of what she was telling him sunk in. He was trapped on a spit of land with a woman who delighted and infuriated him all at once. A woman who refused to behave by any rules, society's or his own. A woman he alternately wanted to make wild love to and throttle.

The storm wasn't over. It had just begun, and he was right in the middle of it.

Thunk. Julia looked out the kitchen window. Brand was still working on the downed paddock fence. Several sections of it were already back in place, and the rest would be soon.

Thunk. Especially at the rate he was swinging that mallet. He was hitting it hard enough to drive a stake a good foot into the ground with a single blow.

The day had turned oppressively warm, and there was a lingering tropical feel to the air. She had all the windows open and had undone the top buttons of her dress in an effort to be more comfortable.

Brand, of course, had the advantage. He was working shirtless, his bronzed chest gleaming in the sunlight.

She was staring—again. Every few minutes she caught herself gazing at him like some addled schoolgirl with no more sense than a gnat.

He had asked her to marry him. And she had said no. Those twin facts, so astonishing as to be almost incomprehensible, kept taking swooping dives through her mind.

Her stomach followed. She felt much as she had three summers before when, on a dare, and without the knowledge of her family, she had gone up in a hot-air balloon.

The experience had been exhilarating but terrifying. Perhaps the excitement had lain in the fear. She had clung to the basket, staring down at the earth, sure that nothing in her life would equal that moment.

She had been wrong. Her hands were shaking. She glanced down at them, realized what was happening and quickly thrust them into the pockets of her dress.

She absolutely had to get control of herself. They were trapped here together, at least temporarily. Despite their differences, which were legion, they were two civilized people. They ought to be able to get along for a short time.

Shouldn't they?

The wave of heat that washed over her warned her otherwise. She was looking at him again, staring at the powerful muscles of his back. Sweet Lord, he was a beautiful man, like a warrior of old, body and mind perfectly honed to triumph against all adversity. To struggle in a harsh world, to take what he felt should be his own, and to protect.

A man a woman would gladly cleave to for her own sake and for the sake of the children she would bear.

Where were such thoughts coming from? What was happening to her?

From the tumult of the storm, a different woman seemed to have emerged. One who was caught between the yearning for freedom and the undeniable attraction of a strong, compelling male.

But it was freedom that mattered most, truly. She couldn't live without it. During the darkest days after her accident, it had been the dream of independence that kept her going. Besides, were she ever to contemplate marriage, it certainly wouldn't be the kind Brand had in mind. He wanted a brood mare, nothing more.

She sniffed and took a quick swipe at her eyes. She had long ago learned to make the most of what life had to offer. In fact, she'd become quite good at it. That, at least, hadn't changed.

He had finished the section and was reaching for the next. Sweat trickled down his chest. She remembered the downy feel of the dark hair that grew there and realized she wasn't breathing.

Quickly she made up her mind. In the root cellar, she cleared straw off a block of ice and chipped pieces from it into a pitcher.

Back upstairs, she squeezed precious lemons brought by ship all the way from Florida, added sugar, water, and the ice. When the lemonade was ready, she took two mugs from the cabinet, and before she could think better of it, went outside.

He had started work on the next section, and didn't see her at first. She forced her gaze to the gleaming blue sky over his perfectly formed shoulder and said, "Would you like a cold drink?"

He turned and shaded his eyes to look at her. For a moment, he said nothing. She could feel his gaze along every inch of her, but refused to flinch. Deliberately she lifted the pitcher and poured a long, cold stream of lemonade into a mug.

Handing it to him, she smiled. "Thank you for fixing the fence, but you don't really have to do it."

He took the mug. Their fingers brushed. Lifting the drink, he swallowed deeply. She watched the play of muscles along his throat with unwilling fascination. When the mug was empty, he held it out to be refilled.

"I thought I should keep busy," he said as she complied.

"Have you seen the inlet?" she asked as she handed the mug back.

He nodded. "It looks as though it could be permanent."

"It wouldn't be the first time. Fifty years ago, another storm cut an inlet about two miles down the shore from here. It's still there."

"What will you do if it remains?"

"Build a bridge, I suppose. The important thing is that the house came through all right."

He glanced toward it. "What would you say to Charles Hewlitt coming out here for a look? Before we start building, I want to make sure he knows how to make a house that will get through that kind of weather."

"I wouldn't mind," she assured him, wondering if he fully realized the implication behind his words, namely that there would be further contact between them. But of course there would. They were to be neighbors.

He, and whoever he eventually married. Inevitably, she would know his wife, watch his children grow. Their paths would cross over and over.

Her stomach twisted. For a horrible moment, she thought she might be ill.

"What's wrong?" he demanded, and reached for her.

"Nothing," she said quickly, but it was too late. He had put down the mug and taken hold of her, as though afraid she might suddenly fall.

The sun was blinding. It seemed to fill all the sky. To fill her. She was hot, so very hot. The need to touch him was irresistible. She brushed his chest with the tips of her fingers, fascinated. It was enough. He groaned deeply and drew her to him.

Sweet relief flooded her. She twined her arms around his neck and clung unashamedly. This was what she had longed for ever since waking in the stillroom to the realization that nothing would ever be the same again.

The world be damned. She needed this man, in ways she had never imagined possible.

But she would have him on her own terms, at least for as long as she could.

He raised his head and stared down at her. A low laugh escaped him. With clear reluctance, he put her from him. "I'm not really fit company," he said apologetically, indicating his sweat- and grime-streaked body.

She smiled shakily. It was on the tip of her tongue to say that she would be perfectly happy to take him just as he was.

But she resisted. She didn't want to seem too shockingly forward and, besides, he did have a point.

"There's always the inlet."

He nodded. Hardly taking his eyes from her, he walked backward to the house until he stumbled, laughed, and went inside. Moments later, he emerged with soap and a towel and headed off toward the inlet.

Joy bubbled up within her. If she'd been wearing a hat, she would have tossed it into the sky. But whatever imp of mischief had come to sit on her shoulder wasn't done yet.

It occurred to her that she was definitely sticky. And why not? She'd been working hard in the hot, humid morning. There was a bathtub upstairs. But it took forever to fill. Another, far more attractive solution beckoned.

Quickly she went inside, but only for a moment. Before she could think better of it, she followed the path Brand had taken.

Chapter Twelve

Water flowed boldly where there had been none. Land Julia had known all her life was gone, possibly for good. She stared at the inlet with wonder.

More than anything else, it revealed the full fury of the storm that had swept over Daniels' Neck. What was now the shore was a good fifty yards away. There was no sign of any activity on the other side.

People must still be trying to clean up and reopen the roads. Her family would be deeply worried. She knew that and regretted it, but there was nothing she could do for the moment. As soon as possible, she would get word to them. But, for the present, her house and land were cut off from the rest of the world.

A snow-white egret lifted its head and regarded her solemnly before darting down to capture a small fish. Other birds fluttered in the trees above. Life was already returning.

She put the towel she had brought on a nearby rock and began unbuttoning her dress. Her daring amazed her, but she told herself she was merely being sensible. The surf along the beach was still far too rough for bathing. This was the only safe place.

Besides, she had no idea where Brand was. None at all.

The air touched her skin lightly. She left her clothes and ran into the water. It was deliciously cool, silky and sensuous. She laughed with pleasure and dived beneath the surface, swimming a considerable distance before surfacing again.

Swimming had always been one of her greatest pleasures. She had learned as a child, and had never stopped. Moving into Amelia's house had meant that she no longer always had to wear the cumbersome bathing garments society insisted on. Many had been the early morning or late evening when she swam naked and alone, unobserved by any but the occasional gull or egret.

Turning onto her back, she floated, gazing at the crystalline sky. After the fury of the day before, the sky looked washed clean. There wasn't a cloud to be seen. The day was perfect.

A branch snapped. She straightened, treading water, and looked toward the bank. Brand stood there, watching her. He had a towel wrapped around his lean hips, but otherwise he was naked. Water sluiced off him.

He did not move, but simply looked at her. She turned over, dived again, and continued swimming. Her heart was beating very rapidly. She was swept by doubt, excitement, fear, all at the same time. But nothing happened. She slowed and let her body drop down, treading water. Only then, when she glanced around, did she realize that she was no longer alone.

Brand was not more than a yard away. He had entered the water so smoothly that she never heard him. In the hushed silence of the newborn inlet, he moved toward her, but slowly enough that, should she choose to stay beyond his touch, she could do so.

She stayed, the water cool silk over her skin, the sky blazing blue. She was hardly breathing, but it didn't matter. Nothing did, except this man and this moment.

His arms closed around her. She was drawn against the steely length of his body. Their legs entwined. She felt the hardness of his arousal and gasped.

He cupped the back of her head, slanting it first one way, then the other, for the devouring possession of his mouth. His passion was raw and untamed. It should have terrified her, but all she felt was surging joy.

Brand took her arms and twined them around his neck. He stroked down her back to cup her derriere. Drawing her legs up around his waist, he rubbed lightly against the soft down of the curls at the apex of her thighs.

Julia cried out. He lifted her high, kissing the high, firm slopes of her breasts. His teeth raked her lightly before his mouth closed around one nipple.

Pressure built in her. Her fingers dug into his shoulders. He seemed the only solidity in a world on the verge of dissolving. Holding her with an arm around her waist, he gently parted the folds of her womanhood and stroked her there, over and over, until she could bear no more.

The climax that seized her was shattering. She screamed his name and, for a moment, almost blacked out. But consciousness returned swiftly, and with it pleasure, mounting again, driving her wild.

Brand groaned deeply. He strode toward the shore and laid her on the mossy shore. Swiftly he covered her body with his own, kissing her again and again, even as he parted her legs. His possession was swift and deep.

She cried out again, her back arching to meet his thrusts. Her womanhood contracted, the muscles spasming rhythmically around him.

Above her, his features tightened. She watched, fascinated, as he struggled for control, waiting, waiting, until pleasure crested within her and she was gone, hurtled into blinding release.

His followed immediately, as he yielded to the power that had become greater than them both. Exhausted, he slumped against her.

Julia held him close. She, too, was dazed by the passion they had shared. But she also felt an overwhelming protectiveness toward this immensely strong, proud man who was suddenly weak and, she sensed, vulnerable. Gently she caressed his back, murmuring to him words that meant nothing—and everything.

They stayed that way for a long time. When they finally stirred, the sun was slanting westward and the air had begun to cool. Brand levered himself off her body and, with his hand, gently pushed the hair back from her face. His eyes were a deep forest green lit by shards of sunlight.

"Are you all right?"

She nodded. Far from all right, she felt marvelous, more alive than she could ever remember feeling. Last night, during the storm, had been wonderful, but this time, without the brief pain and the overwhelming newness—this was extraordinary.

No wonder people tended to make such a great mystery about it. If lovemaking was even half as good for most people, it was difficult to imagine why anyone did anything else.

He rose and held out a hand, helping her to stand. Together they waded into the water and swam. The water eased the sense of unreality that had enveloped Julia since she awoke. But she still had a magical feeling of being not quite herself.

This other woman, this hidden self, was a creature of passion and daring. Julia liked her immensely, even if she was not at all sure what she might do next.

They dressed and walked back toward the house. As they entered the kitchen, Brand touched a hand to her shoulder, turning her to face him.

Quietly he asked, "That...matter we discussed. Have you changed your mind?"

Her throat tightened. It would be so easy. All she had to do was agree, and everything would fall into place. But the price, in pride and independence, was simply more than she could pay.

Mutely she shook her head.

Brand said nothing more. He left her there at the kitchen door. A few moments later, she heard him back at work on the paddock fence.

Their solitude lasted until that evening. Dusk was settling over the house when Julia heard a voice calling to her. She opened the door, thinking it was Brand. But he had put down the mallet he'd been using, and was also listening.

"Julia...are you here?"

The voice was clearer now, dark with worry. And no longer unknown.

"Peter!" Tossing down the towel she'd been using, Julia ran toward the road. A moment later, her brother came through the fringe of trees beyond the house.

He looked exhausted, his hair was disheveled, and there were dark circles under his eyes. But he smiled broadly when he saw her.

"Julia, thank God! We feared—" He choked, and for a moment his eyes shone with tears. Then she was in his arms, held close against him.

Brother and sister hugged fiercely, silently giving thanks. Still holding her, Peter took a quick step back and looked her up and down. "You're unharmed?"

"Perfectly. We were very lucky. Mother and Father—?"

"The same. Everyone came through fine, but the roads are clogged with downed trees and branches. It took all day to get down to the shore. You know you're cut off? I had to go back into town to fetch a boat. Fortunately, Charlotte had a dinghy. She would have come, too, but she's helping with the cleanup in town."

Julia hid a smile. She was now Charlotte, was she? No longer Miss Hemper? Good for her!

"The stable lost part of its roof," she told him, "and a few shutters were ripped off. But otherwise—"

She stopped. Peter was no longer listening. He was staring over her shoulder with an expression of mingled surprise and concern.

"Mr. Delaney—?" he said.

Brand had put his shirt back on and tucked it into his pants. But otherwise he looked much the same—big, hard, tough, unrelenting.

Peter frowned. "When did you—?"

"Yesterday," Brand said. He held out his hand. Peter took it automatically. "I've been in some bad storms," Brand explained, "and this had the look of one coming on. I was concerned about Julia being here alone, and it didn't seem likely that any of you would be able to reach her."

It sounded perfectly plausible, the action of a concerned and conscientious man who was going to be her neighbor. Except for that one small slip, if it had been that—Julia, not Miss Nash.

Julia took a deep breath. She loved her brother dearly, and did not wish to risk his ire. But instinctively she was drawn to stand beside Brand, without any thought to the image that created.

Softly she said, "I'm very grateful to Brand for his help. If I had been here alone, the house would have suffered far more damage." Briefly she explained about the breaking windows and the need to use the wooden boards. "I could never have managed them by myself."

Peter nodded absently. His attention remained focused firmly on Brand. The two men regarded each other silently. Julia looked from one to the other. Something seemed to be happening, but on a purely masculine level she couldn't grasp. Whatever it was, Peter seemed reassured.

"As long as you're all right," he said to Julia. To Brand, he added, "I saw Mr. Hewlitt earlier. He'd already been out to inspect your land, and was relieved that it came through unscathed. Except for a few downed trees, no harm was done."

"I'm glad to hear it. I've asked Julia if Charles might look through this house before we build. For a two-hundred-and-fifty-year-old structure, it came through remarkably well."

They continued discussing the house as they walked back toward it. Julia breathed a small sigh of relief, but she didn't completely relax. In her brother's presence, she could not help but be reminded of her family's love, and her obligations to them. Obligations that certainly did not include throwing away the strictures of a lifetime to embark on an illicit relationship.

Yet she couldn't regret what had happened, not for a moment. So long as she and Brand were discreet, she saw no reason why their actions should hurt anyone.

Besides, she was haunted by the knowledge that they had only a short time to be together. Once he married, they could never again be anything other than acquaintances.

Which made it all the more painful when she realized what Brand was saying. "Charles will see to the house on his own. I have business to attend to in New York."

New York? He was going to New York? He couldn't be.... He... They... She must have misunderstood.

"When will you be back?" Peter asked innocently.

Brand shrugged, as though it were a matter of small importance. Without so much as a glance at Julia, he said, "I have no idea."

Her stomach twisted. She looked away hastily, desperate to conceal the pain that wrenched through her. Her skin felt suddenly cold, and she was swept by a wave of despondency.

Yet what should she have expected? That he would stay with her, content to accept whatever terms she offered? Brand never accepted any terms but his own, and she had no reason to think he would change now. She would have to be a fool even to consider the possibility.

Time passed, although she had no idea how much. Mindlessly she went about the ordinary tasks of cleaning and straightening up. Occasionally she thought she felt Brand watching her, but she steadfastly refused to look in his direction. It would simply hurt her too much to do so.

Peter took his leave, apparently satisfied that his sister was well. He tried to convince Julia to return with him, but he didn't seem too surprised when she refused. In truth, he didn't try all that hard, being anxious to get back into town so that he could check on Charlotte.

He and Brand rowed across the new inlet, Brand bringing the dinghy back before going off to finish his repair of the paddock fence. For a time, she heard the steady rhythm of the hammer as he nailed posts into place, but now it was stilled.

She had to assume he, too, would be leaving shortly. On her knees in the garden, where she was tenderly replanting uprooted shoots, she realized he was nowhere in sight. Surely he wouldn't have gone without a word.

Stumbling slightly in her haste, she got to her feet and stood looking around. It seemed unnaturally quiet, but perhaps that was only the aftermath of the storm. In time, the birds would return, and the forest animals, too. Life would be as it always had been.

And it would be totally different.

Both were true. She had to accept that and go on.

But first—where *was* he?

Slowly forcing herself not to try to run, she walked back toward the house. Opening the kitchen door, she had to bite down hard on her lower lip to stifle the exclamation of relief that threatened to break from her. He was there, standing by the sink, washing the dirt and dust from his hands.

His eyes were shuttered as he glanced at her over his shoulder. Silently he wiped his hands dry and hung the towel on the rack by the window. There was a glass of lemonade on the counter beside him. He carried it over to the table and sat down.

Watching her, he said quietly, "I'd like you to go to New York with me."

Pleasure so intense that it all but wiped out even the memory of rain poured through her. But hard on its heels came caution. She was so horribly vulnerable where he was concerned, helpless in a way she had never before experienced, even during the worst of her recovery. He could hurt her with a word, devastate her simply with his absence, make a mockery of all her proud claims to independence. With him, the very bedrock of her life seemed to shatter.

Instinctively she grasped the only certainty she truly knew, her own courage. "I can't."

"Why not? Surely your family can't be shocked when a young woman who is independent enough to live on her own decides she needs a holiday."

His tone was mild, but his words mocked her, using as they did her own arguments for caution to insist, instead, that she should trust him, go with him, do as he wished.

And truly, as she wished, too. Already he was too wise to her, this man who had lain with her so intimately through the long night of the storm.

Her head tilted proudly. Life had been very hard for Brand Delaney in the beginning, but of late, she suspected, all things had come too easily to him. She would not make the same mistake of being one of those things. "They would still expect me to be properly accompanied. Or are you planning to suggest yourself as chaperon?"

"Tempting though the idea is, I had a different course in mind. Why not ask your sisters to come with you?"

That startled her. Never would she have expected him to suggest such a thing. "My sisters?"

"Daphne and Gloria."

"I know who my sisters are, for heaven's sake. I just can't imagine why they would want to come to New York with me."

"That's because you've led a shockingly innocent life up until now. Not that I'm complaining, mind you. It's merely an observation."

Julia's cheeks warmed. She turned away and tried to busy herself at the stove, to little avail. She could have been stirring soap as easily as soup and wouldn't have known the difference.

"Daphne will jump at the chance because she knows that if she removes herself from Charles now, he will be all the more inclined to pursue her."

Julia whirled. All her good intentions about not looking at him and staying calm were forgotten. "That's terrible. Daphne isn't remotely so manipulative."

Brand's teeth gleamed white against his burnished skin. "She's female, isn't she?"

"Is that your opinion of women, that we're all scheming and underhanded and—"

He stopped her with a glance. "Daphne follows her own course, you follow yours. As for Gloria, I expect she would welcome a change of scene." When Julia remained unconvinced, he added helpfully, "Tell them you want to go shopping. That should settle it."

"It won't," she insisted. "They're not children. Neither, for that matter, am I."

"So I have observed," Brand murmured. He rose and went to her. There were no further arguments—for a while.

"A marvelous idea," Grandmother Sara said. "If I were a few years younger, I would go myself. As it is, while you're away, we can have a bridge built across the new inlet. It can be all taken care of by the time you get back."

Julia opened her mouth to reply, found she could think of nothing to say, and closed it again.

"Shopping," Daphne said. She smiled hugely and whirled around, as though already imagining the new gown she would buy. "What a perfect time to go to the city. There are plays we haven't seen, parties we're sure to be invited to, rides in the park, all sorts of fun."

"I can hardly wait," Gloria chimed in. She, at least, gave her eldest sister a cautious look. "But honestly, Julia, are you sure you want to go? It isn't . . . like you, somehow."

"Of course it is," Grandmother Sara insisted. She looked at the other two girls sharply. "Julia is changing, can't you see that? She's coming out of herself, just as we always hoped. A trip to the city is exactly what she needs to complete the process."

Julia pressed her lips tightly together and prayed that she didn't look as guilty as she felt. It had been two days since the storm. The roads had cleared enough for her to reach her family's home, but she had been spared the effort. They had come to her instead.

Even Grandmother Sara, who at eighty-five could have been excused the trip, had insisted on being included. She claimed to want to see for herself that Amelia's house was unharmed. But Julia suspected she had another motive entirely.

Her wise old eyes twinkled as she said, "I was planning to give each of you girls new wardrobes for the New Year, but there's no reason why you shouldn't have them now."

As Gloria and Daphne were exclaiming their delight, Julia murmured her thanks. She wasn't ungrateful—far from it. But she had a sinking feeling that her grandmother knew—or at least suspected—a good deal more than she should.

That suspicion was confirmed a short time later. Just before she went upstairs for a nap, Sara turned to Julia. "When you're in New York, do give my regards to that nice Mr. Delaney."

"Do you think we'll see him?" Daphne asked, a bit worried.

Sara's eyes twinkled. "It wouldn't surprise me at all."

Daphne and Gloria chattered on about what they would see and do and buy. But Julia's thoughts were elsewhere. Brand had returned to New York the day before without urging her further to join him there. She suspected he already knew that she would, and she resented his confidence.

Remembering what he had said about Daphne maneuvering Charles to pursue her, she wondered if this wasn't the case of the pot calling the kettle black. Had he deliberately put her in a position where she would follow him to New York, unable to accept their separation?

And if she did that, what did it say about her ability to deal with the permanent parting that inevitably must come?

As her sisters chatted about musicales and dances, parties and plays, laces and silks, her thoughts turned to far more serious matters. Chief among them was how exactly she intended to manage the rest of her life.

She had no idea, of course. But she did make herself one promise, that she would live entirely and only for the moment. Nothing else would be allowed to matter.

Starting from the very instant she set foot in the great city between the rivers. Brand's city. His home and his arena. It was a place she had ventured to only rarely and knew very little about, but which she intended, for however short a time, to make her own.

If she could not have the man, she would have the memory. That, somehow, would have to be enough.

Chapter Thirteen

A carriage, racing by, threw up a shower of mud that splattered the skirts of all three young women and made two of them squeal. While Gloria and Daphne were going on about the extraordinary discourtesy of city people, Julia took the opportunity to look around.

They were standing at the corner of Fifth Avenue and Forty-fifth Street, a few blocks north of the reservoir and within sight of the mansion built by John Jacob Astor. Everywhere she looked, there were carriages and wagons in amazing numbers, and in among them, darting here and there, the most harried pedestrians Julia had ever seen.

She had been to New York before, perhaps a dozen times, but not in the six years since her accident. It seemed to have grown amazingly, or perhaps that was only because she was here for the first time without her parents, and was actually responsible for the well-being of her two younger sisters.

They had put up at Hardestys Hotel, just off the avenue. It was a very fashionable, relentlessly proper place where her father stayed when he visited the city. Even the Nashes, careful parents though they were, felt comfortable allowing their daughters to be there.

But then, they thought of Julia as the last word in good sense and propriety. Little did they know.

Feeling she was being incredibly deceitful, Julia shepherded her sisters across the avenue and back toward the hotel. They had been shopping all morning. Her feet throbbed, but, mercifully, her leg felt fine. All the same, she was delighted to be out of the stores, if only temporarily.

"Let's have a bit of a rest," she suggested as they passed through the double doors into the hotel lobby.

Gloria and Daphne agreed, reluctantly. They were brimming over with energy, delighted and excited by everything they did. Only their concern for their sister, and their determination not to let her overtax herself, made them put aside their natural inclination to keep going.

Julia knew that they were willing to take a rest only because they thought she needed it. In fact, she didn't. But she was willing to play on their sympathy, if it meant getting off the city streets, even for a short while.

Her head was spinning. She was having a great deal of difficulty thinking straight. And she wasn't absolutely sure whether she wanted to laugh or cry.

They had been in New York a day. She hadn't heard a word from Brand, much less seen him. So far as she knew, matters would remain that way for the four days remaining of their planned visit.

The lobby was filled with elaborately carved marble columns, potted palms and overstuffed horsehair couches covered in red velvet. Oversize crystal chandeliers hung from the high ceiling. Uniformed bellboys in pillbox caps hurried back and forth, some toting luggage, others carrying boards announcing messages.

Julia stopped at the reception desk for their keys. The slender young man in a stiffly formal collar and carefully slicked-back hair inclined his head respectfully.

"Miss Nash, just one moment, please."

He consulted the assortment of pigeon-hole boxes on the wall behind him. Instead of just the keys, he also handed her a sizable stack of mail.

"There must be some mistake," Julia said. "We've only been here a day."

"They all arrived this morning," the young man informed her. Pointedly he added, "By hand."

Julia frowned. Messengered correspondence? Who could possibly consider it so urgent to be in touch with them?

Her heart beat a little faster as she quickly scanned the engraved names on the envelopes, searching for Brand's. It wasn't there. Her disappointment was not at all relieved by the fact that quite a few of the names she did find were well-known to her, even though she had never met their possessors.

Astor, not once but twice? Gould? Morgan? The cream of New York society seemed to require the Nash girls' attention. How extraordinary!

Without comment, she handed the messages to Gloria. Daphne peered over her sister's shoulder. An instant later, heedless of the requirements of decorum, they were both exclaiming with delight.

"Oh, my heavens," Daphne chortled. "I can hardly believe it. Julia, did you see?"

"I saw," Julia said quietly. She did not share her sisters's excitement, but neither did she begrudge it. Although her own wariness had not eased, she smiled. "Let's wait to open them until we're upstairs."

They agreed, but still only just managed not to rip into the envelopes as they rode up the four flights to their room. The elevator man opened the wrought-iron-and-filigreed glass door and cautioned them to step carefully. Down the hallway they sped, with Julia following more slowly. Gloria's room was first. She had the key in and turned in record time.

The room was large and pleasantly furnished, with a four-poster bed, a mirrored dresser and a brocade couch. High windows gave an extensive view of the street. An inner door connected to the room Daphne was using. Julia's was across the hall.

"I can scarcely believe it," Gloria said as she began opening the messages and passing them to Daphne. "It appears we have been invited everywhere."

Julia accepted one of the heavily engraved cards Daphne held out and glanced at it. "This is very odd," she murmured. "New York is usually quiet at this time of year."

Or as quiet as it ever got. Society tended to congregate around Newport, or at some of the pleasant shorefront villages on Long Island.

"It must have been the storm," Gloria suggested. "It did so much damage, people must have decided to return to the city, at least for a while. Naturally, they'd need to amuse themselves."

Naturally, Julia thought, but that did not explain why they felt they needed the Nash girls to do it. The invitation she was holding was from no less a personage than the fabled Mrs. Astor, doyenne of New York society and the absolute arbiter of who was acceptable and who was not.

How could she possibly have known of their existence, much less decided to acknowledge it?

"A musicale," Gloria said, opening another of the envelopes. "A garden party...horse racing...a private theater performance. It goes on and on."

"Amazing," Julia murmured. Their father had no doubt mentioned to several of his business associates that they would be in the city. He would have asked those gentlemen to keep an eye on his daughters, even as he would have theirs in similar circumstances. Was this flood of invitations and attention the result?

It seemed doubtful, but Julia tried to convince herself. The Nashes were not remotely as wealthy as the cream of

New York society, but they were a very old family whose roots were greatly respected. New money tended to try to legitimize itself by playing court to old.

Or there might be another explanation altogether. New money might respect old roots, but it would positively grovel before wealth and power even greater than its own. Few could claim to possess such raw influence, but Brand Delaney was certainly among them.

She shook her head, telling herself not to be a fool. There was no reason to believe Brand had anything to do with the invitation.

And yet, as her sisters began eagerly to discuss what they would wear when, Julia could not entirely repress a spurt of excitement. She did her best to appear composed, but inside a now-familiar heat began to grow.

Glancing toward the clock on the dressing table, she silently counted off the hours until evening.

Brand glanced at himself in the darkly framed mirror of his dressing room. His evening clothes were impeccably tailored to the unmistakably high standards of Savile Row, and his own. Unrelievedly black except for the brilliant white of his shirtfront and cuffs, the garb suited him. His ebony hair was brushed back from his high forehead and secured in a queue at the nape of his neck.

He reached a hand into an inside pocket of his jacket and removed a silver case. Snapping it open, he chose a cheroot and lit it. A thin tendril of smoke curled upward to the ceiling. He glanced at it absently and smiled. Women were said to object to the smell of even the best cigar, although he personally had never encountered any such opposition. He knew of men—sensible, successful men—who were not permitted to enjoy that masculine pleasure in their own homes.

The thought amused him. He was smiling as he left the dressing room and passed through the luxurious but unrelentingly masculine master bedroom. On his way to the door, he paused to pick up the discreet box covered in dark blue velvet from the bedside table. Slipping it into his pocket, he continued on his way.

The weather was fine, the night sky was clear, and a slight breeze was blowing off the river. Brand chose to walk. His destination was only a handful of blocks from his own residence overlooking Central Park.

The town house he occupied was in fact a small mansion consisting of eighteen rooms and a large garden. He was aware of the various rumors about how he had acquired it—in a card game, in lieu of a large debt, even as the result of a duel.

In fact, he had bought it from the original owner in a simple transaction necessitated by that gentleman's lack of prudence at the races. The price he had paid had been fair—at the time—but, as with many properties close to the park, it had increased in value significantly.

People took that as yet more evidence that anything Brand Delaney touched turned to gold. It was a belief he did not discourage, even as he considered it the height of absurdity.

No man's judgment was perfect. No man slipped through life without mistakes. But it was true that, all things considered, he tended to win far more than he lost.

And when he considered the stakes to be truly important, he simply did not accept defeat.

Tonight was no exception. Striding lithely down the street, he considered his plan. Its appeal lay in its simplicity. Get Julia away from Belle Haven, where family, tradition and memory all supported her notions of independence. Put her instead on his own territory, where he would have the advantage. Show her the life that could be hers, were she to simply acquiesce, as any sensible woman would.

And then let nature take its course.

Simple, practical and, best of all, bound to be effective in the shortest possible time.

Which was fortunate, because he was not at all disposed to wait.

Two days—and nights—without Julia had been enough to convince him that his original response to her was correct. He wanted her, permanently and in the most public way possible. Only marriage would suffice.

She would see that, he was sure. No woman truly wanted independence, but especially not one so innately passionate and giving.

He felt a of twinge conscience. Surely she was entitled to the kind of courtship every young woman supposedly dreamed of—candlelight and carriage rides, roses and ribbons. All that sort of thing. Not the ruthless and speedy campaign he envisioned.

Perhaps she was entitled to all that, but he didn't intend to provide it. Later, after he had her firmly in his bed, he would be more than happy to indulge her in all possible ways. But until then, he intended to take the quickest and most expeditious route possible.

He had a sudden vision of her lying amid silk sheets, her opulent beauty naked except for a strewing of rose petals and candlelight gleaming on her honeyed skin. The hardness that gripped him was almost painful. He stopped, breathing in harshly, and crushed the remnants of the cheroot under his heel.

Moments later, he walked up the steps of a town house not unlike his own and accepted the effusive greetings of his hostess, who still couldn't quite believe her luck at capturing the most talked-about and sought after man in New York under her roof.

Most of the guests had already arrived. There was a small break in the flow of conversation as heads swiveled in Brand's direction. He smiled faintly, accepted a glass of champagne from a passing waiter and nodded to the men, who were eager to display their acquaintance with him.

The women were a different matter. He hardly noticed them as his eyes sought Julia. After a few minutes, he realized she was not to be found.

His eyes darkened. Arranging her entry into New York society had required nothing more than a handful of phone calls. He knew perfectly well that no one would dare to refuse him. No one, that is, except Julia herself.

Was it possible she would decline to accept the invitations he was certain she had received? Yes, entirely possible, given the infuriating stubbornness of a woman who refused to accept her proper place in life. But he had planned for that. While she might decline on her own behalf, he was sure she wouldn't deny her sisters the opportunity to shine in such rarefied realms.

So where was she?

He finished the champagne he had been drinking and took another. Several people spoke to him, and he responded, although with no real attention. All his thoughts were on Julia.

Had something happened to her?

The previous day, he had confirmed her arrival at the hotel along with Gloria and Daphne. Hardestys was a perfectly respectable place, but all the same, he had made it clear to the management that he expected the Misses Nash to be especially well looked after. If anything had gone wrong, he was certain, someone would have contacted him.

Where was she, then? He took a long, slow perusal of the room and relaxed slightly. Her sisters were not present, either. Something had delayed all three of them.

A slight smile touched his hard mouth. He should have realized they would be in an uproar over what to wear. Or at least the two younger ones would be. Julia, kind as she was, would be patient with them. No wonder they were late.

He drank more of the champagne, ignored the pointed looks more than a few of the women directed at him and strolled in the direction of the high French windows that led out to the garden. It was stuffy in the room. Fresh air would be welcome.

Standing with his back to the wall, enjoying the cooling breeze, he amused himself by observing the other guests. Since his meteoric rise to power, he had attended far fewer such events than might have been expected. Until deciding that he required a wife, he had steered clear of as many as possible. But he knew the ritual well enough, the feint and parry of polite conversation, the wandering of eyes to see if anyone more interesting was available, the preening and hooded glares of envy lightly masked by smiles as cold as death.

For the life of him, he could not discover where the amusement was supposed to lie. It was far beyond the understanding of one who sought the wild, open places when he needed to renew his spirit.

Or at least he always had. Just then, he sought Julia. When the minutes ticked by and still she did not appear, his mood darkened.

The champagne continued to slide easily down his throat, and the slanting glances of other women lingered overlong. He was dark and dangerous, leaning against the marbled pillar in a pose of casual indifference that fooled only the most naive.

Brand Delaney was in a mood tonight. No one had the slightest idea why, but each mentally cataloged his or her own behavior and was grateful not to be the cause. The men gave him a wide berth, but the women were drawn closer, tantalized by the wildness and the danger he exuded, like moths—or, more correctly, butterflies, in their lustily colored gowns—compelled to singe themselves in the fire.

Yet he remained aloof, a singularly cold fire, taut with waiting until at last, just when he thought he was liable to march into Hardestys's eminently respectable domain and do something utterly unforgivable, suddenly he caught a flutter of laughter from the reception hall, a glimpse of glowing umber hair, and knew, without knowing how, that she was there.

At last.

He relaxed marginally, a tiny fraction of tension running out of him. Yet the lean, burnished fingers closed around the delicate champagne flute tautly as he raised it to his mouth and drank deeply, draining the effervescent wine to its final drop.

Chapter Fourteen

Everything that could possibly go wrong had. A button had ripped off Daphne's dress. Gloria's hem had sagged. A shoe was missing. A wrap couldn't be found. Getting out the door of Hardestys Hotel and off to the first of the many parties they had been invited to had proven one of the most daunting tasks Julia had ever encountered.

But they were here at last, Daphne and Gloria looking radiant and herself just a bit breathless as she surveyed the assembly and wondered for the hundredth time what precisely she was doing there.

It was for her sisters, she reminded herself, and yet she had to admit to a certain excitement and curiosity about the lavishly dressed ladies and gentleman of high society, about whom she had only read up until that moment.

In point of fact, they looked remarkably ordinary, not much different from the folks at a church social, except for the elaborateness of their dress. But otherwise they weren't more or less attractive than normal people, although the women were definitely flashier, with their hair swept up and diamonds gleaming at their throats. Even the young ones, she noticed, who lacked the practiced demureness of Belle Haven's feminine youth and, instead, seemed to have sharp eyes as fully developed as their mommas'.

Not that she cared. It mattered not at all if her dress wasn't the height of fashion or her jewels were nonexistent. Gloria and Daphne were happy—ecstatic, in fact. As for herself, she could manage to conceal her boredom for at least a few hours.

The room in which most of the guests were gathered seemed immense to her untutored eye. But that was deceptive. One entire wall was composed of gilded mirrors reflecting back the entire panoply of gloriously garbed ladies, high-nosed gentleman, patrolling waiters in livery, gleaming chandeliers, and the orchestra, all in swallowtail coats, providing a musical background for the proceedings.

Such was their tardiness that the reception line had long since finished. They slipped in without being announced and stood at the top of the three steps leading down to the ballroom.

"Just a bit intimidating," Gloria murmured, trying very hard to retain her composure.

"More than a bit," Daphne whispered. She was suddenly pale.

"Nonsense," Julia said quite firmly. She absolutely would not allow her sisters to be overawed. They were going to have a marvelous time, even if she had to drag them into it kicking and screaming.

Even as she was considering how exactly to break the ice—since they seemed to know no one—a plump woman strung with what appeared to be yards of pearls hurried over to them.

"My dears," she exclaimed, her smile broad but her eyes calculating, "how lovely that you could come."

The three Misses Nash stared at her. None of them had any idea of what to say. Clearly, the lady appeared to know them, but, in the absence of scantiest information as to her identity, conversation would be difficult.

Julia took a leap of faith and inclined her head courteously. "How kind of you, Mrs. Dalyrimple, and how kind it was of you to invite us. Your invitation was most unexpected, but all the more welcome for that."

Mrs. Dalyrimple broke off her perusal of Gloria and Daphne and stared at Julia. Whatever she saw, it seemed to satisfy some question within her. Her smile turned knowing.

"Not at all, dear. I'm delighted that you could come. Do allow me to introduce you to a few special people."

The three young women were taken in tow, shepherded here and there, selectively introduced to names that would have taken Julia's breath away if she had been at all susceptible to that sort of thing.

She wasn't, but Gloria and Daphne were younger, and far more the guileless girls they were all supposed to be. They fairly shone with delight, their eyes becoming wider and their cheeks even more becomingly flushed as they were welcomed into a level of society they could only have dreamed of scant hours before.

And always, just beyond her distracted sisters' notice, Julia thought she glimpsed the same surprise, the same assessment, the same knowing conclusions on the other faces that she had glimpsed in their hostess's face. But it was all so quicksilver and subtle that she couldn't be absolutely sure, could almost believe she was imagining it all, until after being presented in quick succession to an oil baron, an English viscount, a renowned explorer and the literary sensation of the moment, she turned suddenly and saw, out of the corner of her eye, a sight that robbed her of breath and set her heart to thudding against her rib cage like a frightened bird caught in a poacher's net.

Brand. A formidable and dangerous-looking Brand, lounging against a pillar at the far end of the room, with a champagne flute in one large hand and a devil's smile on his chiseled mouth.

Mrs. Dalyrimple was talking, something about a terribly old family, among the first, very important in the Revolution, and so on. The explorer was leaning a bit closer than he really had to, apparently focused on the terra incognita of Julia's bosom.

None of it touched her in the least. She could see nothing but the black-garbed man with the burnished skin who was watching her from his pose of indolent ease, hear nothing but the rush of her own breath, feel nothing except the memory of his touch that was running like a sweet, hot languor through every inch of her body.

Heaven help her, she was well and truly caught. But then, she had expected as much, hadn't she? She had come to New York because the time they would have together was too short to begin with. She could not bear to miss a day, an hour, a moment, of it.

And yet she would not let him have it all his way, either, this fiercely proud, indomitable man who had dared the storm for her and demanded a price she could not pay. If she was to be so in thrall to him, then, in all justice, so must he be to her.

For a woman who had been a defiantly plain spinster until scarcely a few days before, and a virgin even more recently, she was surprised to discover the stirring of knowledge deep within her. Knowledge that kept her from throwing aside all caution and speeding to his side. That, instead, made her assess the hungry looks he was receiving from the bejeweled women who had positioned themselves within easy reach of his hand, and match that to his own studied carelessness, the arrogant presumption that radiated from every inch of his splendid body.

Her head, with its mass of dark fire curls piled high, tilted. Her shoulders, bare above the cerulean blue of her gown, straightened. A smile as old as time began to turn her azure eyes to the color of shards of sky as high and vaulting as the path a falcon would climb.

The explorer sputtered into silence. The English lord narrowed his gaze appreciatively. Julia's smile deepened.

Her daring made her almost giddy, as though she were soaring on currents of heated air too high above the earth.

But she didn't care. Nothing mattered on this night, in this place where pride and passion warred and it was impossible to say which would be the victor.

She appeared to be having a wonderful time. Ignoring the obvious invitation of a lushly ripe brunette he vaguely remembered having met somewhere or other, Brand scowled at Julia.

She was far too preoccupied to notice, talking to—what was his name? Oh, yes, Barton, the explorer fellow, the one who kept going off to what he insisted on calling darkest Africa. Nor was he alone.

The Britisher, Viscount Somebody-or-Other, was also hanging on her every word, and there were a number of others, fresh-faced youths and men his own age who should know better, all clustered around Miss Julia Nash.

Not that Daphne and Gloria were being ignored. They had their own admirers, but damn it, they were supposed to. He had made it clear he wanted the two younger Nash girls properly entertained. Nothing had been said about the oldest one, absolutely nothing. He had reserved her strictly for himself.

But that message apparently hadn't gotten across, or if it had, a damn sight too many men were choosing to overlook it.

Julia belonged to him. That she had refused to acknowledge the completeness of his possession made no difference.

The champagne he had imbibed had not dimmed his concentration an iota, and it certainly hadn't softened his will. But it had weakened the hold he always tried to maintain over himself when he was in polite society. The veneer of civilization, never very thick in his case, was wearing perilously thin.

Abruptly he decided that he had been a model of patience and understanding long enough. Straightening away from the pillar, he ignored the mingled looks of apprehension and intrigue that came his way from every point of the room. His stride was lithe, purposeful—the lean-hipped walk of a man sure of where he was going and what he intended to do when he got there.

Julia saw him coming. She paled slightly, but went on chatting with Barton. Not until he was almost on top of them did she acknowledge him.

"Good evening, Mr. Delaney."

Her voice was low and throaty. Her eyes, meeting his, tantalized him. He caught himself staring at the fullness of her mouth, and stifled a groan. "Mr. Delaney," indeed.

"Julia," he said, the use of her given name an unmistakable challenge. His eyes glinted. Ignoring the people around them, he held out his hand.

The gesture was unmistakably a command. Almost any other woman in that room, regardless of her age or her marital status, would have responded to it with alacrity. But Julia wasn't any woman. She was completely and uniquely herself.

Damn her.

Her head tilted to one side. She regarded him with a slight smile. "Have you met Mr. Barton, the viscount—"

"No," he said, making it clear that he did not wish to. The social pleasantries were completely beyond him. Let them gossip all they liked about the extraordinary rudeness of this man who would obviously be so much more at home around a campfire. They would talk no matter what he did. It meant nothing. All that counted was Julia. And the moment.

"Come," he said, making his requirements crystal clear. There was a swift indrawing of breath, not from her but from the people closest.

"Now see here—" the viscount began. Whether by blood or breeding, he was a shade more courageous than the other men. But he wasn't a fool. A single flashing glance from Brand was enough to stop him in his tracks.

Julia swallowed. He could see the battle warring within her. She was Miss Julia Nash of Belle Haven, eminently respectable. The possibility of a scene would dismay her, but that didn't mean she would do absolutely anything to prevent it.

Softening his expression slightly, he made what had to be the greatest concession he could ever recall. His lips formed a single word.

"Please."

She went, even though every remnant of sense she had left was screaming at her not to. The moment his fingers curled around hers, all else was forgotten. She hardly noticed the shocked looks of her sisters or the puzzled frowns of the viscount and the others. None of it mattered. There was nothing except Brand and whatever time they had together.

Or there wouldn't have been if pride, that supremely inconvenient steel that ran through her character, hadn't insisted on intervening.

Yes, she had come to New York essentially at his bidding. Yes, she had ignored every moral imperative to lie with him in shattering intimacy. Yes, he could be pardoned for thinking her completely compliant to his every wish.

But on that score, at least, he would be wrong. As much as she wanted him—and desire was a molten fire coursing through her—she would never, never let him see the full extent of her vulnerability. Not while he sought to bend her to his will so blatantly, to remake her in the image of what he thought she ought to be.

Desire him, certainly. Long for him. Even acknowledge deep within her the stirring of feelings she desperately wanted to deny. But yield to him? Never on his terms. Only and strictly on hers.

Julia smiled. Her head seemed to be sailing ten feet or more above the rest of her. She felt giddy, excited, daring and quite seriously happy.

Until the moment when the music began again and Brand, his tall head bending close to hers, murmured, "Let's dance."

Instantly she stiffened. The sweet, rushing heat of desire was overswept by a wave of embarrassment. She had not danced in more than six years, not since before the accident.

Then she had been barely nineteen, newly fledged in the protective society of Belle Haven. She had danced with her father and brother, with boys who had suffered through dance class with her and with the very few older men Jonathan Nash was willing to trust with his sky-eyed, laughing daughter.

Never, ever, had she danced with anyone like Brand Delaney. Distantly, she remembered that she had loved to dance, but it was an almost forgotten pleasure, long submerged in the struggle to simply be able to walk again. She could not possibly dance now, not in this place. Not with him.

"I can't," she said, and instinctively tried to pull away.

Equally instinctively, his hold on her tightened. His eyes, green as an untouched forest, flared. "Why not?"

Misery swept over her. How could he do this to her? The man who had held her so tenderly, raised her to such heights of ecstasy, repaired a fence for her, for heaven's sake? How could he be so boorishly cruel?

The look on her face must have been enough. Instantly his softened. "I'm sorry," he said contritely. "It's just that I forget."

She stared at him in disbelief. Could it possibly be true? He had seen her stripped of every artifice, without the protection of her clothes or her position, with nothing to hide the results of the accident that had almost robbed her of life.

And he forgot?

Once again he seemed to understand exactly what was going through her mind.

"You are so...complete. You lack nothing. It's difficult to believe that you don't see yourself in the same way."

Her throat thickened. Deeply moved by his words, she managed a tremulous smile. "You're wrong, you know."

"No, I'm not—"

"Oh, yes. I lack obedience, Mr. Delaney. Even you will admit I fail utterly at that."

Laughter tugged at the corners of his mouth, yet there was also a flashing look of regret buried deep within his eyes.

"I stand corrected, Miss Nash. You have indeed identified your single deficiency."

"And I don't dance," she said softly.

"You will," he promised, and drew her implacably toward the doors at the far end of the room. Beyond them, night glittered, and, within its secret realms, all sorts of possibilities.

Chapter Fifteen

Far above the cloistered garden, the moon hovered, peering through the thick-leafed branches of maple trees, peeking through the veil of a passing cloud. A full moon, ripe with promise, luminous with a fall of silver that it generously spread over the darkened world.

How many times had she looked at the moon, Julia wondered. A thousand? Two thousand?

Yet it seemed she had never seen it before. Within the circle of Brand's arms, alone with him in the scented garden, everything seemed new and fresh.

She did not pause to think—overmuch—about why they were left alone. Let society whisper about them in shocked tones of delightful scandal.

Not one of them knew what had happened in the storm and the solitude of Amelia's house. They could speculate all they wanted, but beyond Brand Delaney's obvious— very obvious—interest in Miss Julia Nash, no one knew anything at all.

And besides, beyond her concern for her family, what reputation did she have to protect? It wasn't as though she sought a marriage with one of the rigidly proper sons of great fortune, men so indulged throughout their childhoods that they never outgrew them, but remained little more than self-absorbed boys in men's suits.

Heaven forbid. She had her own land and fortune, which together meant her freedom. And she had Brand. If only for the moment.

This moment, now, beneath the silvered moon with the music drifting all around them and all things possible.

Even dancing.

His arm was steel around her, yet not at all unpleasant. She felt the immense strength and power in him, the driving will, the unrelenting maleness.

It all should have frightened her, but it didn't. Instead, she felt curiously liberated, as though her own fears and hesitations were falling away, one by one.

And she was dancing.

Incredibly, without even realizing that it was happening, she had been lured into the music, her body moving as one with Brand's, perfectly attuned to his superb guidance. A soft, shocked gasp escaped her. Instantly she missed her footing.

"I'm sorry," she blurted.

"Relax, you're doing fine."

And so, it seemed, she was, when she concentrated only on his smile and the incandescent light in his eyes. When she thought of nothing but him. It was all so easy, this surrendering of her will to him. He seemed to understand every nuance of her body, every need. He made her feel enchanted, enthralled, and yet paradoxically safe.

Which she was not. Not at all. The music ended. Julia took a deep breath. Brand was still holding her. He showed no inclination to stop doing so.

"We must go back inside," she said.

He frowned slightly, as though the notion struck him as a singular waste of time. "Why?"

"You know why," she replied with some asperity, hiding her own weakness. He might think that all social norms could be flouted, but he didn't have a family to concern himself with.

Nor did she imagine he would change his mind much when said family was acquired. He would always go his own way, on his own terms.

"I won't be gossiped about," she said, more firmly.

He laughed, that deep, rich sound that never failed to make her skin shimmer. "Dear child, you already are." His expression was almost kindly. "Surely you know that."

She shook her head. "No one knows—not for sure."

Gallantly he agreed.

"But they will if we stay here much longer, or at least they'll presume."

"Heaven forbid." His smile deepened. His arm remained firmly twined around her, holding her in place.

"We must—"

"Of course."

"Right now."

"This very instant."

"Brand, I'm serious." Suddenly she was pleading, not at all like her resolute self. He brought out the worst in her—or was it the best? She no longer knew.

He sighed with unfeigned regret. "All right, we'll go inside. I'll behave very properly, just so long as no one else is rash enough to ask you to dance. But first—"

His arm tightened. Before she could draw a breath, she was pulled hard against his sinewy length. His mouth brushed hers with gentleness so complete it almost made her weep. Again and again, like a bird's wing, until she couldn't bear it any longer.

In the end, it was she who stood on tiptoe, twining her arms around his neck. "I missed you," she whispered, innocent as a young girl, potent as the finest courtesan.

Far in the back of his mind, he savored the contrast. She was so many contradictions, this woman who touched him in ways no one ever had. With her, the cool control that was the hallmark of his character seemed to vanish. He could think only of possessing her utterly, making her his, keeping her. Forever.

But she had made it clear she would not accept such an arrangement. Proud, independent Miss Julia Nash insisted on her freedom. Even as she robbed him of his.

As he had discovered in the two nights since their parting, he could no longer sleep properly without her close beside him. And it didn't end there.

Food had lost its savor. The finest Cuban cigars tasted like so much ash. Even the ruthless combat that passed for the financial world could do no more than weakly stir his spirits.

He wanted her, damn it. All of her, completely. He wanted her waiting for him when he came home—naked on his bed, with her legs spread, or perfectly garbed, pouring tea in the drawing room.

It didn't matter which, or at least not much. Not so long as she was there, close to his hand, where he could see and hear and touch her.

And he wanted her pregnant, swelling with his child, her breasts filled with sweet, life-giving milk. Wanted that with a fierce hardness that would not ease.

Was that so wrong? He had fought all his life without quarter to survive the stigma of his birth, the poverty of his upbringing, the harsh fate life seemed to have chosen for him.

He had triumphed over it all, and now he wanted the rewards. Not merely the wealth and the position, the people deferring to his every wish, the knowledge that he had merely to express a desire for something—anything—and it would be his.

He wanted the future. When the time came to draw his final breath, he wanted to know that it had not all been in vain. That something of his own would survive, down through the river of time, to touch whatever was to come.

But there were any number of women who could give him that, weren't there? That was how he had started out thinking, at any rate. Women of appropriate upbringing, willing to trade their particular female power to create life for a more-than-comfortable existence?

Hell, not just willing, ready to jump at it.

But not Julia Nash. She would tease and tempt, bring him to the gates of paradise and beyond. But she would not obey. She had said so herself.

His hand raked through her hair, closing around the back of her head. Fueled by frustration and anger, fear at the waywardness of his own thoughts and raging hunger, he deepened the kiss. Gentleness fled. There was only savage need and raw, male power.

His tongue thrust deep, sweeping past any resistance she might have offered. At the same time, he pulled her firm against him, his arousal unmistakable.

He felt rather than heard the moan that shuddered through her. And yet, scarcely an instant later, the tip of her tongue brushed his, tentatively, to be sure, but no less evocatively for that.

He started; his body pulled taut. He had known women whose sensual artistry had been honed to the most exacting levels, the modern-day equivalent of houris, perfectly trained and utterly compliant. Yet none of them affected him as Julia did.

He drew a ragged breath, forcibly reminding himself of how close they were to the wide-open doors and the several hundred people immediately beyond them. But they were also conveniently close to a shadowed copse of trees.

How easy it would be to take her there, standing up, if need be, with her skirts bunched up around her hips, her skin pale and glowing in the moonlight. How exquisitely tempting to let the wildness roaring inside him out, and the consequences be damned.

But he couldn't do it, not knowing how she would feel afterward, when the enormity of his use of her sunk in. He simply could not treat her like that.

Of course, if they had been completely alone, it would have been another matter entirely. Then he would have taken her any way he chose, as often as he chose, until they were both satiated and beyond.

He spared a fleeting thought for Daniels' Neck, now so thoughtfully sundered from everywhere else. But that reminded him of the interlude beside the inlet, and his body hardened even further.

He groaned and tore his mouth from hers, pushing her away. In another instant, he would be beyond control. Before that could happen, he said hoarsely, "Inside, Miss Nash, and quickly, if you know what's good for you."

She spared him one quick, startled glance. And then, incredibly, she obeyed.

Which only went to show, he thought with a strange, tearing sadness, that anything was possible.

Julia touched a tremulous hand to her hair. Most of it still seemed to be up, but she could feel the loose curls drifting around the nape of her neck and the shorter wisps around her forehead. She didn't have to touch her mouth to know that her lips were swollen and undoubtedly an even deeper rose than they normally were because of his heated kiss.

And that didn't even begin to consider the rest of her. Her breasts felt almost painfully full, the nipples erect. Every inch of her skin was exquisitely sensitized. Deep within her, a damp, hot aching would not fade.

She bit her lip hard. Somehow she had to get through this, hold her head high and pretend that nothing was wrong. Nash pride came to the rescue, but only just. For a terrible moment, she feared she might burst into tears, so powerful was the unsatisfied hunger coursing through her.

Only the sight of Gloria and Daphne, pleasantly real and familiar, stopped her. They were her responsibility. She could not possibly do anything to shame or frighten them.

Shoulders back, head high, she walked into the ballroom. All conversation ceased, and for a terrifying moment she feared she was about to be denounced. But the murmur of voices picked up again and went on, as though nothing at all had happened.

She released a quick sigh of relief and sought out her sisters again. Their smiles were fading as they eyed her with concern.

"Are you all right?" Gloria asked softly when Julia joined them. "You look as though you might be a bit feverish."

"Nonsense," Julia said briskly. "I merely needed some fresh air."

Gloria frowned. She knew perfectly well the circumstances under which Julia had gone out to the garden. But not for anything would she have mentioned them.

"The punch is excellent," Daphne murmured, and pressed a glass into her hand.

Her sisters' kindness, and the way they closed ranks around her, made Julia's throat tighten. She had always been the one who protected them. But now, for a short time, at least, the roles seemed to have been reversed.

Gloria smiled brilliantly and launched into a conversation about a play she had seen recently. Daphne followed. Julia was given a chance to catch her breath and restore some measure of her equilibrium.

Only when she once again felt in control of herself did she dare glance around to see where Brand had gone. There was no sign of him. He seemed to have disappeared off the very face of the earth.

So be it, she thought with a stirring of vengefulness. Turn her life upside down, shatter everything she thought she knew about herself, and then waltz off without a fare-thee-well. Fine, if he wanted to play games like that, she would do the same.

The viscount had said something amusing. Julia laughed. Encouraged, he went on, his eyes sweeping appreciatively over her. Around her, the party swirled, society at its punctilious best. More champagne and punch were offered, and consumed. She lost track of the time, even, almost, of where she was. And yet she remained painfully alert in every faculty. The light seemed overly bright, the colors too dramatic, the voices too shrill.

And still she smiled, eyes agleam, laughing in all the right places, unaware of how she looked, clothed in azure silk, a glorious jewel fawned over by appreciative, covetous men. She was all quicksilver fire, honeyed skin, feminine challenge and mystery, as beguiling as any woman could be.

Or so she appeared to the man who leaned against the garden doors, just beyond her sight. Brand's expression was jaded, his smile cold. But his eyes, never leaving her, were predatory, and every inch of his body spoke of his determination.

Let the chit enjoy herself. Let her play the flirtatious lady, promising everything and nothing. His immediate presence was not required to remind every other male of how he had looked when he claimed her. No one would overstep society's rigid bounds, at least not if he wished to wake in the morning with all parts of his body still attached.

She could have her amusement. Eventually the evening would end.

And when it did, he would have her. On that score, at least, there would be no argument.

Julia shut the door to her room, leaned back against it and closed her eyes in relief. It was over at last. All the tedious hours of polite conversation and relentless cheerfulness were finally at an end.

Her sisters were snug in their own rooms, where they would undoubtedly open the connecting door and talk happily about what a wonderful time they'd had until they finally fell asleep.

But she was blessedly alone. The social mask she had struggled desperately to maintain could finally be removed. And so could the intolerably fashionable dress.

Fortunately, she had thought to ask Gloria to unbutton her while she still had the chance. Coming farther into the room, she slipped the dress off. It pooled around her feet, leaving her in a delicately spun lace camisole and a froth of petticoats. Picking up the dress, she hung it away in the wardrobe neatly, as she had been taught to do from her tenderest years. That much, at least, of her upbringing she hadn't lost, she thought glumly.

The back of her neck was stiff enough to hurt. She arched it first in one direction, then the other. Her slender shoulders moved with it, her breasts swaying above the rigid bone corseting.

No wonder she'd always avoided lacing. Even though she'd insisted on keeping it fairly loose, it still hurt like the dickens after all these hours.

Quickly she reached around and pulled the laces loose. When the corset was off, she took a deep breath, filling her lungs completely for the first time since dressing for the evening.

Kicking off her slippers, she sat down on the side of the bed and removed her stockings. She was very tired, but doubted that she would be able to sleep just yet. Her mind was racing, and the moment she tried to close her eyes, she was certain, she would think only of Brand.

That simply wouldn't do.

With a sigh, she went over to the dressing table, sat down and began brushing out her hair. It, too, ached after being held up for so long. She shook the auburn mass out before tackling it with the brush. Rhythmically, she began the one hundred strokes she tried to do every night without fail.

It was rather warm in the room, not unpleasantly so, but enough to notice. She puffed out a small exhalation of breath without noticing that one strap of her camisole slid down her shoulder, baring almost the entire curve of a breast.

When her hair was done, she put the brush back on the dressing table and considered what to do. Bed still held no appeal. For just a moment, she wished she were a man, free to go downstairs to the hotel bar and enjoy a cooling refreshment. But that alternative was out of the question for any young woman of propriety. Or any woman at all, for that matter. Hardestys didn't admit the other kind.

No, her room it had to be. She stood and went over to the windows, pushing them open a little farther. The street below was quiet. It was rather late.

But not too late for a bath. Her eyes lit. She should have thought of that at once. A bath was the perfect solution. It would soothe her enough to let her sleep.

Quickly she went into the adjacent bathroom and turned the taps on. The tub was enormous, a claw-footed cast-iron extravagance in the very latest style. It would take a while to fill.

Julia returned to the bedroom. Slowly she unsnapped the wide satin ribbon that formed the waistband of her petticoats and let them fall to her feet. Her eyes were thoughtful as she hung them away with her dress. Standing in the camisole and her pantaloons, she thought back over the evening.

If she was to remain in New York, she would have to be more discreet. No word of her feelings for Brand must be allowed to reach her family. That, above all, she owed them.

She had learned in the past few hours how very good an actress she could be. A few more days of such effort, and she would be ready for a career on the stage. A wistful smile touched her full mouth. Not for the first time, she caught herself wondering how Amelia Daniels would have handled the situation.

A damn sight more adroitly, no doubt. But then, Amelia had enjoyed certain advantages. An untamed wilderness, for instance, where rules didn't seem to matter very much and a man who was willing to sacrifice his own dreams for hers.

Brand wasn't willing to sacrifice anything. He had made that more than clear. He wanted her as a possession, in the same way he had wanted the land he'd bought and the house he would build. She—or any other woman, for that matter—was merely a means to an end.

She was a fool to even be thinking about him. Yet that alone was enough to make her heart quicken. Catching a glimpse of herself in the dressing-table mirror, she realized that her nipples were hardening.

With a curse that would have stunned any member of her family, she turned away. Angrily she snatched the camisole over her head and pulled it off. The pantaloons followed.

Naked, she stood in the center of the room on the delicately hued Oriental rug and contemplated the extravagant mess her life was becoming. She, who had gone from a carefree girl to a cautious but determined woman, now seemed to be neither. She hardly recognized herself, not the sensual woman with the tumbled hair in the mirror or the inner self, confused and crying out for a solution she could not even envision.

A clock ticked in the background, punctuating the silence in the room. Below it she heard a deeper and far older sound—the water running.

She had set the water to be warm verging to hot. Grimly she thought she should have made it cold, instead, to quench the heat building within her. Not that it would.

Only one force of nature could do that, curse his smiling mouth and firestorm eyes.

With a small sob, she stepped into the tub. The water was hot, but not unbearably so. Tendrils of steam rose from it, clouding the air and obscuring her vision.

Slowly she lowered herself. The tub was so large that, even when she was fully stretched out, her feet could not reach the end. She floated, her head supported, as the steam continued to build.

As though in a cloud, she tipped her head back and stared up at the ceiling. A slight sound disturbed her thoughts, but it was gone in an instant. Someone out in the corridor, no doubt.

The strain of the past few hours had taken its toll. She was more tired than she had realized. Dimly she remembered that she must not fall asleep and opened her eyes again.

There was a mirror opposite the tub, but it was almost entirely covered with mist. Even so, she thought she saw something move in it. Something at the door to the bathroom. Abruptly she sat up and turned in that direction. The gasp that escaped her was drowned out by the rush of water. .

Unfastening the top buttons of his shirt with one hand, Brand shrugged off his jacket with the other. His eyes raked over her. "What a marvelous idea," he said. Coolly, he added, "The perfect conclusion to the entertainment you thoughtfully provided."

Julia's breath caught. She was unsure if she was dreaming or if this could possibly be real. Dazedly she asked, "What are you talking about?"

He came closer, pulled the shirt over his head and tossed it away. "Only that before you undress you might want to be sure you're alone. Or perhaps not, as you choose."

Color scorched her cheeks. He couldn't possibly mean... "You didn't—"

"The alcove beyond your bed is remarkably comfortable. Have you tried the chair there?"

She had barely been aware that the alcove existed, having merely glanced at it when she was settling into the room. It would never have occurred to her that anyone could have been sitting there—that he could have been watching her as she disrobed.

"How dare you! Of all the contemptible— How did you get in here?"

He shrugged, as though it ought to be self-evident. "Discreetly, I promise."

She started to rise, reaching frantically for a towel. He caught her wrist in one big, sinewy hand. With the other, he reached for the buttons of his trousers.

"Don't bother, sweetheart," he said. "I like you just the way you are."

"I'll scream," she said, but the words lost some of their effect as she stared, helplessly fascinated, at the unmistakable bulge beneath the finely woven wool.

"Probably," he said, continuing to release himself.

Moments later, he stepped into the tub. Water sloshed over the sides. He drew her to him, hands roaming over her back and down the slender indentation of her waist before returning to her full breasts. He rubbed his palms over her nipples, smiling at her instant response.

"Beautiful," he murmured, and lifted her so that she was half sitting on him, his erection pressing against the downy curls between her thighs.

"By all means, scream" he added huskily as he lightly squeezed and kneaded her breasts. "But not for help."

"For what, then?" she asked, knowing her behavior was insane, but unable to stop herself.

"This," he said, and proceeded to show her.

Chapter Sixteen

"Delicious," Julia murmured. She shut her eyes for a moment, savoring the sensation as the strawberries slipped down her throat. They were small and sweet, just as she liked them.

That they were also served in a crystal dish and accompanied by an excellent champagne added only a little to the experience. It was the strawberries that counted.

That, and the fact that she knew Brand was watching her.

It wasn't necessary for her to turn around to be sure of that. He was always watching her. Everywhere she had gone in the past week—with the sole exception of the modiste, and a few ladies-only tea parties her sisters had dragged her to—he was present.

At every concert and play, every dance and recital, Brand was there. People were commenting on how much more interested in society he had become, but it was impossible to tell if they were serious or not.

He certainly didn't seem interested, giving every impression of being thoroughly bored. Yet he was unfailingly polite, delighting the hostesses who had contested so long for his presence.

And frustrating the men who fluttered around Julia. Men who were attempting to improve their acquaintance with her but were warned off by the always present, always threatening presence of the man who had claimed her as his own.

Not that he did anything untoward. Since the episode in the garden, he had not laid a hand on her in any even remotely public place. But every night, when she bade her sisters sweet dreams and slipped into her room, he was there. She knew she should tell him to go away, or change rooms, or simply go home. But she couldn't bring herself to do any of those things.

When it came to Brand, her will seemed to desert her. That, more than anything, was what she found so frightening. In his arms, she became someone else entirely, a woman of fire and passion whose entire being seemed centered on this single man.

It was as though he held the answer to every question, even to life itself, within his being. He was strength and tenderness, desire and joy. Without him, she would never feel complete.

And so she went to him, her heart thudding each time she turned the key in the lock and stepped inside. Would he be there again, waiting for her? Would he want her as he had the previous night and into the early hours of morning?

Each night, he undressed her slowly, insisting on playing the ladies' maid, even to the extent of brushing her hair for her. Each night they bathed together in the claw-footed tub.

Her cheeks flushed as she thought of the use they had put the tub to, it and the thick rug on the floor beside it. And then there was the bed, huge and welcoming. Only last night he had—

She absolutely had to stop thinking this way. It was broad daylight, for heaven's sake. She was in the midst of a sizable group, all turned out to view the races.

Gloria was there with that handsome young doctor she had met, a surgeon at one of the larger hospitals. He was the son of an immensely wealthy family with roots almost as deep as the Nashes' own, but unlike so many of his kind, he worked seriously at his profession. And he seemed genuinely smitten with Gloria.

As indeed he ought to be, Julia thought loyally. Her sister had never looked lovelier, basking in the attention of a man she plainly liked and admired.

Daphne, too, was radiant. Charles Hewlitt had come down from Belle Haven, apologizing to Brand for temporarily deserting his post, but making it clear he wouldn't go back until Daphne was done with New York and ready to return. He was there now, leaning attentively close as together they shared a bowl of strawberries.

How sweet, how blessedly normal, exactly what love was supposed to be. A pang of envy went through her, but was instantly repressed. She didn't begrudge her sisters anything, not even the happiness that was beyond her own reach.

Besides, she was meeting so many interesting people. Well, men at any rate. Beside the viscount and Barton, there was a poet, a composer, a sculptor, several financiers, and all those sons of the social register whom she would never consider as husbands but who made very pleasant escorts at one or another of the endless events she attended.

Gramma Sara's gift of a new wardrobe was getting a great deal of use. Fashion, she was discovering, had certain advantages. It provided a much-needed armor against the slanted looks and muted whispers that accompanied her wherever she went.

Miss Julia Nash was altogether too popular, too different, too free-speaking and—they all suspected—free-thinking. And then there was that curious business with Brand Delaney. His habit of showing up whenever she did had hardly gone unnoticed. No one quite knew what to make of it, but they were all trying to decide.

Their curiosity was wearing on her. Lately it took more of an effort to smile and join in the meaningless repartee society favored. More and more, she longed for Daniels' Neck, her unspoiled stretch of beach, and her solitude.

Yet that wouldn't last long. Soon Charles would return to Belle Haven. Brand's house would be built. And he would live there—with her or without her. He had made that clear. Some woman would share it with him. Some wife.

She sighed deeply and made an effort to turn her attention to the events on the course. One of Brand's stallions was racing. The crowd cheered as the horses rounded the corner and headed into the straightaway.

Julia strained forward, trying to see what was happening. She was not at all surprised when Brand's horse suddenly surged forward, outstripping all the others and taking the win by a good ten paces.

A short time later, she glimpsed Brand in the winner's circle, accepting the trophy with a faint smile. He looked well pleased with himself, as she supposed he should.

There was a woman at his side, someone Julia had vaguely noticed at the various events she attended. She had blond, almost taffy-colored hair swept up in a chignon beneath her bonnet. Her figure was lovely, slender and graceful. Her gaze, focused on Brand, was warm and very, very familiar. Clearly, she knew him well.

Anger flared in Julia. It was all well and good that he watched her, but she did her own share of observing. Brand was never without his coterie of female admirers, some women well married but bored, others ambitious young things out to snare the most wildly rich and dangerously powerful man to set foot in the city in living memory.

And then there were the rumors she heard, and perhaps was meant to hear. Acidic words dripped within her earshot of his alleged prowess in the bedchamber—to which she could all too well attest—and his indiscriminate fondness for both high-born women and those whose profession required that they please. It seemed there wasn't a clandestine bedchamber or exclusive brothel in the city that hadn't been graced by his presence.

Clearly, Brand Delaney hadn't devoted all his time to amassing his immense fortune. He had found ample opportunity for recreation of a very particular sort.

And yet the dictate he had laid down that first night about no other man dancing with her still held. Everywhere she went, under every roof, once the music began, no man dared to cross him.

If truth be told, she loved dancing with Brand, just as she loved doing so much else with him. But she deeply resented the notion that he somehow owned her. That while he continued to show interest, no other man could do the same.

She popped another strawberry into her mouth and thought about that. It was absurd, almost medieval. But she didn't doubt for a moment that it was also a foretaste of what any wife of his could expect. Especially given his determination to have children. He would insist that their mother be so chaste as not to invite the slightest doubt.

Perhaps, Julia thought with a faint smile, he would adopt the Indian custom and keep her in purdah. Was the house he was building—Summercove, he had called it—going to be equipped for a harem of one? She could ask Charles, of course, but the question would undoubtedly discompose him. She was too thoughtful of Daphne to do that.

Or she could simply ask Brand. Challenge him to defend his notions of matrimony. That might be the far more satisfying course. It might also get just a touch acrimonious. The hotel was no place for that. As it was, each night she had to stifle her cries of pleasure so as not to risk being overheard.

No, somewhere else was needed. Somewhere they could talk openly, holding nothing back.

No possibility presented itself. She was still mulling the problem over when a frisson of sensation rippled down her spine. Julia turned slightly, surprised to see a handsome young man at her elbow. She had been totally unaware of his approach, so engulfed was she in thoughts of Brand.

"Penny for your thoughts," he said, and smiled. His face was open and candid, the kind of face found only on those blessed by fortune from tenderest youth. She had seen him before, at some dance or musicale somewhere. But they had not been introduced.

"Frank Preston," he said, and held out his hand.

"Julia Nash," she replied automatically. His fingers curled around hers for just an instant. They stood, a little apart, regarding one another.

"I trust you are enjoying the city?"

"It's very exciting. Do you live here?"

"Most of the time. We have a place in Newport."

Ah, yes, the Prestons. She did recall hearing about them. Old money, by New York standards, which meant it went back a generation or two. Shipping, she thought, and canal-building. The father was dead, and the management of the businesses was now in the hands of the son. This must be him.

"Do you follow the races?" the younger Mr. Preston inquired.

"Not very often," she answered truthfully. "My sisters and I have been fortunate enough to be invited to a great many events. This happened to be one of them."

"How fortunate. I've been wanting to meet you."

Julia stared at him. He seemed completely sincere and without guile. There was no sign that he had any awareness of the undercurrents between her and Brand, signals other men had picked up on and prudently obeyed.

"Have you?" she murmured.

"Indeed. I'm compiling a study on the settlement of communities in this area. Someone suggested that I talk to you about Belle Haven."

"Who was that?"

"I can't recall. It was only said in passing, but if you could spare a few minutes of your time..."

For this pleasant and undemanding young man. Yes, she might be able to manage that. A glance over his shoulder confirmed that Brand was still busy with his blonde. She looked a bit older than what Julia imagined his taste usually ran to, but perhaps she was just being catty. There was no denying the woman's beauty, or her vivacity. She was laughing at something Brand had said, and gazing at him with such unfeigned enjoyment that Julia's throat tightened.

"I can spare you all the time you like," she said. The younger Mr. Preston looked surprised, but pleased. He offered his arm. With only a moment's hesitation, Julia took it.

Brand frowned. He had caught sight of Julia, but then had been distracted by someone else pressing forward to offer congratulations. When he looked again, she was gone.

That wouldn't have worried him particularly, except that he could have sworn the man she was talking with was Frank Preston. He hadn't gotten a good enough look at him to be sure, but the suspicion was there all the same. Yet more people were crowding around. He felt a pressing need to be away from them, and to find Julia.

"Would you mind, Mother? There's someone I need to speak with?"

Maggie Delaney smiled and shook her head. "Not at all, dear. You go right along. The judge and I are going to have a glass of champagne together."

Brand hid a grin. The judge—a towering eminence on the bench—was one of his mother's many admirers. Better yet, he was a gentleman of the old school, who would never dream of straying from the strictest propriety when dealing with a lady of Maggie Delaney's stature. Mother and son exchanged a quick look of amusement before parting.

The public stands on the far side of the track were beginning to empty out, but people lingered outside the clubhouse and in the private boxes that adjoined it. The races were a pleasant excuse to see and be seen. Several people tried to engage him in conversation, but Brand turned them aside courteously. He kept going, determined to find Julia.

There was no sign of her. Gloria and Daphne were still chatting with friends; he found them readily enough. But Julia seemed to have disappeared. She wasn't in any of the boxes, nor was she under the tent where strawberries and champagne were being served.

Thinking of her love of horses, he wondered if she had walked over to the stables. But when he got there, she wasn't to be found.

His frown was in earnest now. Truth be told, he disliked the thought of her with any man other than himself. But the idea of Frank Preston and Julia together was particularly unpleasant.

More determined than ever, he was heading toward the clubhouse to look there when he caught sight of a flutter of azure silk in the opposite direction. Ordinarily, he would never have noticed it. But the precise shade of Julia's dress had lodged in his memory, as had so much else about her. Turning, he walked in that direction.

A lush, sloping lawn led down from the clubhouse to a small river. Before he reached it, he heard muted voices.

"Yes, actually, it was. But I'm surprised you'd know that. Most people have never heard it."

"Ah, but they should. Belle Haven is the only settlement in this area founded by a woman. It should be well-known."

"I agree, but—"

"Which is precisely why I want to include it in my book. Of course, I'll need a great deal more information to do that."

"Yes, of course. I could—"

"Julia."

She turned, eyes as wide as a startled doe's. They were standing, but Preston was a shade closer to her than was strictly necessary. Brand bared his teeth. He walked forward with the loose, lithe stride of a hunter.

"What are you doing here?" Julia demanded. Her cheeks were flushed. The flash of pleasure she had not been able to deny upon first seeing him was gone, replaced by feminine ire.

"Looking for you." He glanced at the younger man as he spoke, noting that he was only just holding on to his temper. They were distantly acquainted, in the way that Brand knew most people in New York society and they knew him. But he'd heard things lately about Frank Preston, things he didn't like, and he wasn't about to tolerate his being with Julia.

"Is there something you wanted to say, Preston?"

It was a deliberate challenge. Brand wouldn't have minded at all if the younger man lashed out at him. It would have been all the excuse he needed to teach the spoiled, self-centered son of a wealthy family a lesson that seemed long overdue.

But however indulged he had been in his life, Preston did have some instinct for survival. Brand watched the silent battle he waged with himself, pride and anger against common sense. For once, sense won.

"No," Frank said sullenly. "Nothing."

"I don't understand—" Julia began. She looked honestly baffled, as well she might be, this fey creature without experience of the darker side of men.

"Come," he said, and held out his hand. He expected her to take it. She belonged to him, after all, and every night in bed she willingly acknowledged that. But he belonged to her, too. Their passion and joy, their giving and fulfillment, were mutual. Possessing and possessed, they were tied together by silken skeins.

Except that Julia did not appear inclined to admit that, at least not right then. She dug her heels into the soft ground and stared at him rebelliously.

"You are being very rude, Mr. Delaney."

Beside her, Preston looked shocked, but pleased. He was emboldened enough to shoot Brand a look of pure hatred.

"That's it," Brand muttered. He flexed one arm, very slightly. Julia let out a yelp. Apparently she hadn't anticipated being swept off her feet and tossed over his shoulder. So much the better. There was a good deal to be said for keeping a woman off balance.

"What do you think you're doing?" she demanded when she'd gotten her breath back.

"Saving you from embarrassment," he said as he strode up the bank away from the river.

"Saving me...? Are you crazy? People will see...Mr. Preston will..."

"Frank Preston can go to the devil. As for anyone else, if you don't want to make a spectacle of yourself, I suggest you calm down." For a touch of added emphasis, he patted her behind.

Julia hit him, her fist thumping hard against his back. Brand laughed. It wasn't very civilized—or at all polite—but to hell with that. He was enjoying himself.

They were approaching the clubhouse. Much as he would have liked to carry her right through there, her feelings did matter to him. Reluctantly he stopped and lowered her down the length of his body. Her feet touched the ground, but he did not let go of her. Instead, he tipped her head back and, staring into her eyes, said, "Stay away from Frank Preston, Julia. He doesn't mean you any good."

"He doesn't? Why, you—"

Whatever she meant to say, Brand didn't want to hear it. He took her mouth with his, stifling her cry of outrage, and kissed her deeply. She was rigid and unyielding at first, but quickly enough, the heat neither of them could resist engulfed them both. Her mouth softened, pliant beneath his own. A soft moan escaped her as her hands came up to his broad shoulders, clinging.

When he lifted his head at last, her eyes were wide and luminous, but not without a lingering spark of resistance. Through the haze of his hunger for this woman, he thought wryly that he would have been disappointed if she proved too compliant. He liked the sense of a strength to match his own, for all that it was of a completely different nature.

"I mean it," he said quietly. "Preston's trouble."

She took a step back and smoothed her skirts. Her breathing was ragged and her color high, but her voice was steady. "Why? He seems quite pleasant."

Brand sighed. If she meant to goad him, she'd picked the right way to do it. The very thought that she enjoyed another man's company was enough to raise a dark, surging anger within him. He fought it down and eyed her with deceptive calmness.

"Preston's father was a skilled financier. He took good care of his money. The son's different. He wants the same reputation, but isn't willing to do the work for it. He's always looking for the big score."

"He didn't seem like that at all. On the contrary, I thought him very intelligent and thoughtful."

Brand made a derisive noise. There was a great deal he could have said about the susceptibility of women as innocent as Julia still was, but this didn't seem an opportune moment.

Instead, he said, "Whatever you think, take my advice and give him a wide berth."

Her chin lifted. "Is that what you call it—advice?"

"Have you another word for it?"

"Yes. It sounded like an order. And if there's one thing you can't do, Brand Delaney, it's order me around. I've always thought for myself, and I intend to continue doing so."

Before he could reply, Julia picked up her skirts. She walked away without a backward glance.

Chapter Seventeen

By the time she reached the clubhouse, Julia's legs were trembling. She found a chair under the striped awning and sat down quickly. Her stomach was clenched, and she felt vaguely ill.

The scene by the riverbank dismayed her. She supposed there were some women who enjoyed the notion of two men competing for them, but she did not.

Besides, it had hardly been a competition. Whatever Brand might say about him, Frank Preston was far too much a gentleman to be able to deal with a rival who was nothing short of a buccaneer.

She took a deep breath, struggling for calm. Treacherous emotions surged within her—excitement, desire, pleasure. She turned her head slightly, hoping, yet dreading, too, that she would catch a glimpse of Brand. But he was nowhere to be seen.

Neither were her sisters. She was alone in the ebbing crowd, surrounded by people heading for their carriages, talking over the days results and the evening's entertainment to come.

She was suddenly, overwhelmingly tired. The thought of yet another ball or concert or whatever it was she was supposed to attend weighed on her intolerably. And then...

when night came and she stepped inside her hotel bedroom, then...what?

She stood up suddenly, ignoring the weakness that still lingered in her legs. Legs, she noted absently, not one leg but both, a shared weakness that seemed to seep all through her, indiscriminately.

Her smile had a bitter edge.

She was walking toward the carriages, intending to find the one she had come in, when the woman approached her. Julia recognized her instantly. The blonde from the winner's circle, the beauty who had clung to Brand's arm and smiled at him with such familiarity.

Her impulse—her need—was to dislike this woman. Yet it was impossible. The blue eyes catching hers were candid, but not without a certain sympathy. The gentleness of her mouth—she was not quite smiling—was real.

"Excuse me," the woman said. Her voice was soft, slightly husky, appealing. "Would you mind if I walk with you?"

Julia hesitated. The manners bred into her from birth could hardly be ignored. But she did not want company just then, not this woman's or anyone else's. She wanted desperately to be alone, to try to sort out the tangled web of her thoughts.

"I'm sorry—" she began, but broke off. The woman had tilted her head slightly to one side—the better to look at her, perhaps—and now she really was smiling.

"You are lovely, of course," she said to Julia. "But different. I suppose I should have expected that." The notion seemed to please her. She nodded suddenly, as though she had come to some decision. "My name is Maggie Delaney. I'm Brand's mother."

Mother...mother...mother...mother...

The word seemed to reverberate through Julia. She stared at the lovely, serene woman in frank astonishment. "You can't be."

"And why not?"

"You're too young."

Maggie laughed. "Aren't you nice! I was rather hoping you would be. To be frank, my son's taste in women hasn't exactly tended toward anyone I'd care to have a cup of tea with."

"Tea—?" She was sounding like an idiot, but she couldn't help it. That this woman was Brand's mother, that she had sought Julia out and that she clearly wanted to talk with her, was simply too much to grasp all at once.

One moment she'd been thinking of him as a ruthless buccaneer too accustomed to getting his own way, and the next she was confronted by the reality of the good son. Or at least a son who had a mother who worried about him. Which was he really, this astounding, infuriating, magnificent, arrogant man who had turned her life upside down?

"Tea," Maggie said firmly, and took Julia's arm. Moments later, they were seated under the awning. A waiter materialized to receive their order, and as quickly vanished. Maggie smoothed her gloves. She removed a delicate ivory fan from her purse and fanned herself discretely.

"Lovely day, don't you think?"

Julia took a deep breath, determined to get a grip on herself. Above all, she couldn't show by a word or look what she knew about this woman's background. Surely Maggie would be mortified to know what Brand had revealed about her.

Now that Julia thought of it, why had he been so shockingly candid? He couldn't possibly make a habit of discussing his mother's past. Indeed, it had to be a secret between them. If it were not, not even all of Brand's wealth and power would compel society to receive his mother.

The waiter arrived with their tea. Maggie put her fan down to pour. Her hands were steady, and her expression was serene. Julia tried not to stare at her, but she couldn't help it.

The table was small, and they were seated less than three feet apart. Yet even at such close range, Maggie Delaney looked far too young to be who she claimed—older than Julia, to be sure, but certainly not old enough to have borne a child under such terrible circumstances and seen him grow to manhood.

"I was fifteen," Maggie said quietly.

Julia started. She disliked the idea that her thoughts could be read so easily, but she supposed it was to be expected. Maggie Delaney gave every sign of being as intelligent—and perceptive—as her son. It was becoming clearer where Brand had gotten the drive and strength that had taken him so far.

"Brand told me that his father was Cherokee," Julia said quietly.

Maggie nodded. She sipped her tea. Her hand looked delicate against the fragile china, but Julia suspected that, were she to touch it, she would find it strong indeed.

"We were married before his death," Maggie said matter-of-factly, "but afterward I found it more prudent to return to my maiden name."

"I can understand that."

"Can you? My husband was killed because he wasn't white. I couldn't risk the same thing happening to my son." She smiled faintly. For the first time, Julia noticed that there were finely drawn lines around her mouth, the kind that came from frequent smiles over a very long time. Had her smiles begun as rebellion and protection against the harsh hand fate had dealt her?

"I loved my husband quite desperately. Brand is like him in many ways."

It was all Julia could do not to ask what they were. The urge to talk about Brand with this woman who must surely know him better than anyone was all but irresistible. But if she succumbed, her own feelings would be all too clear.

Besides, at the moment, she was more interested in why Maggie had sought her out.

"You come from a very old and respected family, don't you?" Brand's mother asked.

Julia nodded cautiously. "I suppose."

"Just the sort of background Brand would want in a wife."

"He told you that he's looking—?"

"Oh, indeed," Maggie said. "He was very frank about it." She sighed. "Please don't misunderstand me, your background is admirable. Everyone speaks most highly of your family and of you."

"I'm glad to hear that," Julia murmured. Was that what this was all about, then? Brand's mother wanting to get to know a prospective daugher-in-law before having her dropped in her lap by a son who, wonderful though he undoubtedly was, viewed marriage the same way he would any other major acquisition?

"However," Julia went on slowly, struggling to find the right words, "I really must tell you that—"

"Of course, I'm well aware that it isn't any of my business."

"I wouldn't say that. After all, you're his—"

"But when you're a mother yourself, you'll understand how hard it is to just stand by."

"Actually, I don't think I'll ever be—"

"I still remember him the way he was, you see, as an infant and a small boy. He had the sweetest nature. Even during the worst times, he would always smile and pat my cheek, telling me everything would be all right."

Julia swallowed hard. She had a sudden, piercing vision of a small, dark-haired boy with Brand's features reaching out to her. The longing that swept over her was so intense that she gasped. At that instant, she would have given everything she had to reach out to that child, to take his hand, and walk with him wherever he wanted to go.

"Is something wrong?" Maggie asked. Her eyes, gazing at Julia, were suddenly gentle.

"No, not at all, it's just—" Julia stopped, not knowing what to say. She ached inside. It was a dull throbbing, not of the body but of the spirit. "I think you may have the wrong impression about me."

"How so?"

"I—" What to say to this lovely and obviously loving woman? Your son asked me to marry him and I turned him down? I'm Brand's mistress but I have no intention of being his wife? He's fantastic in bed but I think he'd be hell to live with?

The very thought made Julia flush. In almost every situation she had ever encountered, she'd been able to fall back on the social graces but now they failed her. No rule of etiquette she had ever learned seemed useful in the present situation.

Finally, she said, "I'm a rather independent person." It sounded so weak, even a touch absurd, but at least it had the virtue of being true.

Maggie frowned. "I see. . . ."

Julia doubted that she did. Maggie hadn't chosen independence, she'd had it thrust upon her in a tragic act of brutality. How could she possibly understand a woman who feared that marriage would rob her of her identity and strip away the strength that was so essential a part of her life?

"I had an accident several years ago," Julia said quietly. She was surprised by how readily she could speak of it to Maggie. There was an openness about the older woman. Unlike so many people Julia had met, she wasn't judgmental. There was a confidence and serenity about her that Julia instinctively liked—and trusted.

"While I was recovering, I didn't really do the things other young women my age were doing. I couldn't. Instead, I seem to have gone off on a path of my own. I suspect I'm a very different person than the one I would have been if the accident had never happened. But I can't say I regret that."

"You're at peace with yourself," Maggie said softly. "Very few people are, you know, especially the young women I see. They're from what are supposed to be the best families, so you'd think they'd have more confidence in themselves. But instead they seem to worry constantly about what others think of them, or wonder if the right man will come along, or if they will be envied and admired. I used to think money was the answer to everything but since I've had an opportunity to see its effects, I've been forced to change my mind."

"I don't think Brand would agree with you. He seems to think anything can be bought, that in the final analysis everything is a business arrangement."

Maggie's eyebrows rose slightly. "You don't accept that?"

"No, I don't." Softly, but with unmistakable firmness, Julia added, "I won't."

Maggie laughed. She seemed pleased with what she had heard. "I do believe I owe my son an apology."

"How so?"

"For not crediting him with having the sense to prefer a woman who can stand up to him."

"I think you've gotten the wrong impression. He and I—"

"Are the talk of the town. You do realize that, don't you? The inscrutable Brand Delaney finally seems to have met his match."

"He does?" Julia was astonished. She'd had no idea anyone was saying any such thing.

"My dear, believe me, his behavior has been most uncharacteristic. As his mother, I have to say I find it quite refreshing."

She laid her hand gently on Julia's. "When he was a child, I could understand him and reach him. He didn't have to be alone. But since he grew up, there's been a part of him—a large part—that's always closed off."

She withdrew her hand and picked up the silver spoon lying beside her teacup. Slowly she stirred. "Perhaps I shouldn't be telling you all this. I certainly don't want to violate my son's privacy in any way. But there have been times when I was so worried for him, afraid that what he experienced as a child would prevent him from ever knowing the full joy of life."

Maggie raised her head and looked at Julia directly. "Now I no longer feel that necessarily has to be the case."

Julia's throat was tight. "I wouldn't want you to think—"

"It's all right, my dear," Maggie interjected. "I realize you have your own concerns. But now that I've met you, I have to admit that I am greatly reassured."

She glanced toward the clubhouse. An older man was standing by the door, his attitude one of patient resignation.

"I promised dear Judge Harris that I wouldn't be long."

Standing, she nodded to Julia. "I do hope we'll be seeing more of each other, Miss Nash."

Julia rose. "I don't know," she said candidly.

Maggie's eyes were gentle. "Trust is always difficult, isn't it?"

"It's not a question of that. I do trust Brand. It's just that what I trust him to do isn't necessarily what I can find acceptable."

"I didn't mean him," Maggie said softly. "I meant trusting yourself. There's nothing harder than that—or more essential."

Her fingers brushed Julia's. It was the merest touch, but carried a wealth of understanding and comfort. In a whisper of silk, she turned and walked toward the judge.

Alone, Julia stood for several minutes. Maggie and her admirer were gone, and the racetrack was almost empty.

Her sisters would be waiting for her. She shouldn't tarry any longer.

Yet still she stood, lost in thought, until a cloud drifted across the sun and abruptly recalled her to the fading day.

Chapter Eighteen

Rain splattered against the windows. Julia lay in bed, the covers tucked under her chin. It was well after midnight. A lone carriage rattled down the streets, the horse's hooves striking sharply against the cobblestones. In its wake was silence.

The hotel was still. No sound came from the hall beyond her room. The last of the guests had gone off to bed some time before. The front doors would be locked now, and only a single sleepy porter would be posted to admit late arrivals who rang the bell.

Julia was alone. She told herself she was glad of that. Stretched out full-length, her toes straining toward the bed's curved footboard, she tried to take up as much room as possible. It didn't work. The bed felt huge, and far too empty. So, too, did the room, the city, the world, her life—

Absurd. Fed up with herself and the determined waywardness of her thoughts, she pounded her fist into the pillow. The effort didn't make her any more comfortable, but at least it banished the pretense that nothing was wrong.

She was wound tight as a watch-spring, unable to even close her eyes, much less sleep. Yet she was also exhausted, drained by the events of the past several days. With each empty, dragging moment, the rest she so desperately needed became more elusive than ever.

Damn the man. He had no right to do this to her, no right to upset her so carefully ordered life, no right to strip from her the self-possession and confidence that were her shield against the world.

And no right to leave her like this, alone in a silence so profound that her very thoughts seemed to echo.

She hated this, hated the emptiness and the fear as images of where he might be and what he might be doing tormented her. She couldn't believe what was happening to her. That she, Julia Nash, should succumb to such dependency and jealousy, just like so many other women she had seen and mildly despised, was beyond belief. Yet now she was no better than any of them, every bit as subject to the whims of a man. Exactly as she had sworn she would never be.

She threw the covers back and swung her legs over the side of the bed. The room was cool. She was glad of the fringed shawl that she plucked from the chair beside the bed. Wrapping it around her, she went to stand at the window.

Below, gas lamps reflected the puddles of rain collecting amid the cobblestones. She supposed they would all be gone soon, the lamps replaced with electrical lights and the cobblestones buried beneath the asphalt that was appearing everywhere. It was progress of a sort, but she would miss the softer glow of gas and the gently rounded edges of the stones where time and use had marked them.

With a sigh, she leaned her head against the cool wood of the window frame. Tears threatened. She blinked them back, but not before one or two trickled down her cheeks.

She rubbed them away fiercely with the back of her hand. As she did so, she caught sight of her reflection in the windowpanes. The woman who returned her stare looked like a stranger, pale in the rain-washed light. Julia clutched the shawl more tightly around herself and turned away.

There were books on the bedside table. She could read them, write letters, or even try her hand yet again at needlework. Or she could try to sleep. But the mere thought seemed futile. The emptiness of long, silent hours pressed in on her. She had a sudden, terrible urge to flee into the night, to run as far and as fast as she possibly could and not stop until the yearnings that had taken possession of her were as still and silent as the night itself.

But there was nowhere to run to except Belle Haven, and she knew, with the merest flicker of thought, that the peace and comfort she had always found there would be absent now. Not even in Amelia's house would she feel truly whole and free.

A deep sigh escaped her. It threatened to become a sob. She pressed her lips together hard and reached for the first book that came to hand. She was staring at it sightlessly when the silence was punctured by the soft but unmistakable tread of footsteps coming down the hall.

Brand hesitated. He stood in front of Julia's door, his hand raised to knock, and debated what he was about to do. Such uncertainty was foreign to him. He had not climbed so high in the world by being indecisive.

But this woman—alone among them all—made him feel like a green boy again. It wasn't necessarily a pleasant experience. He had not meant to come to her. Indeed, he had considered every distraction he could think of to make himself stay away. But other women had held no charm, whiskey had tasted flat, and the dark, rainwashed streets of the city had only reminded him of his own loneliness.

When had he last felt alone? The emotion was so foreign to him that he could scarcely credit it. Perhaps he had known loneliness as a child; if he tried very hard, he could almost remember it. But at the earliest age, he had determined to seize the world, to stride through it on his own terms and to his own ends. After that, there had never been room for loneliness.

Until now. He stood staring at her door and felt an emptiness inside himself that mocked everything he was or ever had been. The sensation was like falling into a black pit with no bottom in sight.

He took a deep breath and reached for the only safety he knew.

His hand rapped hard on the door. Once, twice, he knocked, short, sharp sounds that punctured the silence of the corridor. Then he waited.

Moments dragged by. He could feel every one of them tugging at him. Impatience gripped him. He was just about to raise his hand again when the door suddenly swung open.

Julia blinked, and her lips parted slightly. She made a sound deep in her throat, somewhere beyond a sob and a moan.

In an instant, she was in his arms, gathered close. Through the thin silk of her peignoir, he could feel every womanly inch of her. She shivered, smiling weakly.

"You're wet." Her hands brushed silver droplets from his hair.

He should step back, be mindful of her comfort, at least take the time to discard the damp overcoat, he knew. But his body would not obey his mind. Instead, he drew her even closer and felt a surge of near-painful pleasure when she made no attempt to pull away.

A few quick steps and he kicked the door shut behind them. The gas lamp beside the bed hissed softly. Rain fell against the windows. Beyond, the city lay wrapped in night. But it had no real meaning for them. They were alone in a world of their own design.

Except for the increasing raggedness of breath and a few impatient groans, silence ruled. Clothes fell away piece by piece. Overcoat and peignoir, trousers and nightgown, shoes, a shirt undone in haste, a hair ribbon, all made a trail to the wide, soft bed.

Their lovemaking was hot and urgent. Naked on her back, with her hair spread in wild disarray over the pillows, Julia clung to Brand. Even as ecstasy hovered on the edges of her consciousness, she was seized by terrifying, inescapable panic. It was all unraveling, coming apart almost in her very hands, time slipping irrevocably past like the grains of sand she had tried to catch as a child. They had escaped her, and so would this magical, mysterious time she had never thought to experience but now couldn't imagine living without.

Tears burned her eyes, slipped down damask cheeks. Brand kissed them away, cursing softly. Tremors tore through him. His high-boned cheeks were darkly stained, and his eyes were glittering. She could feel the iron control he was struggling to maintain, and knew the precise moment when it snapped, the instant she deliberately arched her hips and slowly, purposefully, swayed back and forth against him.

He said her name roughly, yet almost with a note of apology, and pressed her back against the pillows. His thigh, heavily muscled from all his years of riding, thrust between hers.

She moaned, opening to him. All sense of modesty was gone, restraint did not exist. There was nothing but this man, this moment, and the terrible, tearing hunger that was threatening to devour her.

They moved together as one. Her arms, slender and pale in the faint light, held him almost protectively as his strength surged, exploded and at last ebbed.

Spent, he lay against her, unmoving, for a timeless moment, until at last he raised his head and looked into her eyes. She had no idea what he was seeing, but whatever it was, it seemed to confirm something he had been thinking.

With a low sigh, he turned over onto his back, drawing her with him. It felt so natural to lie like this, in the curve of his arm, with the sound of his heartbeat close beneath her cheek. The tremors of passion and fulfillment still resonated within her, but hard on them came an engulfing contentment that in its own way was at least as potent.

Quietly, with a note of self-mockery, Brand said, "You could upset any man's notions about the eternal female."

Julia yawned. She couldn't help herself. Vaguely, in the back of her mind, she thought she ought to pursue that. He shouldn't be able to make so sweeping a statement without contradiction. But somehow it didn't seem worth the effort. Besides, she felt vaguely flattered. Certainly Brand Delaney did not admit to having his notions upset every day of the week. Having accomplished that much, at least, she might be excused if she allowed herself to let the rest slip.

She was so very warm, lying there nestled against him. He had pulled the covers over them both, making a snug nest. Outside, rain continued to hammer against the windows, but inside there was only peace and, presently, the gentle breath of sleep.

Julia stirred reluctantly. Light, filtering in through the curtains, teased at her eyes and finally coaxed her to open them. It was morning. The rain had stopped. She sighed and settled back down under the covers where it was so warm and safe and deliciously—

Brand! He was still there, beside her, dark lashes fanning his cheeks and a night's growth of beard adding to what was already a rakish air.

There, in the morning, well after dawn. At an hour when her sisters might wonder why she wasn't about and come to find out. Panic gripped her. She jumped from the bed, only to yelp when she realized she was naked.

Grabbing the peignoir on the floor, she threw it on over her head. The clock on the marble mantelpiece read 9:15.

A small sigh of relief escaped her. Her sisters had undoubtedly been out late the night before. She had a little more time than she'd thought.

But what to do with it? Waking Brand to urge him to leave was the practical thing to do, but she lacked the heart for it. He looked so endearing lying there, even if *endearing* was a silly word for so strong and virile a man. Still, it fit. He needed his sleep. It wasn't fair to disturb him. And besides, if she did, he would likely have something else on his mind besides taking his leave. Or at least she hoped he would.

Definitely not a good idea, however tempting it might be. She should be just the tiniest bit practical, shouldn't she? Determined to listen to her better self, Julia plucked clothes from the wardrobe. Fifteen minutes later, she was dressed, more or less. Her hair had refused to be restrained in a bun; all she could manage was to scoop it back from her face with tortoiseshell combs. Her cheeks were flushed, her lips were full, and there was a definite glow to her eyes. She could only hope that anyone seeing her would presume she had enjoyed a healthy morning constitutional.

Despite the hour, the hotel dining room was almost empty. Anyone with business to conduct had departed, and visitors bent purely on leisure were not yet stirring. Except for herself, of course. She quickly secured the attention of a young waiter and murmured her requests. He assured her that everything would be seen to most promptly.

Even so, Julia hovered nervously in the lobby until the young man emerged, wheeling a cart laden with a variety of dishes. He was surprised to find her waiting, but hid it well. Together they rode up in the recently installed elevator.

"Thank you so much," Julia said when they stood in front of her door. She quickly signed the check, having added a substantial tip, and assured the young man that she could manage by herself.

If he found that at all odd, he most likely put it down to a young woman's modesty. Wishing her a good day, he was gone. Julia glanced in both directions along the hall, then quickly unlocked the door and pushed the cart inside.

Going slowly past the bed, so as not to let the dishes clank too much, she put the cart near the windows and pulled up the side flaps of the table. Draped in the hotel's monogrammed white linen and set with the finest crystal and china, it looked as proper as anything she might have seen in her parents' own home.

But it was here, in a hotel room that she happened to be sharing with a man not her husband, with whom she also happened to be enjoying—for better or worse—an illicit relationship.

Marveling at the delicious pleasure of the forbidden, she did not hear the almost soundless tread behind her, nor did she sense any movement until rock-hard arms wrapped round her and she was turned against a bare, bronzed chest.

"Where did you go to?" Brand asked, nuzzling her hair. His voice was low and husky, his square jaw pleasantly abrasive. Unlike her, he had not bothered with anything so formal as a robe. Through her flowered dimity gown, she could feel every inch of his magnificent body.

The sensation was almost overpowering. She closed her eyes against a wave of sensation so intense that for a moment she feared her knees might give way. When she opened them again, Brand's attention had shifted to the table.

"Breakfast? How enterprising of you. I'm starved."

He started to pull out the chair for her, saw the look on her face and laughed. "Would you be more comfortable if I put something on?"

She shrugged, trying to appear as casual as he obviously felt. "As you wish."

He shot her a chiding glance, but relented enough to pull on the trousers he had abandoned the night before. Bare-chested and barefoot, he held out the chair.

Julia sat. She tried to look stern, but failed completely. Brand opened the curtains farther before taking the chair oppposite her. Julia poured coffee for them both. There were scrambled eggs perfectly fluffed, crisp bacon, golden toast, fresh fruit, slices of sweet ham, even wedges of cheese. Her stomach rumbled, but her appetite had deserted her.

She looked at him across the table, so familiar to her now and yet still so alien. She had held this man in her arms, welcomed him into her body. He was, if truth be told, a thing of wonder to her. Yet, engaged in the prosaic activity of buttering a slice of toast, he couldn't help but remind her of the world just beyond the hotel room. A world in which young unmarried women of her class did not do what she was doing—not for any reason, not ever. They married. They kept house. They accepted the role society ordained for them and did their best to believe it was all they wanted.

She took a sip of coffee and found it bitter. Brand didn't seem to mind. He poured a second cup for herself, after she demurred, and gave every evidence of enjoying breakfast.

But then, why shouldn't he? It was all so much simpler for him. He had unassailable wealth and power, and better yet, he was a man. He could seriously contemplate acquiring a wife for the purpose of having children, knowing that his own life—his real life—would simply go on unchanged.

Resentment flared in her. It was so unfair. She should be able to be as casual as he was, as confident. Instead, she was plagued with doubts. The moral strictures of a lifetime's training could not be overthrown so easily. Trying to do so brought a heavier price than she could ever have imagined.

Brand glanced up. He saw the look on her face and frowned. "Something wrong?"

What could she say to him? That she felt torn in two? That there seemed to be a war going on within her, between the independent woman she had judged herself to be and some hitherto unknown creature of passion and vulnerability who frankly frightened her?

Instead, she looked away, not meeting his eyes, and murmured, "I'm just tired, that's all. Society wears after a while."

He smiled, breaking toast between his long, strong fingers. "So jaded? Anyone would think you had been doing this sort of thing for years."

"It feels that way."

His dark, slashing brows drew closer together. "What are you saying, Julia?"

He demanded more honesty than she could give just then. But society—cruel, demanding thing that it was—had a solution for that. It overflowed with superficial, shallow details that were like a screen behind which all manner of untoward thoughts and emotions could be hidden.

"The last of the dresses we ordered arrived yesterday." It might have been the only thing on her mind. Casually—she would match him in casualness, if she did in nothing else!—she shrugged. "I think it's time that we went home."

He did not hesitate. Coolly, without a flicker, he said. "I see. Very well."

Her stomach tightened. She hadn't expected protestations of regret, but this calm acceptance unnerved her. Yet why should he mind? Undoubtedly he presumed their relationship would continue when he, too, returned to Belle Haven.

Perhaps he even imagined it would go on after he married.

The urge to flee was suddenly so powerful that she could hardly resist it. Brand must have sensed that, for he reached out, his hand closing on hers with deceptive gentleness.

"Before you go, there's something I'd like you to see."

"What?"

"In time," he said, and stood. Breakfast was over.

The yacht rode at anchor in a private boat basin almost within sight of Wall Street. It was a favorite resting place for the extremely rich, where the Morgans and the Astors and the like kept their vessels when they weren't at Newport or elsewhere. Most of the slips were filled, but none so majestically as the one Brand led her to.

They had come by carriage directly from the races. Julia still wore the flowered dimity gown, but with the addition of a wide-brimmed straw bonnet. Stepping onto the sweeping mahogany deck, she was a sudden splash of color and femininity in an austerely masculine domain.

But one not without its comforts. Having grown up close to the sea, she was no stranger to all kinds of vessels. This one, however, was completely beyond her experience. It looked like something out of an earlier age, when sails ruled the seas instead of steam. Twin-masted, high-prowed, the vessel was clearly intended for the open waters.

"Is this what you sailed in the Caribbean?" Julia asked softly. She told herself that she should be angry at his high-handed method of bringing her here, but she couldn't seem to manage it. Nothing seemed to matter except the knowledge that they were away from all the crowds, away even from her beloved sisters, alone in a place of their own.

"She's called *Wind Dancer*," Brand said, with pride in his voice. "I found her ten years ago in dry dock down in Aruba. It took almost a year to refit her, and I've sailed her ever since."

He didn't add that the great vessel had been little more than a shell when he happened upon her, awaiting the final disassembling. Moved by the beauty of her lines and the power he sensed within her, he had risked far more money than he could really afford at the time to return her to the sea.

He had never been sorry. *Wind Dancer* had carried him through storms that would have capsized a lesser ship, and had also given him the few rare interludes of peace that he had known in his relentless climb to power. When his house was done, he intended to moor her nearby so that he could come and go as suited him best, on the wind.

But he said nothing of this to Julia. Indeed, after a moment, he all but forgot it. Watching her was infinitely distracting. Light never seemed to play the same way twice over her hair. There were times when it appeared so dark that it was impossible to believe it held fire. But there were other times, such as now, when the light hit exactly so and all the buried flame stood revealed.

And then there was her skin... She favored the sun more than most upper-class women. Although he usually saw her dutifully wearing a bonnet, even as she was now, somehow her skin always appeared touched by honey. He especially adored the tiny smattering of freckles across her delicate nose.

He shook himself slightly, searching for the control that had always been his but lately was more and more elusive. Smiling far more pleasantly than he felt, he asked, "Would you like a tour?"

She agreed. They circled the deck, Brand pointing out the adjustments he'd had made to the winches to make them easier to operate and the hatch that led to the compartment containing the steam engine installed for those few instances when even *Wind Dancer* could be becalmed.

Belowdecks, the vessel was even more magnificent, perfectly restored to the highest standards of elegance. Julia's eyes widened as she took in the main salon, luxuriously outfitted with built-in cabinets and furniture that would not have shamed the finest home.

"Is it all like this?" she asked.

He looked abashed. "I'm afraid so. Once I got started, it didn't seem right to stop before she was back the way she was meant to be."

"She?" Julia asked with a smile. "Why is it that men always refer to ships as female?"

"Perhaps because they can seduce and betray us with equal skill."

Immediately he regretted the words. They were too frank, too honest. They spoke too clearly of what was in his soul.

He turned away toward the bar outfitted in one of the cabinets. "Would you like a drink? Or perhaps tea?

"No, thank you."

Her voice was soft, little more than a whisper. But it held a thread of steel. He splashed brandy into a glass for himself and took a quick swallow.

"Is that what you really think of women?"

The words hung between them, impossible to ignore. He sighed and set the brandy down. If he was nothing, he was an honest man. He had known this moment was coming. Perhaps he had deliberately brought it about by bringing her here, where they could confront one another without hindrance.

All the same, he would have welcomed a bit more time to get his thoughts in order. The years had accustomed him to relentless effort, but they had also made him used to winning. He had a sinking feeling deep inside himself that this time he might not.

"Is what?" he asked, knowing full well what he had said and how it must have sounded to her.

The shadows of her delightfully feminine bonnet obscured her face. He could not see her expression, but he could imagine it well enough from the stiffness of her shoulders and the distance she had put between them.

"That we seduce and betray. Is that your assessment of women?"

"Not at all. You misunderstood me."

"It seemed clear enough."

"We were speaking of *Wind Dancer.* She may be like a certain type of woman, but not every woman is like her. In fact, damn few are."

He didn't add that the male gender should be grateful for that. It might make life less interesting, but it did make it a whole hell of a lot more predictable.

"Type?" Julia repeated. The way she said the word, it sounded like an insult. But he hadn't meant it like that, not at all. He was simply being forthright.

"Excuse me," she said, "I didn't realize we came in *types.* But how naive of me. Of course, men would think that way."

Despite himself, Brand smiled. She looked like a honeyed piece of confection, her frothy dress standing out startlingly against the dark-paneled walls.

They were alone on board. He had given the crew the day off. It would be so very easy to go to her, ease her down on the conveniently nearby couch, and slowly strip the dress off every delectable inch of her. So very easy.

Or not. If he gauged her mood correctly, he might very well have a struggle on his hands. The thought held a certain primal compulsion that shocked him.

He had never hurt a woman in his life, and certainly had no intention of starting now. But the thought of bending Julia to his will was all but irresistible.

And that, he supposed, lay at the heart of the problem. Control had always been important to him, but never more so than with this passionate, enthralling woman who valued independence above all else.

He took another swallow of the brandy, but hardly tasted it, so completely did she absorb his attention. "Aren't you generalizing? If men all thought the same way about everything, the world would be a damn sight more peaceful."

"Excuse me—some men, those who see women as commodities to be neatly labeled."

"Don't kid yourself. All men do that, at least to some extent. Moreover, women do the same to us. We're seen as amusements, or providers, or protectors. Whatever the woman happens to want or need at the moment."

Julia turned away. It was either that or risk having him see the sudden sheen of tears in her eyes. She had known all along that he had a ruthless, even cynical, view of life—hardly surprising, considering how he had grown up. But she had also experienced enough of his gentleness to make her hope for something more.

Foolish hope. Foolish woman. All the wanting in the world wouldn't make it so.

"Not everyone sees things that way," she said softly. "My parents, for instance. They love each other."

"You said yourself that your mother was the kind of woman who made a good wife."

It was true, she had said that. Heather Nash's nature was vastly more compliant than her own. She could be strong when she chose, but very often she put her own wishes aside for those of others.

Or perhaps the wishes of those she loved became her own. It was difficult to tell.

"All the same," she said faintly, "it is possible." But not for her, an inner voice insisted. Not unless she was willing to make a choice that would cost her nothing less than her truest self.

If her life had been otherwise, she might have done it. But she had fought her way back from near-death, overcome a disability that could have crippled her, and, in the process, become the woman she was. She simply could not go back.

Besides, in the most secret places of her soul, an unavoidable truth had to be confronted. She loved Brand Delaney, and would give up anything for him except her own self. But that was what he wanted, nothing less.

Love did not demand such sacrifice. It nurtured the soul, it did not destroy it.

"*Wind Dancer* appears ready to sail," she said quietly.

He inclined his head slightly. "As you said, society palls after a while."

She almost asked where he was going, almost pleaded to go along. But pride stopped her, that and the certain knowledge that she could not be what this magnificent but ruthless man demanded.

"My sisters will be wondering where I have gotten to."

He put the brandy snifter down and took a step toward her. "They can see to themselves, don't you think?"

The look in his eyes was all too familiar, and too enticing. Yet below it, just out of her sight, there was something else, something watchful, waiting. Almost hoping.

She told herself it was a trick of the light. He could never look at her like that, so filled with yearning.

She took a breath, almost surprised that she could do so. It hurt, but then, so did everything else.

"I must be going."

His eyes met hers, dark, fierce, demanding. "Must you?"

"Yes, I think so. I've tarried too long as it is." Too long beside the fire, and far too close to it.

She had only herself to blame, for hadn't she known all along, since that first night when she glimpsed him on the moon-draped shore, that this was a man who would rob her of all peace?

He hesitated and, for an instant, she thought he meant to block her way. If truth be told, a part of her wished that he would.

For the first time in her life, she understood why some women found the notion of being overpowered so pleasant. It eliminated the need for decisions that could be agonizing.

What more could she say? Thank you for a pleasant week? For the hours of ecstasy? The days and nights of joy? The dream of possibilities?

Her throat felt clogged. She was dangerously close to tears. Her legs felt like lead, and yet they moved past him. Her skirts brushed against his trousered leg. She was close enough to touch him—one last time.

Her fists clenched, hidden in the folds of her gown. She smiled the best, most polite, most impeccably social smile she had ever managed and walked out the door.

Chapter Nineteen

Brand leaned back in his chair, stared at the water immediately beyond the porthole and scowled. *Wind Dancer* would sail within the hour. The weather was fair, the wind brisk. It would be a relief to shake the dust and grime of New York from his heels.

The crew had sensibly made itself invisible. The hapless young man who dropped off the business correspondence he'd demanded had scurried away as soon as he was able. Brand was alone in the salon, alone with his own company, exactly as he told himself he preferred to be.

Besides, it was only temporary. He'd give Julia some time to think things over. Maybe her temper wouldn't have cooled entirely when next they were together, but he was willing to bet that when she'd been without him for a while, she'd be at least a little more reasonable.

Without pausing to consider the misleading effects of male ego, he told himself he was doing the right thing. If ever a woman needed to be reined in, she was the one. But he meant to do it gently, letting her come to it of her own free will.

She...liked him. The thought made him smile. This time vanity played no part in his calculations. Julia responded to him with incandescent passion. She was the most instantly responsive and sensually generous woman he had ever encountered.

And she had been a virgin. He was still more than a little amazed at that. Like any sensible man, he'd made sure he gave inexperienced women a wide berth. Not until he met Julia had he bent that rule. Bent it? Hell, he'd thrown it out the window.

The mere thought of how she had felt in his arms, in his bed, moving beneath him in the sweet release of passion, was enough to make him almost painfully hard. He cursed under his breath and stood up, going over to the porthole.

The tide was turning. He needed to tell the crew where they would be going. It would be hot in the Caribbean, but his home in Jamaica was in the mountains, where cooling breezes always blew. Ten days' sail down, a week or so to catch up on that end of his business, and then back to Belle Haven. Call it a month altogether.

Not long, by any measure, save for the hunger of his body and the bleakness that threatened at the edges of his soul.

All right, not a month. Somewhere closer to hand—the Carolinas, perhaps, or Bermuda. Either could be very pleasant. Or he could sail north to Boston and renew some old acquaintances. Or even farther, to Maine, where there was an island he was considering buying.

The island could wait. Boston was far enough. He picked up the speaker to inform the captain, then sat down again to continue going over his correspondence.

But his attention strayed. Two days to Boston, two days there, two days or less coming back. Under a week.

Would that be sufficient to convince Julia that the life he offered her was the one she should want?

He had no answer for that, save the simplest. It would have to be. He very much doubted that he would be able to wait any longer.

Grimly he pushed the papers aside and propped his long legs up on top of the desk. Anyone who glimpsed him at that moment would have seen a powerful, virile man apparently taking his ease. The appearance could not have been more deceptive.

Behind the carefully maintained facade, hunger dwelled, the all-consuming need of a man for the only woman who made him feel complete.

A week, not more. And then, by God or the devil, Miss Julia Nash would bend to his will.

He would insist on it.

"To where?" Brand asked. He was standing near the town green, where such a short time ago he and Julia had listened to the pleasant summer concert and sipped punch together.

Peter Nash faced him. Their paths had crossed by accident. Brand had been back in Belle Haven scarcely a day, having wrapped up his business in Boston a bit earlier than expected. But then, he had driven three secretaries and two bankers into such a frenzied panic over the possibility of displeasure that it was perhaps understandable that everything had been finished quickly.

Now he was here, on this well-tailored green in this pleasant little town on this lovely day, listening to a courteous young man with wariness in his eyes explain where his sister had gone.

"Europe," Peter repeated. "She had a long-standing invitation from cousins, and finally decided to take them up on it."

"I see..." In fact, he did, although it hurt him brutally to admit it. All the days—and nights—since Julia walked off *Wind Dancer,* he had wondered if he wasn't making the worst mistake of his life by demanding so much of her. Trying to hold her fast was like trying to catch the wind itself. Inevitably, it died in the hand.

His only comfort had been the knowledge that she was nearby, safe in the place where she surely belonged. Not any grand house he might build, but at the heart of her own heritage and her own freedom, Amelia's house.

Except she wasn't. She was gone.

"For how long?" he asked, and was surprised that his voice sounded so normal, not at all as though he were being rent in two.

Peter shrugged. "I've no idea. She'll stay for the fall season, I suppose, now that she's—" he hesitated "—become more sociable."

"In New York, society bored her."

Peter's eyebrows rose fractionally. Julia had said nothing about the city when she came back. Only Daphne and Gloria had gone on and on about all the parties they'd attended and how wonderful it had all been. Julia had been strangely quiet, drawn more into herself than he had ever seen her, until she suddenly announced she was going to Europe.

"Did it?" he asked, staring at the powerful, enigmatic man before him. The man he had found with Julia after the storm.

Brand nodded once, no more. He sensed the questions building in Peter, and had no intention of answering them. It was enough that he knew Julia had left. That seemed a final and irrefutable answer to the question he had asked her after that night of fire and passion.

Julia Nash would not bend to his will. She would not accept the life he wanted her to lead. Rather than do so, she had left him entirely.

His body tightened against the pain, but also with anger. So be it. She had made her choice, and while he might be hurt by it, he would certainly survive. If she imagined he would come after her, she was mistaken. There were other women as beautiful, as passionate, as desirable.

A harsh laugh escaped him. No, there were not. Not for him, at any rate.

"Is something wrong?" Peter asked.

Slowly Brand shook his head. "Nothing. Kindly give my regards to your family."

The young man assured him that he would, and took his leave. Brand lingered a little longer by the green before abruptly turning away.

At the stables behind his rented house, he saddled the big stallion without really thinking of where he was going. But there was really only one direction. Mounted, he rode out and took the fork toward the shore road, toward his own land and Julia's.

The bridge was in place across the new inlet, but he did not cross it. Instead, he continued on until he reached the site where he planned to build.

Charles had been right—the land was almost intact—despite the storm. It was a sheltered spot, perfect for raising a house. He sat, holding the reins loosely, and stared out across the place where land and water met.

Seabirds circled in the almost cloudless sky. A fresh wind blew, scented with the ocean beyond the sound. The ocean Julia had crossed.

It would be so easy to follow her. He had only to give the order, and *Wind Dancer* would be readied at once. Even under sail, she would make England or France in no more than two weeks, and if that was too long, he could order her put under steam. He had agents throughout Britain and the Continent. Wherever Julia had gone, he was sure he could find out and track her down.

But to what end? Again he had the sudden, flashing image of trying to catch the wind, and realized the terrible futility of it. She had flown from him, determined to be free. He could let her go, wait her out, let her try her wings until she tired of it and decided to return home. As a boy on the plains, he had waited through entire days and nights on the hunt, drawing on immense reserves of patience to finally catch his prey. He could do it again if he had to.

But Julia wasn't prey. She was a beautiful, passionate woman who refused to be what he wanted her to be even more intensely than he had realized. Surely she did not deserve to be hunted.

He could leave Belle Haven himself. It might be the sensible thing to do, for the place seemed to have lost its charm. There were other places, thousands, where he could choose to settle eventually.

Go? Stay? Pursue her? Wait for her? None of his choices held much appeal. But when all was said and done, he had no other alternatives.

Except one. It came to him gradually as he sat on the stallion, watching the sun turn the water to diamonds and listening to the call of the seabirds on the wind. Whether out of male vanity or the strength of his own need, he had misjudged Julia. He had refused to accept how much she truly needed to be herself, the strong and capable woman she was, and not merely the appendage of a man.

But he could learn from his error. He could stay and try to understand the woman who had turned his expectations upside down and left a void within himself that seemed nothing and no one else would ever be able to fill.

Slowly he turned the stallion back toward the road. Doubt, anger and resentment all continued to war within him. But beneath them, stronger than everything else, was the conviction that he had to let his beautiful woman of the wind fly free if he was to have any hope of ever winning her back.

The thought was humbling—not a common experience for him. But then, nothing in his life was as it had been only a short time ago. Everything was new and surprising, and not always pleasantly so.

In the distance, the bridge across the inlet gleamed. It had the new, raw look of something that has not yet settled onto the land. But that would change. Time and weather would age the wood, take from it the fresh-cut paleness and add a richer patina. Before long, it would look as though it had always been there.

As did the house he glimpsed through the trees. Everyone else called it Amelia's house, but to him it was Julia's. Was and always would be.

He came to a sudden decision and touched his heels to the horse's sides. Moments later he was galloping back up the road toward town.

Brand leaned back in the chair beside the kitchen table and slowly put down the book he had been reading. He was surprised to see how the light had faded. The book had so absorbed him that he had lost all track of time.

But then, it did the same whenever he read it. No matter how familiar the carefully penned passages became, they never lost their ability to fascinate him.

Slowly he put the leather-bound volume aside, but he made no attempt to stand. His mind was still focused on the scene he had just heard described for him in the words of a woman who had lived two and a half centuries ago. A woman who had loved deeply, despite her determination to be free.

Garrick Marlowe had returned to Belle Haven, giving up his dreams of the sea, to find his Amelia and make a life with her. The entry was short, penned by a woman at the end of one part of her own story and the beginning of another. A woman who had been frustratingly discreet.

Brand was sure there were more details. So vital a moment couldn't have remained lost to time. Only yesterday, he had asked Gramma Sara about it.

They had been sitting in the parlor of the Nash's house, his presence there no longer a surprise since he and Sara had hit if off so well. He had taken to visiting her regularly, ostensibly to report on what he was learning about Amelia's house.

She had graciously given him permission to examine it for himself, to better understand the construction that had allowed it to endure for so long and in the face of the greatest adversity.

And she had suggested he read Amelia's journal.

Indeed, her wise old eyes had twinkled when he came, humbly asking her permission, since Julia was away and, after all, the house still technically belonged to her. He had thought she might refuse, or at the very least demand some detailed explanation. But she had done neither. She had merely looked at him for a long moment before smiling gently and agreeing.

On the condition that he come back to her with any questions he might have.

He'd had more than a few, but none he'd felt comfortable asking the elderly woman, except for those directly related to the journal.

"When Garrick came back, how exactly did he do it?"

"What do you mean?" she had asked, her eyes alight with amusement.

"Overland from New York? It would have been New Amsterdam then. The going would have been hard."

"Heavens, no. He sailed his ship, the one Amelia had bought and given to him, right up to the beach. Or at least as far as it would go." She laughed softly. "Amelia saw him and waded out into the water. His crew could have put a longboat down, would have if he'd given the word. But he was too impatient. Dived right in, he did, and swam to her."

She sighed, lost in the memory of an event that had happened generations before her own birth, yet remained remarkably fresh and real. "It was right there on Daniels' Neck, not far from where the house stands. Nothing much has changed. I daresay, you walk along that beach now, you'll be seeing it just as they did.''

It was a tempting thought. He stood and stretched, trying to get the knots out of his shoulders and back. Inactivity was unusual for him. He was too accustomed to hard physical work to be content with sitting still. But he had forced himself, determined to learn and understand all he could.

Slowly he walked down the path that connected the house and beach. The evening was clear. He could make out the first few stars, just coming into view.

In the distance was the land on which he intended to build. Or did he still? He had told Charles to hold off on the house, and asked him instead to consider the design of the hospital Brand had promised Belle Haven. Gloria's doctor friend was helping with it, and both young men were completely absorbed in the project.

Whether Brand remained in Belle Haven or not, he would keep his promise to the place Julia called home.

And then he would—what?

Deep within him, he sensed that the time had come when he had to act. For a man who had never been much for waiting, he'd been remarkably patient. But his patience was wearing very thin.

Doubt moved through him. It was his unfamiliar bedfellow these recent nights. He viewed it coldly, knowing that doubt could paralyze him. That it had already, to a certain extent. He'd put the time to good use, but he wasn't kidding himself. He would have been after Julia days before if he hadn't been so damned scared she would refuse him again.

It had all been about winning, but it wasn't anymore. Now it was simply about living. He needed her the same way he needed air and water, food and warmth.

And he would have her. On any terms. Including her own. High above, the stars gleamed more brightly. Brand didn't notice them. He was striding up the beach, back toward the house.

A short time later, a horse clattered across the bridge. Not long thereafter, *Wind Dancer*'s decks were alight as she made ready to sail.

Chapter Twenty

Julia dismissed the maid, who, despite her instructions, had felt compelled to sit up for her. When the girl was gone, she let out a sigh of relief and kicked her slippers off. As she did, the soles flapped loose.

A faint laugh escaped her, but it held little humor. Yet again she had danced until she should have been exhausted. This was the third pair of slippers she had worn out in the past fortnight. At this rate, she would have to start buying them by the cartload.

As it had for hundreds of years, and would probably continue to do for hundreds more, society insisted on keeping late hours. Since coming to stay with her British cousins, she had learned to breakfast at eleven, shop and receive calls until four, dine until nine or ten, and only then begin the true business of the day in the endless round of late theater parties, balls, routs, and so on.

She had even gotten good at it, or so everyone seemed to think. No one rode harder, danced longer or chatted more wittily than Miss Julia Nash. She was a tremendous success. Not one person suspected that she did it all for the single purpose of wearing herself out enough to get a decent night's sleep.

So far, she hadn't managed it. There were delicate violet shadows under her eyes. When she was most tired, which was more and more often, she had a strangely incandescent aura men seemed unable to resist. She was like a candle burning fiercely at both ends, yet unable to burn herself out.

Her gaze drifted toward the bed. It was so high she required a stool to climb into it, equipped with an overstuffed mattress and more pillows than she had bothered to count. Surely no bed in all of creation could be more comfortable.

She hated it. It was the setting for her worst torments, during the endless hours when she tossed and turned, longing for Brand. Every nuance of his touch remained vividly imprinted on her mind. No matter how she tried, no matter how attractive the men she met, she could not forget him. Not even for an instant.

Heaven help her.

Wearily she sat down at the dressing table and undid her hair. Brushing it soothed her a little, but her lack of rest was becoming increasingly evident, even to her young maid. Only yesterday the girl had gently suggested to Julia that she might wish to try a bit of laudanum to help her sleep.

That she had actually been tempted, if only for a moment, told her all too well how close she was to the end of her reserves. Staring at herself in the mirror, she saw a woman who was barely recognizable with wide, haunted eyes and a vulnerable mouth full of wanting.

It was all so terribly wrong. She had more freedom than she had ever truly dreamed of having. Her cousins had made it clear she was welcome to stay as long as she wished. Or if she preferred, she could travel on the Continent, even go as far as Egypt for a sail down the Nile. Much of the world lay open to her, in all its fascinating diversity.

Nor did she necessarily have to see it alone. With her newly awakened senses, she was well aware that several of the men she had met were very serious in their regard.

Courteous and respectful though they were, their interest was evident.

None struck her as particularly demanding or ruthless. None seemed like a misplaced warrior from another time who would expect his wife to sit home, safe behind high walls, breeding babies for him. They were modern men like Charles Hewlitt and Gloria's doctor beau, men attuned to the notion of marriage as a partnership.

Not at all like Brand, who saw it as a form of barter.

The mirror misted. She blinked hard, driving away the tears she would not allow to fall. Weariness washed over her in a wave. Slowly she rose and managed to get off the frilly silk-and-lace ball gown she had worn. She even hung it away neatly, even though her maid had said she needn't bother. Old habits died hard.

Wearing a nightgown of alençon lace, she slipped into bed, but made no attempt to turn off the light. Darkness was worse. In it, she could almost see the hard planes of Brand's face, the deep secrets of his eyes, the powerful muscles of his taut body moving rhythmically beneath her hands as he claimed her.

A moan broke from between her lips. She pressed her fingers to them and turned her head into the pillow. There was a great roaring in her mind, like the storm that had swept over Daniels' Neck, like the wind calling to her.

Softly, a single tear slipped from beneath her lashes and down her cheek. It was followed by another.

The wind blew, hard and fierce, mocking her hopes, demanding her surrender. Long before dawn, her pillow was soaked.

Julia greeted the morning with a throbbing headache and reddened eyes, but greet it she did. The long, anguished night was over and she was still there, still in London and still resolved to stay. Her refuge was pride. It was all she had left. She would hold on to it come hell or high water.

And even through breakfast, taken mercifully alone, for none of her cousins was as yet awake. She managed to choke down a cup of tea and a single scone with only a few thoughts about the hotel breakfast she had shared with Brand. She had already replayed that scene too many times in her mind. She simply couldn't continue to do so.

Neither could she sit around the house, waiting for someone to wake up and suggest something to do. Smoggy, rainy London had reversed itself suddenly and produced a day of near-incandescent brilliance. The sky was blue, the sun golden and the breeze balmy. She would go for a walk.

Her mind made up, Julia saw no reason to delay. She had dressed in a pretty mauve suit with a long tapered skirt and matching jacket. Her hair was swept up under a pert little hat, of the kind that was all the rage that season. She had even had the foresight to put on a comfortable pair of boots, pampering her poor feet after all the dancing.

As yet, she'd had no chance to see much of London, beyond the great society houses and the most popular—and exclusive—shops. She thought she might visit Hyde Park. It was a green and peaceful sanctuary in the midst of the bustling city that reminded her just a little of the unspoiled woods and open fields around Belle Haven.

She was at the door—indeed, she almost had it open— when the butler suddenly appeared. From the Olympian heights of the truly superior, he surveyed her expressionlessly.

"May I help you, miss?"

Julia restrained a sigh. She wasn't completely ignorant of servants; her parents had a cook, and several young girls came in regularly to clean and sew. But this was an entirely different matter. She had never before encountered such a politely tyrannical being as the English butler.

Still, she supposed he meant well. Mustering a smile, Julia shook her head. "No, but thank you."

His gaze slipped to her hand on the doorknob. Quietly, with a note of forgiveness for her obvious ignorance, he said, "You should have rung, miss."

"To have someone open the door?" Julia laughed. "I'm not quite that helpless, Mr. Carmichael."

"Just Carmichael, miss. I meant to have someone accompany you. None of the others are awake as yet, but one of the maids can certainly be spared." He turned smartly on his heel, approached the velvet cord concealed in a recess of the wall and gave it a firm tug. In the bowels of the house, a bell rang.

"That isn't necessary," Julia protested, too late to stop him. "I prefer to go alone."

"Alone, miss?"

"Yes, by myself." As he continued to stare at her, she felt compelled to add, "Only as far as the park."

Carmichael nodded, as though it all made perfect sense now. Of course he understood, his expression said. "I perceive things are different in America."

Different did not appear to be a compliment. Indeed, he pronounced it as a man might when contemplating a fish that had been deceased for several days.

"Perhaps they are," Julia said. "But I find it difficult to believe that London is so uncivilized a place that a woman cannot stroll unmolested through a public park in full daylight."

The butler's eyebrows shot up to meet the fringe of hair decorating his forehead. "London, uncivilized?"

"Isn't that what you imply, Mr. Carmichael?" Proper forms of address be damned. He was "mister" to her, and so he would remain. "Surely, I didn't misunderstand you. You couldn't possibly have meant to suggest that my own behavior was less than trustworthy."

He flushed, this epitome of the starch-souled English butler. His cheeks actually turned red.

"I don't believe I actually said any such thing, miss."

"I'm sure you didn't." Julia turned the doorknob. "Have a pleasant morning, Mr. Carmichael."

The corners of the butler's mouth quirked. He almost smiled. "And you, miss."

Julia's step was light as she walked down the cobblestone street. It was a small victory she had won, to be sure, but it made her feel better. That and the brilliance of the day combined to make the long night seem a little less painful.

Elsewhere in London, gentlemen in frockcoats were descending from their carriages to begin another energetic day conducting business in the great banks and trading houses of the Empire. But in Hyde Park there was only solitude and blessed quiet.

Julia strolled undisturbed, save for the occasional squirrel that ran across her path. She breathed deeply, glad that she had bothered with only the lightest corset. Her leg was not troubling her at all. That was more often the case now that she thought less about her disability and worried not at all that other people would notice it.

All the same, she wasn't so foolish as to press her luck unduly. Having walked by her own estimate slightly over two miles around the Serpentine, the winding pool that bisected this part of the park, she decided to sit down for a few minutes.

She had just taken her place on one of the ornamental wrought-iron benches when a shadow fell across the gravel path near her. Looking up, she was surprised to see a familiar face.

"Why, Mr. Preston. Is it truly you?"

The young man she had met at the horse races smiled disarmingly. "It is indeed, Miss Nash, and may I say I am delighted to find you here?"

Julia laughed. She couldn't have said exactly why, but the sudden appearance of someone from home made her feel better. The hollow ache inside her eased a little. She moved over on the bench, making room for him.

"What brings you to London, Mr. Preston?"

"Business. I have dealings with several of the trading houses here." Settling himself beside her, he cleared his throat self-consciously. "But, to be truthful, Miss Nash, I didn't just happen by. I saw you entering the park and took the liberty of following you." His brow knit as he looked at her. "I hope I haven't been too forward?"

Had he? On the one hand, the thought of someone following her was disconcerting. On the other, such a courteous, even diffident, young man couldn't have been less like Brand, and, at the moment that was exactly what she needed.

"Not at all," Julia said. "In fact, I'm delighted to see someone from home."

"Have you been missing it?"

"I suppose. London is wonderful, of course, very exciting and energetic. But I have to admit, I've been a little homesick from time to time."

"I know exactly how you feel. Sometimes there is no substitute for what you know best." He thought for a moment. "I'll tell you what. If you don't mind a suggestion, I'm off to the American Restaurant for breakfast."

He laughed, a little apologetically. "It may sound silly, but what I miss most whenever I'm away from home are the simplest things—food cooked the way I'm used to, familiar voices, people who follow the same sports teams, that sort of thing. You can find it all at this place, but I assure you it's quite respectable. Ladies go there, as well."

"I'm sure they do," Julia said, wondering why she hadn't heard of it. But then, her cousins were veddy, veddy British. They surely wouldn't frequent any place so blatantly American.

Besides, she'd managed very little breakfast. At the mere thought of flapjacks and real coffee, her mouth watered.

"I'd love to go," she said before she could think about it any further.

"Great." Frank's open enthusiasm was a further reminder of how far she was from home. Everyone was so restrained here, so terribly careful not to show any emotion beyond mild amusement. It was refreshing to find someone who could actually enjoy himself.

"Off we go, then," he said, and held out his arm.

Julia took it with a smile. Under other circumstances, she might have paid scant attention to Frank Preston. But here, miles from everything she knew, she saw no possible harm in his company. They would have breakfast together and then take their leave, she to return to her cousins' home and he to attend to his business.

If he stayed in London long enough, perhaps their paths would cross again. Indeed, she might even look forward to it. He was an enjoyable companion, kind and undemanding. She saw no reason not to go with him. None at all.

Frank had a carriage with him. It was waiting for them at the entrance to the park. The driver was a dour-faced man who inclined his head but did not speak.

"The American Restaurant," Frank instructed as he handed Julia up. He followed her in, took a seat on the opposite side and reached across to grasp the leather handle of the door. Pulling it closed, he said, "I really couldn't be happier to have run into you like this."

Julia's smile faltered slightly. Again she felt faintly uneasy at his having followed her. But it seemed such a small failing in a man who otherwise seemed impeccably polite.

"London is so big," she said. "It's really amazing that you happened to come across me."

"Amazing," Frank agreed. He sat back more comfortably against the bench.

The carriage rattled along. They were going rather fast for the narrow cobblestone streets. Julia glanced out the window. There seemed to be fewer other vehicles than she would have expected at this hour.

When she mentioned that to Frank, he said, "We're skirting the City itself. This way is slightly longer, but actually takes less time."

"Where is the American Restaurant?"

"Not far from Mayfair, actually."

Julia frowned. She had walked all over Mayfair with her cousins, it being one of the few parts of London they thought proper for her to be shown on foot. They had never come across any American Restaurant. But then, he hadn't said it was in Mayfair, only not far from it. Still, she couldn't help but wonder why no one had mentioned the place, especially since her homesickness had not been as perfectly concealed as she would have liked.

"Something wrong?" Frank asked.

"I was just wondering why none of my cousins mentioned the restaurant." She shrugged apologetically, embarrassed by the strange doubts that suddenly assailed her. "They've told me about so many places. I can't imagine how they missed it."

"An oversight, no doubt," Frank said. He reached into the inner pocket of his jacket.

"I suppose." Julia glanced out the window. That was odd. She knew the direction to Mayfair, and they didn't seem to be taking it. Indeed, the sun was on entirely the wrong side of the carriage. Unless she was very much mistaken, they appeared to be heading south, instead of north.

"Mr. Preston, I..."

She had no opportunity to finish the sentence. Frank withdrew his hand. In it were two objects—a white linen handkerchief, and a small brown bottle, the stopper removed. The stain on the handkerchief appeared to indicate that it had come in contact with the contents of the bottle.

Julia stared at it in amazement. She could scarcely credit what she was seeing. What could he possibly intend?

"You're too clever by half," he said. His pleasant smile was gone now, and his voice was harsh. "But it won't do you any good."

Before she could reply, he lunged across the seat at her. Julia was strong for a woman, and she did not hesitate to fight. But it availed her little.

Though she did manage to land a blow to his cheek that made him cry out, Frank had all the advantages. He shoved one arm against her throat, slamming her back into the leather bench and pressed the handkerchief over her mouth and nose.

The sickly-sweet smell of laudenum made her gag. She kicked out at him, but the effort suddenly seemed to belong to someone else. She was floating away from herself, being sucked into darkness. A soft cry of despair drifted behind her, somewhere back there in the light. The darkness thickened, and she knew nothing more.

Chapter Twenty-One

Brand stepped onto the dock at Southwark and surveyed his surroundings. It was midmorning, seven days after he'd left America. They had made excellent time. He made a mental note to award a bonus to *Wind Dancer*'s captain and crew.

Even so, the days had passed with excruciating slowness. Try though he had to distract himself, he could think of little other than Julia. She occupied his every moment, waking and sleeping. He smiled ruefully as he recalled the dreams that had plagued him. Never had he been so entirely absorbed in a woman. The experience was at once exhilarating and terrifying.

Still, he had made his choice. He was here. Now all he had to do was find Julia, convince her to see things his way, and set *Wind Dancer* asail once more, this time with her to occupy him rather than mere dreams.

It was a pleasant thought. He was smiling as he crossed the cobblestone road opposite the docks and lifted his hand to summon a coach. There were always several loitering in the area, hoping to pick up passengers of the more affluent sort.

The driver took one look at Brand, tipped his hat cordially and asked, ''Where to, guv'nor?''

Brand did not have to consult the small slip of paper in the watch pocket of his vest. He had long since committed the address to memory. Giving it to the driver, he sat back and did his best to relax.

He knew London well. There had been a time when the city had offered many pleasant diversions, as well as opportunities to increase his fortune.

But none of that concerned him now. He watched the passing streets, thinking only of how much longer it would be before he reached the home of Julia's cousins.

The driver was skilled and aggressive. He deposited Brand at his destination a good quarter hour before what might have been reasonably expected.

"Good day to you, sir," he said as his hand closed around a silver guinea, extravagant payment even for exemplary service. But Brand was in an extravagant mood. He would see Julia soon.

The door knocker was made out of a brass shaped to resemble a lion's head. It made a satisfyingly urgent sound. Brand let it drop, expecting to wait the necessary minute or so for a servant to respond.

But the door was wrenched open almost instantly, not by a servant, but by a young man dressed much as Brand himself was, with a pale, strained face and anxious eyes. He stared at Brand.

"Oh, it's you." The young man's disappointment could not have been more evident. Brand frowned. Perhaps he had come to the wrong address, after all.

"Mr. Nash?"

"Yes, that's right. Derek Nash. Who are you?"

"Forgive me, but I assumed you knew who I was from the manner of your greeting."

The young man sighed. He stepped aside and gestured for Brand to enter. "I'm sorry. Everything's rather confused today."

"So I see," Brand murmured. The center hall appeared to be filled with people, servants hurrying to and fro and others standing about with serious faces. From a nearby room, a woman could be heard weeping.

"I've come at a bad time."

Derek made a harsh sound. "I'm afraid so. My cousin is missing."

A wave of coldness washed through Brand. Hardly aware of what he was doing, he reached for the young man, took hold of him by his jacket and jerked him forward. "What did you say?"

Derek stared at him in disbelief. Like a sleeper half emerging from a deep and disturbing dream, he took hold of Brand's hand and endeavored to release himself.

His point made, and not especially pleased at having come so close to losing control, Brand let him go. But he offered no apology. Instead, he said again, "What did you say?"

"My cousin is missing, if that is any of your affair, Mr.—?"

"Delaney, Brand Delaney, and if the cousin is Miss Julia Nash, I assure you it is very much my affair."

The shock present in Derek Nash's eyes when he opened the door had given way to anger at Brand's presumption. The anger, in turn, yielded to shrewd consideration.

"Mr. Brand Delaney of New York?"

"Yes, that's right. I came here to see Miss Nash. Is she—?"

"Missing, I'm afraid, since yesterday. Was she expecting you?"

"No, she— Yesterday? Why the hell aren't the police here?"

"The authorities have been informed. They are doing everything possible. If you would care to leave your place of residence, we can keep you informed."

"No, I don't care to do that," Brand said. He bit out the words. Derek Nash's seeming calmness infuriated him, until he remembered how haunted the younger man had looked when he flung open the door.

"You were hoping she'd come back, weren't you, just now, when you opened the door?"

Derek took a deep breath, as though struggling for calm. Slowly he nodded. "It was a foolish thought. At any rate, we truly are doing everything. Now, I don't wish to appear rude, but I really must get back to my mother. She is quite distraught."

"You do that. Just tell me who I can talk to."

"Talk to?"

"About where she was last seen, what areas of the city have been searched, who's been contacted, that sort of thing."

"I really don't see why you should—"

He had to be patient, had to stay calm. But these damn British aristocrats, with their exemplary manners, would drive him mad. Anything could have happened to Julia. She might be anywhere, and they were standing around and talking about the proper authorities being notified.

Damn them all to hell and back again.

"You are going to accept my help, Mr. Nash," Brand said. He forced himself to speak slowly and softly, but his intent was clear all the same. No one was going to prevent him from joining the search for Julia.

Derek hesitated. He looked at Brand for a long moment. Whatever he saw must have satisfied him. Quietly he said, "As you wish, Mr. Delaney. Come into the study. I will bring you up-to-date on exactly what has been happening."

Within the hour, another person arrived at the Nashes' London house. He was considerably different from those who had gone before, being altogether rougher in his dress and manner. Not even Carmichael could hide his dismay as he ushered him into the study.

Brand was seated behind the desk, Derek having ceded it to him when he realized that, like it or not, leadership of the search effort had passed from his hands. The American was now in charge.

"This is Docker," Brand said, introducing the new arrival. "He's going to be assisting us, aren't you, Docker?"

The man grinned, exposing widely spaced teeth. He cast a wary eye at Derek, but appeared at ease with Brand, as though he knew what to expect there. "Anything you say, sir. What's the play?"

"A young woman is missing. She went out for a walk yesterday morning and failed to return."

Docker frowned. "Lady, sir?"

Brand nodded. "She went alone, in the direction of Hyde Park."

"Shouldn't have come to any mischief there."

"That's what we thought when we heard," Derek said. "Carmichael reported it at once, of course, but I really thought she would be all right. She'd put on quite a valiant front, but I had the sense that she wasn't happy." He looked at Brand. "Perhaps she needed time to herself. There's nowhere safer than Hyde Park at that time of day."

Docker nodded. "I've got to agree with you, sir." He sucked air in through his teeth, thinking hard. "You sure she got to the park?"

"No," Brand said. "We aren't. The fact is, we're not sure of anything. The authorities are putting on a great show, but so far they've been useless."

"Aye, I can see how they would be. If someone's snatched her, isn't likely anyone would blab to the coppers. But here now, wouldn't you have had word? A ransom demand, or something of the like?"

"We've been expecting it hour to hour," Derek said. "But there's been nothing."

"Then maybe she just took herself off. You said she wasn't happy like. Anybody thought to check the river?"

Derek reddened. "For God's sake, she's done nothing of the sort. Julia is a perfectly intelligent and sensible young woman." He turned to Brand. "I fail to see how this is helping."

"That's because nothing's happened yet." Brand stood. He looked at Docker, almost pleasantly. "But it's about to. Spread the word. I'll pay ten thousand pounds for the information that leads to her recovery."

Docker's mouth dropped open. He stared at Brand in disbelief. "H-how much, sir?"

"You heard me. Ten thousand pounds."

"Sweet Lord, the city could be torn apart for that money."

"Don't restrict yourself to London. She could have been removed from it. Get the word out as widely as possible." Docker nodded vigorously. "Yes, sir. I got mates everywhere. You can bet they'll jump on this." He whistled softly. "Ten thousand pounds. Never heard the like, I didn't. Man can do anything with that kind of money."

"But first he has to earn it," Brand said.

"Yes, sir, right you are." Docker jammed his grimy cap back on his head. He reached for the door. "I'll be going now, but I'll be in touch, I will. Ten thousand pounds. I wouldn't want to be whoever took her, that's for sure. His own mother would sell him out and be glad of it."

His voice faded away into the hall. A moment later, the front door slammed.

"Was that really necessary?" Derek demanded when he and Brand were once again alone.

Brand struck a match and held it to the tip of a cheroot. He took his time replying. "Was what?"

"Putting a price on her head, and a frankly obscene one, at that. If you imagine that only the criminal classes will hear of it, you're very much mistaken. It will be all over town before nightfall."

"I'm counting on that."

Derek's eyes widened. "You are?"

"Of course. Docker and his like may be able to help us, but I have no illusions that any of them are involved in this. As he pointed out, if it were a straightforward kidnapping, you would have received a ransom demand by now."

"But then what—"

"I don't know," Brand said softly. "But I intend to find out." He strode toward the door. "Come on."

Derek hurried after him. "Where are we going?"

"To your clubs. You belong to several, don't you?"

"Yes, of course, but I hardly think—"

"It's not enough to spread the word at Docker's level. It's got to go a lot higher."

They had reached the street. Brand raised his hand to summon one of the carriages that were always in easy reach.

"You can't possibly mean—" Derek began.

A driver spotted them and immediately urged his horses forward. The wheels were still rolling as Brand opened the carriage door and stepped up. Derek followed automatically.

"If you want to believe no one of your own class could be behind this," Brand said as they settled themselves, "go right ahead. But I lack your confidence. It seems far more likely to me that Julia went with someone she knew."

"Surely not—"

"Your clubs. Name one."

"White's, but—"

Brand leaned his head out the window. "White's," he told the driver.

They were off.

Julia woke from the light sleep she had drifted into scant hours before. Her first thought was that she'd had a terrible nightmare. But all too quickly she realized that was a blessing to be denied her.

She sat up slowly on the narrow cot and looked around. A small sigh of relief escaped her parched lips as she realized that she was alone.

For hours she had struggled against exhaustion, loath to become even more vulnerable. The thought of sleeping while Frank Preston watched her made her skin crawl. But he had not returned to the tiny room. By the dim light filtering in through windows near the ceiling that were little more than cracks, she could see only the single chair he had occupied, the cot where she lay, and the heavy metal door.

Despite cramping in her arms and legs, she got up quickly and hobbled over to the door. Reason told her it was locked, but she had to try it all the same. With her hands tied behind her back, getting hold of the handle was difficult. She managed it at last, only to confirm what she had expected. She was locked in what seemed to be a cell buried almost entirely underground.

How exactly she had gotten there escaped her. She remembered nothing after the moment in the carriage when Frank had pressed the laudanum-soaked handkerchief to her nostrils. After that, there had been only darkness until she awakened in this room, probably sometime the previous day, to find him gloating over the success of his scheme.

"You are entirely too gullible, my dear," he had said, smiling broadly. "Or perhaps I'm even cleverer than I give myself credit for being. At any rate, you're here, and that's what counts."

"To what end?" Julia demanded. "You have to be mad to have done this."

"Mad? On the contrary, I may be the only sane man left in New York—or London, for that matter. Everyone else is so beguiled by the marvelous Mr. Delaney—or so afraid of him. But not me. I see him for what he truly is, an upstart deceiver who doesn't hesitate to ruin men better than himself.''

"Brand? This is about Brand?"

"Oh, yes, Miss Nash, the same person with whom you are so very familiar. Did you think anyone has failed to notice how extremely friendly the two of you have become? All society is talking about it, gossiping about how Brand Delaney has finally met his match. I can only assume that your sensibilities are coarsened beyond repair, but that doesn't concern me. I had been searching for a weapon against him, and you finally provided it."

Julia shook her head, hardly crediting what she was hearing. "You are mad if you imagine you can use me somehow to hurt Brand. Why, the fact is—"

"You are about to claim that he doesn't truly care for you. It's only to be expected that you'd say that under the circumstances, but it makes no difference. My course is set. Brand Delaney is going to find out what it means to lose something he truly cares about, just as I did."

"What did you lose?" Julia demanded. "Money? If you did, it was through your own foolishness. Why didn't you try doing your own work, researching your own investments, instead of just jumping on something because you heard Brand Delaney was interested in it?"

Frank flushed. "Because I am a gentleman, something with which you are only distantly acquainted. I don't soil my hands with that sort of thing. It never occurred to me that he would deliberately give the impression of being interested in one firm when in fact his interest lay in an entirely different direction."

"Then you're a fool," Julia said bluntly. "Brand Delaney isn't responsible for your well-being, much less for the safety of your investments. If being a gentleman means being greedy, arrogant and lazy, you fill the bill nicely."

"Be careful," Frank snarled. "I have suspicions about exactly how far your dealings with him have gone. If I'm right, you have put yourself outside the bounds of consideration normally given to a woman of your class.''

A retort sprang to Julia's lips, but she wisely restrained it. The threat to her person was very real. She was tied up, confined and helpless. The horrible truth was that Frank Preston could do anything he chose to her, and she would be extremely hard-pressed to stop him.

Mercifully, he seemed to take her silence for deference. Satisfied for the moment, he left. Sometime later, Julia at last allowed herself to drift into exhausted sleep.

But now she was awake again and painfully alert. Thirst plagued her, as did the pain in her limbs. She forced herself to keep moving, walking up and down the narrow cell, until some ease returned to her muscles. Still, her hands remained tied. Without their use, there was very little she could do.

She looked around quickly. Now that her eyes were better adjusted to the dark, she could see more. There, on the far wall beneath the windows, she thought she saw a glint of metal.

It was. In some forgotten time, there had been a bracket there, perhaps to hold a lamp. It had broken off, leaving a sharp edge ideal for cutting ropes. Except that the bracket was far above her, too high to be reached.

Quickly she went over to the chair and, with an effort, pushed and nudged it into the proper position. Standing on the chair and raising her bound hands painfully as far as she could was just enough. She was able to make contact with the sharp edge.

Even then, it took long minutes to cut through the ropes. By the time she was done, her arms were throbbing and tears blurred her eyes. When the ropes finally snapped open, she sobbed in relief.

Jumping down, she quickly undid the loops around her wrists and threw the ropes aside. Then she began looking for something she might be able to use as a signal.

Beneath the mattress of the cot were wooden slats. She removed one, and thought hard. Without knowing where she was, she had no way of guessing what might attract attention. Still, there was an item that no one could possibly be used to seeing fluttered about in public.

Quickly she removed her lace petticoat and tied it to one end of the slat. Using the chair again, she was able to poke it through the narrow window. She could just see it begin to flutter, confirming that it was, indeed, outside.

That done, there was nothing more she could do except wait for her captor to return.

Chapter Twenty-Two

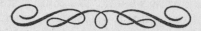

"This is pointless," Derek insisted. "All we're doing is attracting unwanted attention to ourselves."

Brand ignored him. They were at Lamb's, the third club on their list. At the first two, Julia's disappearance had already been well-known, but no one had anything of use to contribute. Not even after Brand had let drop that he was paying well for genuine information. Several eyes had gleamed avidly, for ten thousand pounds was not a small sum, even to members of the upper class. But the plain fact was that no one knew anything.

Still, Brand wasn't about to give up. He leaned against the mahogany bar that took up the main room at Lamb's and glanced at the men coming and going. Except for the servants, they were an interesting assortment.

Some appeared to be taking a brief break in the midst of an otherwise busy day devoted to banking, trading, politics, or whatever. But there were others who were clearly idlers, men living off inherited wealth who had nothing of any importance to do. Most of them were at cards or were fitfully chatting. A few appeared to have been drinking heavily, although it wasn't yet noon.

Whatever their preoccupations, the members did take notice of Derek and his American companion. Brand heard his name whispered as he entered, but wasn't surprised. He had been at Lamb's twice before, during earlier trips. And besides, he was too well-known on both sides of the Atlantic to hope to be anonymous.

Indeed, it was the hint of notoriety that hung about him that he intended to exploit to the fullest. Men began clustering around the bar, ostensibly out of sudden thirst. But many knew Derek, and none was shy about striking up a conversation.

Before long, Brand found himself in a circle of some of London's wealthiest and most powerful men. Their desire for his company did not surprise him; nor did their fondness for gossip.

Here, too, Julia's disappearance was known. Each man took pains to express his shock and offer assistance. Derek's expression made it clear he found all this painfully uncomfortable. But Brand did not hesitate to make use of it.

"As it happens," he said, "we believe the whole thing may be a misunderstanding. Miss Nash may very well be in the company of someone she knows. It's perfectly possible that she sent a note regarding her plans to be away temporarily but it has gone amiss."

The men exchanged glances. None was fooled but, then, that wasn't Brand's intention. He merely wanted to get them talking. Exactly as he had at the previous two clubs, he spun a polite fiction of a young woman of perfectly proper behavior who had simply been mislaid, or had mislaid herself, all through some oversight they would all undoubtedly laugh about when it was revealed at last.

The pretense allowed the perfectly proper gentlemen, in turn, to make a show of helping out, all the while enjoying the delectable scent of scandal at close range.

As it had before, the ploy spurred much conversation, but it seemed to yield little else. Until, that is, a white-haired gentleman put down his port long enough to recall something that had happened several days before.

"Pettifort," he said by way of introducing himself. "Hamden Pettifort. Served with young Nash's father, a century or two ago." He paused just long enough for the young men to chuckle politely. "Now that I think of it, there was a chap asking after Miss Nash. An American fellow."

"When?" Brand asked. He managed to frame the question almost casually, despite the tension roaring through him.

"Four, perhaps five days ago. I'd gone to Margaret Hamilton's for dinner. She sets a very good table, don't you know. We had lamb, and an excellent cherry tart. But that's beside the point. It was the day before, or after—? No, wait, it was the same day. Yes, it was, because I came back here thinking perhaps I'd overindulged just a bit and was hoping for a nod in the library. But this young American chap was there, asking after Miss Nash, wondering if anyone knew her whereabouts."

"Did he say why he was looking for her?" Derek asked, his reluctance suddenly evaporating.

Pettifort pondered that. "Said they were acquainted in New York. He'd heard she was visiting here and wanted to look her up. Pleasant chap, though, can't have anything to do with this."

"What did he look like?" Brand demanded.

"In his thirties, tall, slender, well dressed, fair-complexioned. A gentleman, I would say."

"Did he give a name?"

"He may have. It's customary, after all. But I'll be danged if I can remember it." One glance at Brand's expression was enough to convince Pettifort that he should try.

"Nestor... Pestor... Pester? Yes, I remember thinking he was pestering me when I wanted to sleep. But that's not it. No one's named Pester."

"Preston?" Brand suggested softly.

"What's that? Preston? Why, yes, it could be that. Preston something or other, or something Preston. Hard to say, I'm afraid. Memory isn't what it used to be." He shrugged apologetically.

"Never mind, you've done quite well. Come on, Derek. Please excuse us, gentlemen."

"How did you come up with Preston?" Derek asked when they stood out on the sidewalk again. "And who is he?"

"Frank Preston. He's from New York. I could be wrong, but he's someone I've been having problems with."

"That hardly explains why he'd abscond with Julia."

"Do you imagine anything in her own life explains it better? She grew up in the midst of a loving family. She spent almost her entire life in a peaceful, protective community. Until she met me, she—"

"She what?" Derek asked. His voice had gone dangerously soft. "Why exactly do you think that someone would try to strike at you through Julia?"

"Because they'd be wise to do so," Brand said bluntly. "Nothing else would be remotely as effective."

The anger that had been stirring in Derek faded, replaced by understanding. "Is that how it is?" he asked quietly. "I did wonder."

Brand shrugged. "There's no point talking about it, at least not now. We have to find Frank Preston, if he's in London."

He was, staying at the Staffordshire Hotel, one of the best in the city. They had started looking at the top of the list of places where a gentleman who wanted to present an appearance of wealth and position would choose to stay, and they got lucky on the first try.

"Indeed, Mr. Preston is with us," the majordomo informed them. "But I regret he is out at the moment. If you would care to leave word—"

"We would care to see his rooms," Brand said. He ignored the man's look of shock and laid a thick wedge of bills down on the desk. An instant later, they were gone.

"This way, sir," the majordomo said as he reached for a key.

"Are you accustomed to buying everything?" Derek asked as he and Brand followed along behind the man.

"I was."

"This way, gentlemen." A door opened before them. They stepped into an ornately furnished parlor. Just beyond it was a bedroom.

"I'll just wait outside," the majordomo said. "If I might request a certain discretion—?"

"Of course," Brand assured him. He went over to the desk and began going through it quickly.

Derek hung back. He clearly found the entire exercise distasteful. "Do you really expect this to help?"

"It may. At any rate, we have no other leads."

There was a sheaf of papers in the center door of the desk. Brand began flipping through them. As he'd suspected, Preston had lost heavily on investments. He was typical of a certain type of wealthy individual who regarded success in life as an entitlement. It must have come as a profound shock to him to discover that that wasn't the case.

Derek put aside his distaste to join in the search. But, though they examined every part of the suite, nothing else of substance turned up. Or at least not until Brand spotted the leather satchel on top of the armoire in the bedroom. It was unlocked.

"Probably empty," Derek said.

"Doesn't feel like it."

Whatever clothes it had held had been removed, but a small cloth-bound book remained. Derek flipped it open. "Addresses, most likely. Could be useful, but— By God!"

"What is it?"

The younger man's face had gone white. "It's a diary, started in New York and then kept up here. He's been following Julia around, recording her every movement, where she went, who she saw. Listen to this, from three nights ago. 'J at the theater. Didn't appear to enjoy the production, but then little seems to please her these days. Pining for Delaney? Hah-hah. She wore the blue silk. A good color for her.'

"And then this, just from two nights ago. 'J dancing at the Blanchards. She really should get more rest. Sleeping badly? Damn family all around her. I must find her alone.'

"And he did," Brand said grimly. "When she went out for a walk yesterday, he must have been waiting."

"He's a madman. We must go to the authorities at once."

"With what? A diary we're not supposed to have, and my own suspicions? They're supposed to be doing everything they possibly can as it is. This won't help."

"Then what?" Derek demanded. "We can't simply wait for Docker or one of his ilk to turn something up."

"Keep searching," Brand said. His eyes were bleak, but his resolve never wavered. "If he planned this all along, then he must have made some preparation to take Julia where he believed she couldn't be found. There has to be some record of that."

"Unless he—"

Derek broke off. Both men stared at each other. Unspoken between them was the knowledge that there might be no such place to be found. Julia had been missing over twenty-four hours. If all Preston intended was revenge, she could already be dead.

With even greater urgency, they resumed their search.

The child was small and dirty. She had not been fed yet that day, and her stomach hurt. Earlier she had been drifting with a group of other children, but she'd sat down to rest for a few minutes and lost sight of them. Now she was alone.

Or as alone as anyone could ever be in the crowded, twisting streets of Southwark. Tenements pressed in close upon one another. Sewage ran in the open gutters. Even in broad daylight, rats scrambled among the few scraps of garbage that eluded the human residents.

The little girl was named Megan. Her parents had come to England from Ireland, seeking a chance for a better life. They had not found it. Late at night, when Megan and her four brothers and sisters were asleep, there was talk of returning home. But to what? Land was scarce, hope scant. And hunger was ever-present.

A breeze fluttered through the dank alleys and lanes. Megan raised her head. Riding above the usual stench of unwashed bodies, molding buildings and refuse was the scent of the sea. She loved that smell. When she closed her eyes, she could imagine herself on a great ship, sailing away to a beautiful world so much better than this one.

But her eyes were open now, and something flashed before them, white against the background of unrelenting gray. It was delicate, and pretty-looking.

Megan stumbled to her feet. She crossed the road slowly, eyes locked on the strange white thing. If she blinked, it might disappear.

But it didn't. She got close enough to see that it was silk trimmed with lace. Her eyes opened wide with wonder. She had never seen such things, except once when her mother had taken her through the back alleys and byways to a different part of London, where the gentry lived. They'd stood hidden, in the shadows watching the grand folks come and go, before weariness finally drove them home again.

But Megan remembered the beauty she had seen. Whatever this lovely thing was, it didn't belong here. She bent over, trying to see where it came from. There was a bit of wood poking out of a tiny window.

Being so small, Megan was able to peer through the dirt-encrusted glass. It was very dark on the other side. She could see little, and she was about to give up when a sudden movement stopped her. Somebody was there, down in the cellar on the other side of the window.

"You there," Megan called, her voice very tiny and uncertain. It came out hardly more than a whisper.

But it was enough. A face appeared suddenly, as white as the pretty thing, except for the huge eyes that stared at Megan in disbelief.

"Oh, thank God," a woman's voice said. "Please, listen to me, it's very important."

The woman had a nice voice, very soft and gentle, for all the urgency in it. Megan listened.

Frank Preston's mood was sour as he returned to his hotel. Merely capturing Julia had not been anywhere near as satisfying as he expected. She was too defiant, for one thing, not cowering and pleading, as he had expected. He would have to do something about that.

But first, he needed a proper meal and a rest in decent surroundings. And he needed to scrub the stench of Southwark off himself.

He entered the lobby and collected his key from the desk. His imagination must have been working overtime, for he could have sworn that the majordomo looked at him oddly. Not that it mattered. Little people like that never did.

The key turned readily in his door. He entered, deep in thought over whether he should eat first or bath. A bath seemed more appealing, especially since the hotel was outfitted with the finest indoor plumbing, superior even to any found in New York. He would luxuriate in a hot soak while contemplating what he would like for a meal. All the while, he would think of poor Julia, trussed up like a chicken. She must be very thirsty by now. He would have a particularly nice bottle of wine in her honor.

He was halfway into the bathroom when his eye fell on the leather satchel on top of the armoire. It was pushed farther back toward the wall then he remembered it being. Surely he had left it closer to the front, within easier reach?

His brows drew together. The bath forgotten, he began looking carefully around the room.

"I'm sorry, sir," the factor said. "There are no fewer than thirteen Chatham Lanes, Alleys, Roads and the like in London. And that's before we even consider the outlying districts."

Brand shook his head in disgust. He didn't doubt the accuracy of the man's statement. He was Brand's own factor in London and, as such, expected to be accurate at all times. But he had hoped that the search would be narrower.

"Take a look at this," he said, handing over the document they had found lodged between a drawer and the inner side of the desk. Actually, Derek had found it, as he all but tore the suite apart in his determination to help. It had taken them some time to put things in order again.

"Interesting," the factor murmured. He adjusted his spectacles. "A rental agreement drawn up one week ago for a basement flat on Chatham—the rest is blurred. It appears the ink ran."

"We were able to deduce that for ourselves," Brand said.

His forced patience did not escape the other man. He applied himself to the lease with renewed vigor. "Hmm, this part might be helpful."

"What's that?" Brand demanded.

"Here, beneath terms and conditions, et cetera, et cetera. The part setting out the rental payment. It was paid one month in advance, for a total of twenty pounds. Curious."

Derek took a deep breath, visibly fighting for control. "Why?"

The factor removed his glasses, folded them and put them away neatly in his coat pocket. "It's either too high or too low, depending on which Chatham is meant. For the better districts, a two-room flat, as this is described, would rent for considerably more. But in the poorer areas, twenty pounds a month would be out of the question."

"Unless," Brand said, "whoever was doing the renting suspected that the apartment would be used for an illegal purpose."

The factor nodded. "Possibly."

"Chatham Lane," Derek said. "Over in Southwark. It's one of the worst parts of London. Not even the police venture there."

"Here now, have a bit more, there's a good girl." Megan's mother was coaxing her to finish the small bowl of broth that was her teatime meal. It was weak stuff, made from the few leavings they'd been able to afford. But it was the first food anyone in the family had had since the day before. Only Megan wasn't eating.

"She's poorly, Jack," her mother said, despair making her voice break. "I just know it."

"Easy now, Deirdre, you know no such thing. Our Megan's a fine girl, isn't she? Come on then, love, tell your Da what the matter is."

Megan crawled onto his lap. She laid her head against his chest, feeling as though she might go to sleep. But first she had a story to tell.

Brand and Derek had just stepped out onto the street in front of the factor's office and were in the act of summoning a carriage when a bedraggled urchin ran up to them.

Gasping for breath, he said, "You be Mr. Delaney, sir?"

"I am. What do you want?"

"Message from the Docker. Come at once to Chatham Lane over to Southwark. Little girl there's seen your lady."

* * *

He would kill her, Frank decided. It was the simplest way, really, and the safest. He should have done it at once. After all, there was no point to keeping her alive. He'd have to kill her eventually, anyway. It might as well be now.

It was just as well he had rented the place in Southwark. It was convenient to the river. He had the sheets he'd thought to take from his bed shoved into the satchel, along with a supply of rope. He'd wait until nightfall to dispose of the body. Then he could sit back and enjoy the spectacle of Brand Delaney twisting slowly in the wind, helpless to know the fate of the one woman who had finally pierced his invulnerable heart.

It would be a most satisfying spectacle. He could hardly wait for it to begin.

Julia was lying on the cot when she heard the footsteps. Exhausted though she was, she got up and ran to the other side of the cell. Pressing herself against the cold wall, she listened, hardly breathing, as the steps grew closer.

A key turned in the lock. The door was thrust open. Julia waited one moment, another. Sweat trickled down her back. Her heart was pounding so quickly, she was certain he must hear it.

Frank walked into the cell. The smile on his face was chilling. She spared it only the briefest glance before darting forward. Exactly as she had planned, she used the brief moment when his back was to her to race for the door.

She almost made it. Daylight was directly in front of her, the way to the street clear up a short flight of steps. If she could only—

She couldn't. Frank was on her in a second. He grabbed hold of her with both hands and slammed her against the nearest wall.

"You bitch! Think you can get away from me? I'll teach you—"

She struck out, frantically, kicking and hitting, but it was no good. He was stronger by far, and unrestrained by any consideration of morality or law. Again he threw her hard against the wall. Her head struck it. A sudden, loud buzzing filled her ears. She feared she would lose consciousness again.

If she did that, she would lose everything. Fighting with all her strength against the waves of darkness that threatened to engulf her, Julia stumbled to her feet. She had to try one last time—

She got only a few feet before Frank caught her again. His face was contorted with rage, and his eyes were gleaming with the unholy light of madness.

"I won't wait until tonight. Now's as good a time as any." His hands closed around her throat, and he began to squeeze the life out of her.

With the last faint, flickering remnant of her strength, Julia raised her knee. It felt weighted down by lead and, at the same time, a vast distance away from her. But raise it she did, slamming it hard against him.

Frank screamed. His grip on her throat relaxed, but he did not release her.

Out in Chatham Lane, Brand bent down to look the little girl in the eyes. "Are you sure?" he asked gently.

She stared at him in somber fascination. Her parents stood to either side of her, clearly stunned by what was happening. The sudden appearance of gentlemen in their midst would have been enough to cause tongues to wag for days. But that one of them bore the dark strength of an avenging angel made them vastly more afraid.

Jack put a hand on his daughter's head. "Go on then, Meg, tell the gentleman."

"She said her name is Julia and she needs help."

"You're a good girl, lass," Brand said softly. He stood and glanced at the family, who continued to stare at him with mingled wonder and disbelief. Behind them, Docker grinned. He was already counting his commission, if only mentally. But for the good Irish family, the reality of wealth had yet to sink in. They would be rich beyond their wildest dreams. Brand would see to it.

But first—

A scream tore through the lane. Megan flinched and instinctively reached for her father, who also gathered his wife to him. Derek froze. The sound was bloodcurdling, madness mingling with deadly rage.

Only Brand did not hesitate. He raced toward it. The scream had come from behind the very door Megan had indicated. Brand hurled himself against the old, cracked wood. It shuddered, but did not yield.

Again he threw all his weight against it. Still the door held. His shoulder throbbed but he scarcely felt it. Once more, with his full strength heightened by terrible fear of what he might find on the other side, he slammed against the door.

Metal screeched as the hinges tore loose. He all but fell into a small, sparsely furnished room. On the far side of it was a small flight of steps leading downward.

And there, at the base of the steps, was Julia, lying limp on the ground, her face ashen and all sign of life in her gone. So overcome was he by the sight of her that he scarcely noticed the man who pushed past him and raced out the door.

Gripped by a terror more profound than any he had ever known, Brand knelt beside her. He gathered her still form into his arms. This could not be. No deity, no matter how uncaring, could let this happen. If anyone had died, it should have been him, not beautiful, brave Julia, with her valiant spirit and generous heart.

Hardly knowing that he did so, he touched his mouth to hers, pleading, ''Julia, my love, don't do this. Don't leave me. Please, I can't bear the thought of being without you. Julia—"

Scalding tears fell against her pale cheeks. He clasped her to him fiercely, as though he could impart some measure of his strength into her.

Other people were pouring into the room, but Brand didn't notice them. Dimly he was aware of Derek saying something, but the words made no sense. Nothing mattered, nothing was real, except Julia in his arms.

Slowly he rose, holding her. The crowd parted before him. Her glorious hair tumbled free in a pool of fire. Heedless of the tears that still coursed down his cheeks, he carried her out of the hovel that had been her prison to the waiting carriage.

Chapter Twenty-Three

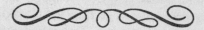

Julia stepped off the train before it came to a full halt. She ignored the pain that shot up through her ankle when it made sudden contact with the platform, and looked around anxiously.

The telegram she had sent ahead from New York had asked Peter to meet her. She did not want to say or do anything that would upset her parents or sisters, and she trusted Peter to be discreet.

Relief flooded her when she saw him only a few yards away, hurrying toward her. His face was creased with concern. "Are you all right?" he demanded. "That was a damn foolish thing to do."

"Only one of many," Julia murmured. She gave him a reassuring smile. "I'm sorry, it's just that I'm—"

"Exhausted, by the look of it. I wish you hadn't insisted on traveling alone. Any one of us would have come for you."

"I know," she said softly. "I just needed some time to myself." After a week of being cosseted by her cousins in London, for which she was duly grateful, she had been relieved to close the door on her solitary cabin and shut out the world. Except for walks by herself around the deck, she hardly left it. Not even an invitation to the captain's table had lured her out. She had been content to be the mysterious Miss Nash in Stateroom B, who was rarely seen and spoke even less.

In fact, her throat was almost entirely healed. It was her spirit that still ached. Barely had he confirmed that she lived and would recover when Brand vanished. Neither she nor anyone else had the slightest idea where he had gone.

Off on some new adventure, she supposed. He had come on the wind, and he seemed inclined to go the same way. Could she blame him? After all, she had refused to bend to his will, rejected his proposal of marriage and left him herself to go off to London. She could hardly claim now that she was sorry. It was much too late for that.

"I just want to go home," she said.

Peter nodded. He had a great capacity for silence when it was most needed. Julia had never appreciated that as much as she did now. His hand was warm and strong on her own as he led her away.

Daylight flickered at the edge of the water. Julia raised her head wearily and looked toward it. She had been sitting on the beach for more than an hour, driven there when she could no longer stand the confines of the too-silent house.

The beach that had always been her sanctuary was scant comfort now. She felt alone and empty. A sob escaped her. She pressed her lips together tightly. She was Julia Nash, damn it. She would not sit there crying over a man she had lost through her own stubbornness.

She'd go inside and cry.

But first, standing there on the edge of the world, she stared out at sea and sky. A few stars could still be seen, just winking out. Softly, on a breath of sound, she whispered his name.

Nothing more, only that, but with it all her hopes and prayers, her regrets and longings. All her love. Out over the silent sea, beneath the fading stars. The sound was gone in an instant, yet it lingered within her. As it would forever.

Brand swung his legs over the edge of the stateroom bunk and stood up. It was pointless to try to sleep. Despite days at the wheel of *Wind Dancer,* he could not rest.

Shirtless, wearing only breeches, he went up on deck. Dawn was breaking. The wind was fair, the sails were unfurled. They were making excellent time. He would be in New York in a few hours.

And then?

He braced his arms on the brass railing and stared out into the growing light. The air was chill, but it blew away the demons that had been haunting him. He felt far more himself, however changed.

His thoughts slammed to a halt. Instantly his head came up, his eyes narrowing. What was that? Just then?

There was nothing, only the soft *soosh* of the water as the proud vessel cleaved through it. That, and the whisper of the wind. The newborn day was completely peaceful.

But his spirit was not. Resolved on his course, he was suddenly uncertain. Hardly breathing, he stared out at the sea. Surely he was mistaken.

He'd had so little sleep lately, worrying about Julia and all he had lost. Wondering if she would refuse him again. It was understandable that he might be fooled by a murmur of the wind or the water.

But he hadn't been. Slowly the conviction grew in him, becoming stronger by the moment. He wasn't mistaken. Something ancient and powerful had touched him.

He waited a moment longer, breathing slowly, as he had been taught, feeling the day in all his senses. It was there again, the faint, elusive, but undeniable urging, touching him almost like a woman's caress.

One particular woman.

The day crew was stirring, preparing to relieve those who had been on watch all night. In another few minutes, the captain would be in the deckhouse.

Brand took one last long look toward the horizon. They were still out of sight of land, and yet he could have sworn that he saw, shimmering there in the far distance, the faintest hint of golden beach, and beyond, the dark, eternal green of sentinel pines.

It was madness, a trick of the mind. Or of the heart. He was playing the fool, wasting valuable time, acting like an addled boy.

But if the captain thought so when he heard Brand's orders, he was careful not to show it. Commands were shouted, startled looks exchanged.

Before the cook had brought the breakfast porridge to a boil, *Wind Dancer* had altered course just slightly, a bare fraction on the nautical charts, but enough to make a world's difference.

Julia meant to set the kettle back on the stove. Instead, she bumped against it, splashing the scalding water over her hand. A soft scream escaped her. She put the kettle down quickly and went to the sink, running cold water over the burn. It wasn't particularly bad, but it was the third accident she'd had that day, and her clumsiness was getting to be more than she could bear.

She had intended to fix a cup of tea and eat a few biscuits, but her appetite was gone. Leaving the house, she went into the kitchen garden. It was still coming back from the storm, but the plants were doing well. There was nothing for her to tend there, and nothing to distract her from the terrible hollowness deep inside that seemed to grow with each breath.

Inevitably she turned toward the beach path. Slipping off her shoes, she dug her toes into sand still warm from the sun.

As always, the beach was empty. She began to walk, her long skirt blowing in the wind. It billowed out around her like a sail, making her think of times as a child when she—

Like a sail. There was a sail within sight. Shading her hand, she looked out across the water. No, not one sail, several. A double-masted vessel of great majesty and power, coming directly toward her at a considerable speed.

The nearest harbor was a mile closer to town. She expected to see the ship tack at any moment, but it did not alter course, instead continuing to come straight at her. Only when it was close enough for her to see the proud, sleek lines of a mahogany deck and the brass fittings gleaming in the sun did she realize what she was looking at.

Wind Dancer.

Her hand flew to her throat. She couldn't believe what she was seeing. Brand was gone. Miles away, not here, coming ever faster, directly toward Daniels' Neck.

But he was, it was real, it was truly happening. And it was oddly familiar.

Her throat tight, the wind loosening her fire-touched hair, she stared at the mighty ship and the man she could now see clearly silhouetted on the prow. A sudden fear gripped her, like cold iron against the burgeoning warmth of her relief. Surely he knew the anchorage was too shallow? If he brought *Wind Dancer* in much farther, she would be beached.

His crew must have known that, for she could see them scurrying to ready a dinghy. But before they could, before she could get her breath, he caught sight of her. A slashing smile broke across his burnished features. For an instant, he stood, poised between sea and air. Then he dived, knife-smooth, into the water and swam toward her.

Laughter bubbled up in her. She suddenly knew—and dared to believe—exactly what he was doing and why. Without pausing to think—for, indeed, what more was there to think about—she ran into the surf.

Her dress was of summer-weight cotton, but it held the water and threatened to drag her down. She didn't care. Joy filled her, radiant as the sun, powerful as the wind. Joy to last a lifetime.

He came up out of the water suddenly, bronzed as an ancient god, dark and resolute. And laughing.

"I think," he said as his arms went around her, holding her upright, "that I prefer you to swim in somewhat less." His eyes met hers, forest depths against clear sky. "That is, if you don't mind a suggestion?"

Julia stared at him in wonder. A suggestion, from her autocratic warrior? Sweet heaven, he almost sounded docile. Happily, his body felt anything but. He swept her high against his chest, laughing into her eyes, and, with her close against him, strode up the beach, for all the world like a conqueror claiming it as his own.

Or like a lover entering his beloved's abode, with strength and tenderness to last through all eternity.

Gently he set her down, until her feet touched sand, but he did not let go of her. Cradling her chin in his hand, he said, "I want you for my wife, Miss Julia Nash, but I also want more." His mouth brushed hers, warm and seeking. "I want a friend, a helpmate, someone to get through storms with and welcome the dawn beside. I want a lover, in every sense of the word, to love and be loved by."

Her hands ran over his broad shoulders. She could feel the tremors racing through him and knew they were matched by her own. Slowly her mouth curved in a smile. She touched her lips to his and whispered, "I think I know someone perfect for that position, Mr. Delaney. Would you care to discuss her qualifications?"

"No," Brand said, his eyes so fiercely tender that they took her breath away. "I think a demonstration would be more in order."

Julia nestled her head against his shoulder. Arms around each other, they walked up the beach and into the future.

* * * * *

Author's Note

This is the third book I've written about Belle Haven. With each visit there, it becomes more real. I feel as though I should be able to take a turn on a road, wander down a lane, and find it there waiting. Even as Julia and Brand's story ends, I'm looking forward to the fourth and concluding volume in the Belle Haven Saga, *The Surrender of Nora,* for Silhouette Intimate Moments. It will bring the story of Amelia Daniels and her remarkable descendants into the present day. Please be there to enjoy it with me.

COMING NEXT MONTH

#247 DESIRE MY LOVE—Miranda Jarrett
In the continuation of the Sparhawk series, Desire Sparhawk enlists
Captain John Herendon to rescue her brother, but finds the captain's
motivation far different from her own.

#248 VOWS—Margaret Moore
The seventh book in the Weddings, Inc. promotion, *Vows* is the story
behind the legend of Eternity, Massachusetts, the town where love lasts
forever.

#249 BETRAYED—Judith McWilliams
Coerced into spying on her British relatives, American heiress Eleanor
Wallace finds herself in a trap that could cost her the man she loves.

#250 ROARKE'S FOLLY—Claire Delacroix
When obligations force a landless knight to become a weaver's
apprentice, he discovers he has an affinity for trade, as well as for the
man's fiery daughter.

AVAILABLE NOW:

Award-winning author

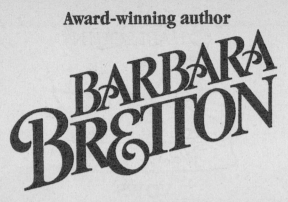

BARBARA BRETTON

Dares you to take a trip through time this November with

Tomorrow & Always

How fast can an eighteenth-century man torn with duty and heartache run? Will he find the freedom and passion he craves in another century? Do the arms of a woman from another time hold the secret to happiness? And can the power of their love defeat the mysterious forces that threaten to tear them apart?

…Stay tuned.

And you thought loving a man from the twentieth century was tough.

Reach for the brightest star in women's fiction with

MIRA™

VOWS
Margaret Moore

Legend has it that couples who marry in the Eternity chapel are destined for happiness. Yet the couple who started it all almost never made it to the altar!

It all began in Eternity, Massachusetts, 1855.... Bronwyn Davies started life afresh in America and found refuge with William Powell. But beneath William's respectability was a secret that, once uncovered, could keep Bronwyn bound to him forever.

Don't miss **VOWS**, the exciting prequel to Harlequin's cross-line series, **WEDDINGS, INC.**, available in December from Harlequin Historicals. And look for the next **WEDDINGS, INC.** book, *Bronwyn's Story,* by Marisa Carroll (Harlequin Superromance #635), coming in March 1995.

WED7

Maura Seger's
BELLE HAVEN

Four books. Four generations. Four indomitable females.

You met the Belle Haven women who started it all in Harlequin Historicals. Now meet descendant Nora Delaney in the emotional contemporary conclusion to the Belle Haven saga:

THE SURRENDER OF NORA

When Nora's inheritance brings her home to Belle Haven, she finds more than she bargained for. Deadly accidents prove someone wants her out of town—fast. But the real problem is the prime suspect—handsome Hamilton Fletcher. His quiet smile awakens the passion all Belle Haven women are famous for. But does he want her heart...or her life?

Don't miss THE SURRENDER OF NORA
Silhouette Intimate Moments #617
Available in January!

1994 MISTLETOE MARRIAGES
HISTORICAL CHRISTMAS STORIES

With a twinkle of lights and a flurry of snowflakes,
Harlequin Historicals presents *Mistletoe Marriages*, a
collection of four of the most magical stories by your favorite
historical authors. The perfect way to celebrate the season!

Brimming with romance and good cheer, these heartwarming
stories will be available in November wherever Harlequin
books are sold.

RENDEZVOUS by Elaine Barbieri
THE WOLF AND THE LAMB by Kathleen Eagle
CHRISTMAS IN THE VALLEY by Margaret Moore
KEEPING CHRISTMAS by Patricia Gardner Evans

Add a touch of romance to your holiday with
Mistletoe Marriages Christmas Stories!

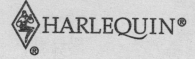

MMXS94

"HOORAY FOR HOLLYWOOD" SWEEPSTAKES

HERE'S HOW THE SWEEPSTAKES WORKS

OFFICIAL RULES — NO PURCHASE NECESSARY

To enter, complete an Official Entry Form or hand print on a 3" x 5" card the words "HOORAY FOR HOLLYWOOD", your name and address and mail your entry in the pre-addressed envelope (if provided) or to: "Hooray for Hollywood" Sweepstakes, P.O. Box 9076, Buffalo, NY 14269-9076 or "Hooray for Hollywood" Sweepstakes, P.O. Box 637, Fort Erie, Ontario L2A 5X3. Entries must be sent via First Class Mail and be received no later than 12/31/94. No liability is assumed for lost, late or misdirected mail.

Winners will be selected in random drawings to be conducted no later than January 31, 1995 from all eligible entries received.

Grand Prize: A 7-day/6-night trip for 2 to Los Angeles, CA including round trip air transportation from commercial airport nearest winner's residence, accommodations at the Regent Beverly Wilshire Hotel, free rental car, and $1,000 spending money. (Approximate prize value which will vary dependent upon winner's residence: $5,400.00 U.S.); 500 Second Prizes: A pair of "Hollywood Star" sunglasses (prize value: $9.95 U.S. each). Winner selection is under the supervision of D.L. Blair, Inc., an independent judging organization, whose decisions are final. Grand Prize travelers must sign and return a release of liability prior to traveling. Trip must be taken by 2/1/96 and is subject to airline schedules and accommodations availability.

Sweepstakes offer is open to residents of the U.S. (except Puerto Rico) and Canada who are 18 years of age or older, except employees and immediate family members of Harlequin Enterprises, Ltd., its affiliates, subsidiaries, and all agencies, entities or persons connected with the use, marketing or conduct of this sweepstakes. All federal, state, provincial, municipal and local laws apply. Offer void wherever prohibited by law. Taxes and/or duties are the sole responsibility of the winners. Any litigation within the province of Quebec respecting the conduct and awarding of prizes may be submitted to the Regie des loteries et courses du Quebec. All prizes will be awarded; winners will be notified by mail. No substitution of prizes are permitted. Odds of winning are dependent upon the number of eligible entries received.

Potential grand prize winner must sign and return an Affidavit of Eligibility within 30 days of notification. In the event of non-compliance within this time period, prize may be awarded to an alternate winner. Prize notification returned as undeliverable may result in the awarding of prize to an alternate winner. By acceptance of their prize, winners consent to use of their names, photographs, or likenesses for purpose of advertising, trade and promotion on behalf of Harlequin Enterprises, Ltd., without further compensation unless prohibited by law. A Canadian winner must correctly answer an arithmetical skill-testing question in order to be awarded the prize.

For a list of winners (available after 2/28/95), send a separate stamped, self-addressed envelope to: Hooray for Hollywood Sweepstakes 3252 Winners, P.O. Box 4200, Blair, NE 68009.

CBSRLS

OFFICIAL ENTRY COUPON

"Hooray for Hollywood"
SWEEPSTAKES!

Yes, I'd love to win the Grand Prize — a vacation in Hollywood —
or one of 500 pairs of "sunglasses of the stars"! Please enter me
in the sweepstakes!

This entry must be received by December 31, 1994.
Winners will be notified by January 31, 1995.

Name _____

Address _____ Apt. _____

City _____

State/Prov. _____ Zip/Postal Code _____

Daytime phone number _____
(area code)

Account # _____

Return entries with invoice in envelope provided. Each book
in this shipment has two entry coupons — and the more
coupons you enter, the better your chances of winning!

DIRCBS

OFFICIAL ENTRY COUPON

"Hooray for Hollywood"
SWEEPSTAKES!

Yes, I'd love to win the Grand Prize — a vacation in Hollywood —
or one of 500 pairs of "sunglasses of the stars"! Please enter me
in the sweepstakes!

This entry must be received by December 31, 1994.
Winners will be notified by January 31, 1995.

Name _____

Address _____ Apt. _____

City _____

State/Prov. _____ Zip/Postal Code _____

Daytime phone number _____
(area code)

Account # _____

Return entries with invoice in envelope provided. Each book
in this shipment has two entry coupons — and the more
coupons you enter, the better your chances of winning!

DIRCBS